SPARK

WEST HELL MAGIC - 2

Also By Devon Monk

West Hell Magic:
Hazard

Ordinary Magic:
Death and Relaxation
Devils and Details
Gods and Ends
Rock Paper Scissors (novella collection)

Shame and Terric:
Backlash

House Immortal:
House Immortal
Infinity Bell
Crucible Zero

Broken Magic:
Hell Bent
Stone Cold

Allie Beckstrom:
Magic to the Bone
Magic in the Blood
Magic in the Shadows
Magic on the Storm
Magic at the Gate
Magic on the Hunt
Magic on the Line
Magic without Mercy
Magic for a Price

Age of Steam:
Dead Iron
Tin Swift
Cold Copper
Hang Fire (short story)

Short Fiction:
A Cup of Normal (collection)

SPARK

WEST HELL MAGIC - 2

DEVON MONK

Spark Copyright © 2019 by Devon Monk

Paperback ISBN: 978-1-939-853-14-1

Published by: Odd House Press
Art by: Kanaxa Design
Interior Design by: Indigo Chick Designs

DEDICATION

To my family and hockey lovers, young and old.

1

"DUNCAN. HEY. HEY, DONUT. Dunc." Hazard, my best friend brother, smacked my skate with his stick. "Game. Now. Focus."

Right.

My opponent, my enemy, my obstacle, was six and a half feet of pissed-off Russian with anger issues and a deadly weapon in his hand. He had the too-much-white-in-his-eyes that would have looked a little extreme on a serial killer.

Sweat poured down his face as he growled.

He wanted my blood.

And I mean literally my blood. He was a fourth-marked Felidae shifter. A cat of some kind. Smelled like tiger. I was second-marked Canidae shifter. One-hundred percent wolf, baby.

Me and kitty did not get along.

But here at the ass end of the third period in West Hell hockey, all I cared about was dragging my team out of this one-nothing hole we'd suicided into.

"We got this," Hazard at my right panted, sweat dripping off the ends of his dark hair under his helmet. "Just keep your head in the game."

Wizards were not as fragile as everyone thought. Or at least Hazard wasn't.

He'd pulled a storm of knives out of a clear sky. He'd snapped thirty shifters back into human form mid-shift. He'd caught a hundred mile an hour puck with magic to keep it from killing a guy.

I loved the hell outta him. In a brotherly way.

Our crowd screamed for us. The rolling chorus *Thunder-heads! Thunder-heads! Thunder-heads!* pulsed and pounded, punctuated with two stomps and a clap. That battering, bolstering wave of sound was so thick, I could feel it in my teeth.

I shivered beneath the heat of it, the thrill of it.

I grinned, happy to be here, surrounded by the stink of sweat, exhaustion, adrenalin and blood, tied together with the hoppy tang of beer, brats, and violence.

Our right winger, Johan Jorgesen, or JJ, a third-marked who had a sensitive's knack of knowing where the puck was going to be and when, took the face-off.

I planted myself outside the circle, knowing he was going to shuck it toward our D-man, Graves, if he won the drop.

The Tide asshole, Paski, covering me took his spot right up my ass.

I made kissy noises at him. "Here, kitty, kitty."

"Fuck your face," he snarled.

There was a lot of cat in those words. Which meant he was gassed, worn out. The human in him was losing control to the cat inside him.

Wouldn't want him to lose his temper, now would we? Wouldn't want him to shift and force a break in the game so they could throw him out.

I mean, there was only one minute left.

We wouldn't want things to get chaotic, now would we? Wouldn't want to break their fucking stride so we had a fucking chance to bury that puck in the net.

"You ain't got the bone for it, boy," I chirped. "I've had cat. Tastes just like pussy."

There. That was the blood-berserker rage I was looking for.

Tension in his muscles, check.

Lowered shoulders, check.

Snapping his damn hockey stick in half with his bare hands? Well, now. Check and double-check.

Upside? We were going to get a break in game play and that would give us a better chance to score.

Downside? This was about to turn into a freak-on-freak brawl.

No, never mind. There was no downside to that.

Commie Kitty dropped gloves and barreled toward me with a roar.

A literal roar.

The terrifying screech cut through the rest of the heat and anger and exhaustion on the ice.

It was the kind of sound that brought a loud auditorium to full silence.

Music to my fucking ears.

I laughed, the only sound in the place, and it echoed off the rafters.

The wolf in me wanted *out, out, out. Blood, blood, blood. Kill, kill, kill.*

Not today. The only way we were getting through this game without our team being penalized for fighting was if I kept my shift buried.

Good thing the human in me enjoyed fighting just as much as the wolf in me did.

We were a good pair, my wolf and me.

I dropped my stick, and cocked a shoulder down so I could catch the Russian under his charge and either flip him, or get a punch into that broken rib he'd been favoring for the last two periods.

"Kneel!" The league sensitive demanded over the arena speakers. "Players will take a knee now."

A reasonable request. Too bad none of us were all that reasonable.

I dropped my gloves.

The crowd, which had spent all of three seconds silent, went absolutely wild. They wanted Comrade Kitten to shift. Wanted me to shift.

The chant, *Shift, shift, shift* rocked the walls.

As soon as my gloves hit the ice, the chant became *fight, fight, fight.*

Oh, yeah. There was gonna be a fight all right.

Players lunged. Someone got slammed up on the boards, snarling, cursing. Refs hauled ass that way, stun prods in hand, ready to throw a few thousand watts of electricity into every shifter who wouldn't drop knee.

I wondered who was about to get zapped.

Then I ran out of time to think about anyone else because there was a fist the size of a...what's a large Russian thing? A bear? A tank? A Kremlin?

Yeah, a fist the size of a Kremlin eclipsed all the light in the room and barreled down toward my face.

I ducked and blocked. Slid forward and grabbed his jersey. It was hard to pound the ever-loving sand out of your opponent's bags when you were on ice. Hanging on to his sweater locked us into place.

I twisted away from the follow-up punch and jack hammered my fist into his broken ribs.

His groan was not human. Neither were his eyes. They carved wide as his face expanded, reshaped.

And then it all went to hell.

The first blow hit the side of my head like a freight train with a cut brake line. And that freight train had claws.

I blocked, tucking the juicier bits of me out of reach, then pushed back.

The wolf in me gave me strength no human could achieve.

But then, the Russian wasn't human either.

I heaved and twisted sideways to use the half-shifted cat's greater weight and mass against him. He outweighed me as a human. He was even heavier as a cat thanks to magic's screwed up mass-to-weight ratios.

Full shift now, his jersey ripped at the seams, his shin pads, elbow pads and skates broke free as they were designed to do. Then his base layer stretched and shredded.

His massive muzzle pulled back from huge teeth, and he snarled like a chainsaw in need of a tune-up.

He stank like pissed-off tiger.

No, he stank like prey.

My wolf shoved for the shift. Sharp, heated claws scrabbled everywhere underneath my skin, digging for a way out. I breathed heavily and asserted control, feeling my muscles ripple and flex. Controlling a shift was nearly impossible when a person was angry, hopped up on adrenalin, or exhausted.

So, you know: exactly the state of every player in the third period of every hockey game.

Good thing? I kept the wolf in check.

Bad thing? I went down under a couple hundred pounds of fur and muscle and fangs and claws. Hit the ice hard.

Catski landed on top of me and reared back to angle a swipe at my chest.

I was pretty sure he was aiming for my neck. But he hit too low and his claws got caught in all that protective gear under my jersey.

"You can't even hit a jugular vein," I grunted. "No wonder you can't score a goal."

I slammed my fist repeatedly into his side. Just because he was a cat didn't mean his ribs were unbroken.

"Get the hell off, dude," I snarled. A snarl that was edging closer and closer to wolf. "Get. Off."

The snap of a stun prod crackled through the air and Kitty kitty went stiff. Even as he toppled slowly and bonelessly off of me, his eyes never left mine, nor did the anger and hatred in them fade.

I had not made a friend today.

Oops.

"Stay down!" This was a new voice, strong. Male. I looked up into the ref's face. You'd think he was angry, but no, not really. He shook his head and pointed the prod at me, not close enough to touch.

"Spark, you are a pain in the ass. Do you always have to stir up trouble at the end of every goddamn game? Some of us want to get home before midnight."

I gulped down air. "Sorry, Hartman. How's the family?"

He blew out a breath. "Get that face looked at."

"What's wrong with my face?"

"You're bleeding, son."

Oh. Well, yeah, of course I was bleeding. I'd just been mauled by a cat. I levered up to sit under the watchful eye of the ref and got my first look at the ice.

Everyone, and I mean shifters, humans, sensitives, and the one wizard in the entire freak league was kneeling.

Hazard watched me, his expression intense. Fierce.

People who said wizards were too weak to play contact sports had never met Random Hazard. He looked like he was about to punch his fist through reality and pull the guts of magic out of it.

He looked like he was going to fold the world in half and hit the entire Tide team over the head with it.

I was pretty sure he could do it too. He was terrifying with magic. Tested so far off the charts, they had to make new charts and they still hadn't found his limit.

He was also super-protective of me, which was kind of cute since I was a lot bigger than him and—remember—a wolf.

It was *my* job to protect him.

He was the little brother I'd brought home from school, and who my awesome parents had immediately adopted.

What I'm saying here is, I'm a really great brother. And he is a pretty great brother too, even though he worried too much when I started fights. Like I couldn't handle a knuckle buster.

He said, "Okay?"

I heard him, even over all the noise. Wolf hearing was awesome. Plus, I'd know his voice even if I was at the bottom of the ocean and he were on top of the moon.

I nodded. He only had regular human hearing, poor thing.

Then he said, "Idiot." And, "Good fight."

I smiled with all I had, and that included my wolf. He smiled back.

The crowd—which I'd blocked out since, hey, busy not being eaten by a tiger—was still chanting and cheering and stomping.

As I gained my feet they went balls-out wild. Some of the wolves out there even howled.

I raised one hand in acknowledgment to my violent, violent people. They shouted even louder and banged the glass like they were in a zombie movie.

I laughed and skated off the ice, the ref moving with me to make sure I wasn't going to beast-out.

"Never seen a kid covered in so much blood look so happy about it," Hartman muttered.

"What can I say?" I shot back, the adrenalin, the surge of the crowd, the heat and hope and power of the game pouring through me like lightning frozen in my lungs, shooting down my spine, burning, burning until I was on fire, alive. "I love this game!"

He tapped me on the ass as I stepped over the boards where our trainer, Leon, waited for me. "Let's get you cleaned up Siegfried and Roy."

I laughed, because, c'mon, that was funny. I loved this game, loved this team. Hell, I loved my life.

And I would do anything to make sure it never changed.

2

"SPARK, MY OFFICE," COACH Clay ordered.

The guys didn't give me shit for being called out of the locker room.

Random nodded though. He had my back. If there was anything left of it by the time Coach got done chewing my hide.

I wiped the towel over my hair—rusty-brown just like my mom's—and scrubbed fingers through it to smooth it down.

I was careful mopping my face. Kremlin Kitty had gotten in a lucky claw. Or maybe it was just his big dump truck fist that had split skin under my eye, lip, and weirdly, by my ear.

Things were a little leaky on the face front even though Leon had disinfected, glued, and taped me.

By tomorrow, these cuts would be scratches.

By the next day, the black bruises would be yellow.

By the day after, it would all be gone and I'd be my handsome, healthy self again.

Shifters bounced back quickly.

I chucked the towel on the pile and headed down to Coach's office.

The door was open, but I knocked anyway because I had manners and I respected Coach. He'd taken a chance on both Hazard and me this year. Picked us for the team. That gave me all kinds of warm, loyal feelings toward him.

Dad always told me I was too quick to adopt people into my close circle. I just thought I found good people easier than most.

I'd adopted Hazard—given him my old hockey gear when we were still in first grade and forced him to learn the game so we could play together. Told him he was my brother and he was never going to be alone again.

Gave him my parents since his were always absent, and along with them, gave him a home. His mother had been out of the picture pretty much since he could dress himself.

I hated that he'd been without family for six years before I'd met him. It was hard to even imagine what that would be like. My family was solid. My mom and dad were stable as stone.

And that was good. Every wolf needs family. Every wolf also needs an alpha. It grounds us. Helps us make good, human choices. Keeps our brains clear.

Here, in my hockey life, with my hockey family, Coach was as close to an alpha as I could find. Even though he was a fourth-marked Felidae shifter. And yes, him being a cat made it a little weird.

"Come in, Spark." Coach stood behind his desk and that meant this was going to be a serious talk. When he sat, that was a let's-work-together talk.

But standing Coach was irritated Coach.

Standing Coach was a retired right wing player.

Standing Coach was a snow leopard, deadly and cold.

I could see the beast in him now. Could smell it, that slightly sweet spice that was particular to snow leopards. Coach always smelled like cedar and sunshine, salt and honey. His eyes flashed lighter blue between blinks.

"Sit. I'm not going to bite your head off."

I guessed I was throwing off a little more wolf than I thought. I was healing, and it took wolf to do that quickly.

He didn't sit, which put him in a position above me. But I was okay with that because he was pack. He was as close to an alpha as our team had.

I did sit in the chair closest to the door, though.

Coach noted my choice. Probably noted my body language—uncomfortable, but trying not to be—and adjusted his own stance in response.

Like I said, he was the kind of man I respected.

"Let's talk about the fight first." He was all California cool, but I could tell he was angry that we'd assed up the end of the game.

I'd fucked up out there. I expected him to penalize me for it. That was fine. That was right.

I could take my lumps just like any other guy. Maybe better since I tended to get into lump-worthy situations with some regularity.

"Sure, Coach. I'm sorry I let it go that far."

He nodded. We both knew I had no control over Paski's shift. The only thing I had control over was my own shift—and I'd kept that shit locked down.

We both also knew I'd totally provoked that dude. I'd seen him teetering on the edge of beast and threw him a verbal elbow-to-the-face and one between the legs just for good measure.

No regrets.

"Fighting is not the answer, Duncan."

That startled me. He never used my first name unless something was really serious. Unless something was really personal.

"Sorry, Coach. I shouldn't have run my mouth."

"We still lost. You understand that, right? You got mauled and we still lost."

I opened my mouth to argue.

"You got mauled by a cat, Spark. Face that or we aren't going to be able to go forward."

I inhaled logic, exhaled my habit of brushing everything off as a joke to redirect conversations.

"Okay," I said. "Yeah. He got the upper hand. Can't argue with his work." I waved a finger in a circle around my face to indicate all the bleeding I'd been doing.

"You hit back, which I expect," he said. "And you did not shift, which I did not expect. So, good job on that. That's the kind of control I want out of my players, and doubly want out of you."

"Thanks, Coach." My cheeks and neck flashed warm. Yes, I was blushing. Pleased. I was a sucker for praise.

"But you were the cause of that circus. You, Duncan. One minute before the end of the game. Do you want to explain to me what the hell you were thinking?"

This was normal, this was how things went in hockey. In life mostly too. If I screwed up which I did occasionally (okay, constantly) I paid whatever price made sense. Hopefully, I learned from my mistake, and went forward from there.

"He was edging beast, and we were down by one," I said. "We couldn't huck anything past that Iowan giant they have in net. But if we broke their stride, we could have gotten a goal in. Maybe two. Except the Great Wall of Russia out there was in front of the net every time we got in the zone."

"China," Coach said.

"What?"

"It's the Great Wall of China. Russia doesn't have a wall." I couldn't tell if he was amused or irritated.

"Gee, Coach. If they don't have any walls, how do they keep their roofs from falling down?" I delivered that with the puppy head tilt that almost always made people laugh.

Coach gave me one slow blink and the corner of his mouth twitched up.

Score one for the Donut.

He rolled his finger in a little circle telling me to wrap it up.

"So I thought I'd get him off his game. Get in his head a little."

"A little?"

"Tomato, too-much-o. He snapped, so of course I pushed. But I didn't think he'd go beast. I thought if he went claws, he'd keep it to himself. But he wanted blood. Weird, right? I mean, they were winning. What did he have to be pissed about?"

"You."

"Me?"

"What did you say to set him off?"

I looked up at the ceiling trying to remember. There was a brown water stain in the corner, a sort of wavy circle that looked like the chalk outline of a dead jellyfish. Like a jellyfish had floated all the way down the Columbia River just to land in that ceiling corner and die.

"The usual," I said.

"Which is?"

"Whatever crosses my mind. Made fun of him being a cat—no offense, Coach. I don't have anything against cats, but you know how it goes on the ice."

"And did he say anything back?"

"He expressed displeasure with my face." I grinned. The edge of the tape under my eye stabbed into my skin and stung a little. "Which explains why he rearranged it to his taste. He apparently likes his Duncan Spark bloody."

Coach stared at me. Hard.

"I'm sorry," I said. "I read the game wrong. I thought a little scuffle would rev up the crowd and give us some gas going into the next game. Thorn was hating that she let that one puck past her and I wanted to get some energy onto the ice."

He was quiet long enough I started worrying I'd been wrong to apologize.

But I'd told the truth, and really what more could I do?

A fight wasn't always about winning. Sometimes it was a statement saying that even if we lost, our fans, and any of the other teams we were going to face, would know that we were not beaten. The Thunderheads did not go down with a whimper. We went down swinging.

"I also, uh, kind of wanted to see if the big Russian knew enough English that I could get under his skin. Because I am *crap* at learning other languages. Those guys from outside the US can throw insults in three languages. It's not fair."

I grinned again and coach finally breathed out. He smiled. "You are a hard guy to hate, you know that?"

"You hated me?" It came out a little cracked. Like I was a kid, which I most certainly was not. I was one of the toughest, hardest-hitting offensemen out there. A fourth line left winger any team would love to have on their roster.

"No. I've never hated you. Stretch out your attention span past that five second loop and listen to me. You are a hard man to hate. Everyone on the ice likes you, even though you are constantly talking, just constantly talking. So much *talking*."

"You should hear all the things I don't say."

"The only reason you don't say them is because you run out of oxygen."

19

"Oooh. Nice chirp, Coach."

This was good. This was right. This was me and Coach figuring things out. Getting the world back to square. Back to where it felt right and made sense.

I liked this.

"But you took a chance out there that I don't approve of." Coach dipped his head to look me in the eye. "Are you listening?"

I nodded, giving him all of my attention.

"When we are down by one—that's not the time to stop playing. That's the time to play harder, play cleaner, play our game. And our game is about hockey, Spark. Putting that little black disk in the back of that big, wide net. That's our game.

"There's a time for fighting, I have no argument about that. There is a time to do just what you did tonight. A time to push another player until they have to decide how much losing control is worth. There is a time to play the player."

"Yeah," I breathed. Because I was ready for this. For some of that wisdom I knew he had stored up inside him. He was filled with high octane Zen. He saw the world with a cold-eyed clarity a wolf shifter, a regular guy like me, would never have.

"Tonight wasn't it, Spark."

I waited. He was waiting too. Maybe for me to talk?

"I should have hit hard, but stuck with the play?" I didn't want it to come out as a question, but hey, I was feeling my way through this.

"That's right," Coach encouraged.

I got that electric happy tingle in my stomach and chest that made me wish I had a tail in human form so I could wag it.

"He probably would have shifted anyway, Coach. He was that close."

"I know. I saw it. Leon saw it too."

Leon was our trainer and also a sensitive. He knew when players were going to shift, could see the way magic worked in the marked: people infected by magic.

The way Joelle Thorn, our goalie who was also a sensitive explained it, a sensitive saw the way magic worked inside of everything. Even rocks and trees and French fries and sunsets.

I knew because I'd asked her about each one.

"So here's what I need you to do for the team, Spark," Coach said. "I need you to play like hell out there. You're strong, you're fast. You can keep up with Hazard, which is no small feat. But I need you to play *smart*. Smarter than you have been playing. I need you to think like a man, and not like a wolf."

I could take that as an insult, because wolves were amazing. In the wild, they had complex groups that hunted together, employing a lot of strategy and teamwork. Wolves were the perfect animal to represent hockey. Fast. Strong. Team players.

Apex predators, baby.

But this was Coach. I had to trust him. He'd been in this game, in this pack longer than I had. He knew strategy I'd never heard of. And if he wanted me to learn something new, then by Gretzy, I'd learn.

"I understand, Coach. Stay in control. Don't start fights?"

He nodded. "Don't assume starting a fight is the first thing you should do. I want you playing on the ice and on my team for a good many years. And at the rate you're going, *rookie*, you aren't going to have a larynx by the end of the next game."

I barked out a laugh. "Losing my voice box won't stop me from talking out there. I know how to swear in American Sign Language."

"Of course you do. All right. I'm not going to make you grind out a bag skate because you would probably like it."

He was right. I would. Bag skates were absolute hell. So hard and long, they usually only stopped when someone barfed.

"You are going to go to a meditation class instead." He grinned serenely.

I groaned and went boneless in the chair.

Coach had made me and Random meditate at the beginning of the season when our team was losing every damn game. Back then Hazard was having a hell of a time controlling his magic.

He'd spent all his life hiding it. So once he actually used it, magic sort of took over his control. Like a dam breaking under a wrecking ball impact, magic had roared out of him in a torrential flood. He'd almost drowned under it.

The meditation helped him. I had told coach it was great for me too.

I had totally lied.

I hated holding still.

Hated being quiet.

Hated emptying my mind, which frankly was like scooping out an ocean, one teaspoon at a time. In a monsoon.

Meditation made me feel alone. And I hated being lonely. It was one of the worst things that could happen to a wolf shifter, to me. I needed contact, people, noise.

"It's at the local health food store," Coach went on like meditation was just some kind of regular thing anyone could do. "Tomorrow night. You will show up on time, you will behave as I expect a player who is representing this fine team should behave. And by that I mean you will be on your best damn behavior. No fights."

I groaned again, still boneless in protest.

"*And* you will follow what the instructor tells you to do. Respect the students, the teacher, and the art of inner peace. Understand?"

"Yes, Coach," I muttered.

"Didn't hear you, Spark."

I opened my eyes. Stared at the ceiling. Wondered if the jelly fish had felt like this right before it had just dried up and died.

"Yes, Coach," I said clearly. "I understand."

"It's a three week class."

He was enjoying this. I could tell from the gleam in his eye.

I pressed my lips together hard enough I felt the bite of my busted skin against my teeth and the pulse of blood behind the swollen, healing knot.

Exhaled through my nose.

"Yes, Coach." I could do this. Now that the shock of it had dulled down, I figured it wouldn't be the worst thing I'd ever had to do for hockey. And if it made Coach happy, then it made me happy.

3

"THE HELL WAS THAT out there, Dunc?" Random asked as soon as I was out of the arena. He wore a hoodie and leaned against my Chevy Vega, his arms crossed. It was the middle of December, and cold enough most nights that we frosted.

Already the blacktop had gone all diamonds and stars, glittering, twinkling, silver and black.

The air smelled of exhaust from the roads surrounding the Veterans Memorial Coliseum and that weird tang of the electric trolley MAX that ran nearby.

This late at night, my favorite Portland smells were the rich, savory scents of garlic and beef and butter wafting out of the restaurants and bars filled with party people and night owls.

My mouth watered—I last ate hours ago, and that fuel was long gone.

I could really go for a greasy burger and fries dripping in cheese. But I needed something protein heavy and carb light if I didn't want to skate like I had a ten ton slab of concrete in my gut tomorrow.

"Duncan. Are you listening to me?"

"Of course I am idiot. I can hear a fly fart."

He smiled and rubbed his jaw where his manly stubble was stubbling.

I had been growing a beard since I was thirteen, pretty common among wolfies. So I'd had years and years to absolutely tease the ever loving shit out of Random about his baby smooth face.

"Why did you start the fight, dude?" he asked. "Did Coach scratch you for it?"

I checked the way he was standing.

Shoulders back and a little too tight, chin up, legs spread. He was bent just slightly to his left, favoring that hip shot he'd taken in the first that had painted a black bruise across the side of his ass and all the way down to the outside of his knee.

"How's the hip?" I asked.

"Killing me. Now it's your turn to answer."

I waved him out of the way so I could open the door and we could get out of the cold. Cold didn't bother me as much as him, but Dad would give me hell if Random came down with pneumonia. Also, we had a hard game coming up.

I did not want to go into that without Hazard at my side.

On the ice we were like honey and bees. Sweet and deadly.

Some people thought he was the sweet one and I was the deadly one. And yeah, they weren't wrong. He was smooth as cream over glass on the ice, and handled the puck like it was magnetically attached to his stick. Sweet.

I got into a lot of fights. Enjoyed doing so. Deadly.

But my boy Haz could kick any ass out there and hand out seconds. Hell of a player and not afraid to get physical.

That made him deadly.

When I was on fire, when I was all blood and soul thrumming and alive, heartbeat set to the pulse and breath of the team around me? When I was a part of the thing that was so much bigger than me?

There was no one as fast, no one as dirty, no one as good as me on the ice.

And that made me sweet.

He punched me in the arm. "Talk."

"Ow. That almost hurt, Ran. Did you up your weights from tuna cans to chili cans? 'Cause it's paying off, buddy."

Random locked his stance, refusing to move from between me and the door.

I could wrestle him for it. Wouldn't be the first time we ended up fighting in the middle of the night in an empty parking lot.

We weren't related, but we'd been brothers for so long, we both knew how to deliver a hit and how to take one. We were also maybe a little bit competitive.

Hockey players, right?

"Oh, that's how it is, huh?" I asked. "You want to fight? Think you can take me?"

"I am not going to throw down with you in the parking lot," he said. "But I will turn your Vega into a potato." He raised one hand, fingers loose, ready to casually gather a handful of bombastic magic out of the air right then and there.

"Really?" I tipped my head and sniffed the air a little, trying to sense the lie or truth of him. "Can you do that? Magic my Vega into a spud? Because: cool dude. And you should just go all the way and make it a pile of French fries. No, wait. Chili fries. I'm starving." As if to prove it, my stomach growled.

"Maybe I'll just freeze the carburetor."

"How you gonna get home?"

"I have a cell phone and a girlfriend. You have neither."

"Ouch. Owie. Kick a guy when he's down. Coach just chewed my hide. And my cell phone's at home."

He sighed, loudly. "Tell me the details. What are you going to have to do? Sit out a game?"

"No." I decided to give him this one since, okay, it was starting to rain frozen pellets and I was getting tired of standing in the parking lot. "He wants me to play smart. *Smarter.*"

Hazard rocked his head back and forth. "Can't squeeze blood out of a stone."

"And he said I have to go to a class."

"A what?" Random leaned forward as if he hadn't heard me. Which he probably hadn't because I'd sort of mumbled it.

"A class, you ass," I enunciated.

"What kind of class?"

"Just. A class."

"Hockey class? Skills? Conditioning?"

"Meditation. Okay? Is that all right with you? I'm going to go chill and peace out and find my inner goddess or something, all right Random? You have a problem with that? With my inner fucking bliss?"

25

My voice rose with each comment, but that was only because he'd started snickering, then chuckling, and finally laughing.

"What is so damn funny?"

"I love how angry you are about a meditation class. You're gonna have to Google Map to find your inner bliss, Goddess." He wiped his fingers over his mouth. "Okay, is that it?"

"Is that what?"

"Is that all he talked to you about?"

"Yes?"

Everything in him relaxed. His eyes, his breathing, his heartbeat, which, yeah, had been running a little fast. That was…weird. I hadn't been paying attention, but he'd been tense. Defensive.

He must have expected Coach to say something else. Something bad.

"Talk, Ran."

"I am." He unwound his arms from where they were locked across his chest. "Let's go home. I'm hungry."

He walked to the back of the car where his duffle and mine were tossed on the ground. I unlocked the trunk and we both heaved in our gear.

"Why are you acting weird?" I asked.

"You're weird."

"You're worried."

He shrugged. "Not really."

And that was a lie. I stared at him over the top of the car, but he ignored me and ducked down into the passenger seat.

"Random, Random, Random." I lifted the door to ease the weight off the sagging hinges, then pulled it open, and cringed at the loud metal squeal.

He continued ignoring me, jamming the seatbelt lock into place until it clicked.

"Talk," I said.

"Drive."

"Talk."

He stared out the window, mouth closed.

Fine. Like him not talking would make me stop pushing. I'd get it out of him. I shivered as ice pellets melted against the back of my neck. Time to get the car, and maybe even heater going. "C'mon, baby. C'mon, pretty girl."

"You need a new car."

"I like this one."

"This one doesn't drive."

"This one drives faster than you can walk, which is what you'll be doing if you keep up the Vega shade."

"She was old when you got her years ago."

"If by old you mean mature and experienced, then hell yeah, she's old." I patted the dash fondly.

"I just mean old, Duncan." He rested an elbow on the windowsill and wiggled around in the seat. Probably trying to avoid that one spring that got pretty up there if you didn't sit just right.

"She still has plenty of good years left in her," I said.

"Yeah, and I think we're gonna spend all of them in the parking lot."

I made an offended noise and gave him the chew-toy glare. The key caught, *finally*, and the engine rattled to life.

"Ha!" I cried shoving a finger at him. "She lives! She lives! The old lady is a-live!"

"Want me to get out and help the old lady cross the street?"

I laughed. "Cruel. So cruel." I jiggled her into gear and we shot off at a respectable three miles an hour.

Hazard pulled out his phone and got busy texting.

"How's Genevieve?"

"Good. She's got a gig in Seattle over the next couple days."

"Tell her I love her," I said.

"No. Shut up."

"Tell her I really love her. I love you, Genny-vieve!" I yelled.

"This is text, idiot. She can't hear you."

"This is love, my dude. She will hear its wild call across the miles. We don't need no phone!"

"Oh my god you are so annoying!"

Sure, that's what he *said*, but he was grinning and texting and pushing away my hand when I tried to grab for his phone— a maneuver I would never try at the speed of a normal car. But

27

my sweet Vega hadn't made it over ten miles an hour yet because she was cold and had been waiting out in the parking lot all alone for hours.

I wouldn't feel like zipping around after being abandoned for so long either.

He jammed his phone into his coat pocket, mostly out of my reach.

"Since we have a ways to go before we get home," I started.

"It's under a mile," he said. "If you'd step on the gas…"

I pulled my foot off the gas and the Vega sputtered and shook, gasping like a vaudeville starlet shooting for an Oscar.

"What is wrong with you, Duncan?"

"Me? Oh, I'm fine. What are you hiding from me, Random?"

"I don't even know what you mean."

"What did you think Coach was going to talk to me about?"

"Nothing."

He said it too quickly, avoided looking my way too studiously. He was a terrible liar.

"Talk, Wizard."

He didn't say anything. I added a little gas mostly because we had rolled to a startlingly slow crawl and I didn't want to get rear-ended.

"All right," I said, "if you're not going to talk, I will. You know I can talk. Like it's one of the best things I do. I mean, I do lot of things better than other people, but talking is right up there as the best thing that I can do for as long as I have to do it even if I have to talk about absolutely nothing other than how amazing and great I am and how I know you think I am the most amazing and greatest person you've ever met because you tell people all the time that I am amazing and great, like all the time.

"I shall now count down all the times that I've been amazing and great. One hundred. That time when you got lost in the campground and I found you crying in the outhouse and led you back to our tent which was like right there in front of you. You have a terrible sense of direction. Ninety-nine. That time when you barfed on Dad's Warhammer figures and I told him about it so I could get your share of ice cream that night and you said 'thanks a lot, Dummy,' but I knew you were glad because you were sick and ice cream would have made you sicker. Ninety-eight…"

His hand whipped out and smacked down over my mouth. Which: ouch, because that cut wasn't healed yet.

I must have made a sound.

He snatched his hand away. "God, sorry. I forgot you had tape and stuff. Someone with a broken lip should not be able to talk that much. For real."

"Tell me."

"No."

"Tell me."

"There's nothing to tell."

"Tell me what you thought Coach was talking to me about. Tell me. Tell me. Tell me."

He inhaled. I could sense it, the way his heartbeat *thunked* harder. The slight rise in his pulse. Then it was gone. Whatever he didn't want to talk about was big.

"Is this about the game? About the one we have coming up with the Brimstones? Do you think he's going to switch up our line? He's going to switch up our line, isn't he?"

I was really gaining steam now. "Fuck no. No way. I am not playing first line with Baller and Cha-cha. I am not. I'll refuse. Coach can healthy scratch me before I'll switch lines.

"Right? Right, Random? It's me and you, buddy. Fourth line for life, right? Or at least through our rookie year. That's the deal. That's how it's going to be. You're not leaving me, are you, Hazard? You wouldn't switch lines and play with Captain Swedish Cookie and the Crunchberries, would you? You wouldn't leave me alone?"

"You really…" Hazard shifted in his seat to better glare at me, but winced when he remembered just how personal that broken spring could get. "You really think you'd be sent up to first line *before* me? You're out of your mind. I'm a way better player than you."

"And yet I've never been kicked out of the NHL."

I held my breath to see how he'd take that last jab. We didn't talk about it a lot, but his dream had always been to play in the pros. He had hidden magic from his family, from himself, from everyone and the world for that one chance to play in the NHL. And he'd been kicked out.

Marked don't play hockey with the real players. Marked aren't human enough.

This was a tender-as-hell subject. But I always thought heartbreak was like other injuries: it only got better when you got some rest, did something to numb it, and kept it protected until it was strong enough to bear weight. As soon as you could, you got back out there on it, as if it had never been broken.

Maybe standing on broken dreams made the new dreams you built even stronger.

"Jerk," he said. No heat. It was his shortcut for "I love you" 'cause he didn't like to admit it very often. "At least I made it into the NHL before I got kicked out, loser."

"Then, just..." I huffed out a breath. "God, tell me. I'm really starting to worry here. What's wrong?"

He wiped his hand over his mouth again, thinking. When he nodded to himself, all the lines of him, all the tension of him, settled into his decision.

I had worn him down. Because I am amazing like that.

"It's Dead Man's week."

Oh. *Oh.*

Dead Man's week wasn't something that happened in the NHL.

Back in the early days, it wasn't uncommon for grudge matches in West Hell to end with a severely injured player. But after Johnny Morton, a star player for the Bismarck Boilers was killed on the ice for nothing more than running his mouth, the entire league lost its shit.

The only way to even the race for the Cup was to allow the Boilers to choose any player in the league they wanted to replace the superstar they'd lost.

It had become a tradition every year since. The losingest team could snipe a player—a Dead Man—from any other team, death or no death.

"Who's at the bottom?" We were still a couple slots away from making the playoffs ourselves. But I knew we weren't in the last spot.

Not anymore.

Not since Wiz here had finally brought his A game. He really was good. NHL good. They never should have gotten rid of him.

"It's not the Brass is it?" That would be a huge upset. They were in the lead, and I had no idea how they could have fallen down so far. But only something like that would be a big enough shake-up to make Hazard act so weird.

"The Brass are in first place." He picked at the crumbled remains of weather stripping around the window.

"So who is it?"

"The Tide."

I stared at the streetlights inching by, and took some time to watch a snail lose its lead on us.

"Okay," I said, slowly. "Tacoma doesn't like us."

"They hate us, Duncan. That coach. Nowak." He scowled and wiped his mouth again, then tugged his hair. "He wants our blood. My—all of our blood. Wants us dead."

He'd told me what happened with Nowak. The threatening letters, the attempt at blackmail.

Death threats.

The *hell*. I'd about lost my shit. And I'd done it loudly. We'd told Coach everything. Mom and Dad too. They had been the ones who talked me out of driving up to Tacoma and breaking Nowak's knees.

Prick.

Coach had taken it up with the people in power in the league. We hadn't heard if or what action they might take against Nowak yet.

After I'd finished yelling at Random for keeping another huge damn secret from me, he'd explained that he had no actual evidence to take to the police or the league. So, yeah. It was a he said/he said problem with no evidence to back it up.

"The Tide's record isn't that bad," I said.

"Before tonight, they lost the last four in a row."

How had I missed that? Maybe I had been a little distracted lately. "Holy shit. How did that happen? I hate to say it, and I mean I really *hate* to say it, but they are not that bad of a team."

He dug fingers into his thighs, gripping at muscle like he was bracing for a crash. This car couldn't manage a crash if it was full of explosives, going down hill on ice.

"I think they've been throwing games." He said it quietly, stoically. Like he'd been thinking about this for a while. He didn't look my way.

"That's not... I can't even...wait. Okay," I said. "Why would they do that?"

"Nowak wants a shot at our team. Wants to take a...a p-player off our team so he can hamstring us."

"A player?" I pushed.

Yeah, I'd noticed the stutter. He did that when facing the big stuff, the life changing stuff.

He'd done it when he was a kid, abandoned by his useless mother, standing in our living room asking if it was okay if he could have dinner if he washed all the dishes. Because he'd been out of food at his house since like a couple days before.

Random and I were a year apart and it had always been my job to protect him against bigger, older, badder things.

That's what big brothers were for.

"A player," he said.

"Which player? Who do you think Coach No-sack is after?"

Silence. We'd made it to my parents' house and I parked against the curb.

"I don't know."

Liar liar, wizard on fire.

"No. Nope. Tell me. Who do you think he wants, Ran?" I used Dad's reasonable tone that always worked on me.

"You can*not* pull that off like your dad," he said.

"What are you talking about?"

He dropped his voice to a fake low octave. "Who do you think he wants, Ran?"

"Shut up. I don't sound like that."

"Neither does your dad, you doof." He smiled, but it was a little watery and his heartbeat was all over the place.

"Fine. I'll just start guessing. Is it me? Or maybe me? Do you think it's me? Oh, god, I bet it's me. Because I'm like the greatest and everyone loves a donut and that's my nickname,

Random. Coach Nowak is hungry for the donut, and okay, that sounded dirty, but still. Me. He's gonna pick me out of the whole league for his Dead Man just to give Coach Clay a hard screw. And yeah, I heard how that sounded too, get your head out of the gutter. And then I'll be gone and you'll all cry and wail and stuff because you won't have no donut either and that's sad. The saddest. Wait. Maybe it's JJ. Holy crap. It's JJ. Is it JJ. Do you think it's JJ. Because everyone wants the J, am I right?"

"Duncan…just…" He scowled out the window. "It's me. Okay? I think he threw games to take me. His rivalry with Coach Clay…"

"Which everybody knows about. The Tide hate the Thunderheads. Always have. So what? Why would Nowak submarine his chance at the Cup just to steal you? I mean, no offense man. You're good, but let's face facts. We are both rookies. This is our first season in West Hell. We aren't the hottest shit in the shed."

"No," he said, "but one of us is the only wizard to ever play hockey. One of us is a fad. Pop fucking Rocks."

I waited a second. Instinct told me this was the core of what he had to say to me and it was important, and any minute it would make sense. Pop Rocks?

Nope. I still didn't get it.

"Your wizardly greatness will sell candy?" I guessed.

"It doesn't matter if I'm great or not. He wants me off the ice."

I groaned and tugged on my ear, which was at the itching and aching part of healing. "But why? That doesn't make any sense. They can go for the Cup. Why go for you instead? You're no superstar. His team doesn't need you."

"It's not so I'll make his team better. It's so he can keep me under his thumb. Those death threats? That hit he called on his own player, Steele? I can sink his reputation. Maybe his career."

I growled. "You should."

"No proof. Remember?"

Yeah, I remembered.

"Even if he took you." I swallowed to keep the wolf down, to keep the protective growl out of my voice. Because the wolf did not like the idea of Random being taken from him. From family, pack. "Even if you weren't on our team, we'd still win. We've proved that. When you were suspended, we were winning."

"It's not about winning."

"It's about having a wizard," I stated even though it was still a question.

"It's about having a new *thing* no one else can have. An idiot wizard who threw magic around to save an NHL player's life, to save a WHHL player's life too. I was big news," he said, like announcing a terminal disease had been named after him. "Hell, I'm still big news."

He wasn't shouting, he wasn't frantic. He was steady, accepting this truth as if there were nothing he could do about it.

Bullshit. There was always something to do. There was always a choice.

"We don't have to worry about it," I said. "Coach didn't mention Dead Man."

"He wouldn't. He probably won't even tell me until it happens."

His distress was so thick, the sharp vinegar and pepper coated my nostrils. It bothered me, and made the wolf stretch outward, twisting to escape my control. The wolf needed to defend and protect Random just as much as I did.

"Look," I said. "You need to stop stressing so hard, dude. You're killing me here. Until it happens, until *anything* happens, all we need to do is play our game. It's gonna be okay."

I patted his shoulder, awkwardly, since there wasn't room to bend two elbows in this car.

"Yeah," he said, not even a little convinced. "Sure. It's gonna be okay."

He didn't believe it, but that didn't matter. I had his back. And I was determined to do anything necessary to make sure he remained a Thunderhead, right here alongside me.

THAT NIGHT, AFTER FLOPPING around on my bed until I couldn't stand it anymore, I did a little research.

Started with the background on Clay and Nowak. Moved on to articles that were long and boring so I didn't read them. Finally thumbed to videos, watched a couple games Clay and Nowak played against each other.

It was pretty normal West Hell hockey, which is to say brutal. The two men hated each other. It was obvious their coaches tried to keep them from being on the ice at the same time.

But every time they ended up playing the same shift, the crowd got worked up to a lather.

Because when those two were on the ice, fists flew.

"Holy Gordie Howe. Look at you, Coach Zen-is-in. You know how to bring the pain." I watched a younger Coach Clay get his hate out on the younger Coach Nowak.

Nowak was giving it back as hard as he got it. Body checks that could break a human's spine, elbows and head shots and cross-checks that would knock a non-marked off their skates and straight into the morgue.

Every time they hit the ice, players shifted so quickly to beast, the refs had to get off the ice, had to get the humans and sensitives off the ice, and had to electrocute the ice itself.

Electrocute. The. Ice.

Which: okay, that was balls-out metal. It was hardcore shifter management right on the edge of abuse.

Maybe that was the way it was done back then, but there hadn't been an ice electrocution in years. And there wouldn't be.

Even a guy with my attention span (short) could read through a contract and tell if it mentioned something about group electrocution fun times. Mine didn't.

Watching the players in beast form stagger and fall on the ice, snarling and twitching and thrashing, was rough.

That video wasn't hockey. It wasn't even freak league hockey. I didn't know what it was, but the crowd ate it up like bacon-wrapped candy.

The camera panned the ice, littered with ripped jerseys, gear, and skates. Looked like a tornado had blown the roof off a Laundromat. And right there in the middle of it all lay the shifted, bloody snow leopard—Coach Clay—and another shifted, bloody snow leopard.

Holy shit, Coach Nowak was a snow leopard.

All the jokes about cat and dog behavior didn't really apply to shifters. Nor did birds of a feather always flock together. But enemies were enemies, no matter what kind of marked they were.

This was more than just two men hating each other, which, yes, happened in any sport. This was war.

I flipped through a few more vids of them together. None of their games were as violent as that one with the mass electrocution. But none of the other games put Nowak and Clay on the ice at the same time for long.

"Did you two ever get along?" I wondered out loud.

I did some deeper digging and found a single short, grainy old clip of the two of them on the ice playing on the same team back when they'd just started out in the league. They played on the same line, actually, two wingers for a center I was going to have to look up since I didn't recognize her.

Even though it was only thirty seconds of ice time, one thing was so very clear.

Clay and Nowak were amazing together. If two players could be perfectly matched, if two players could work the ice like they were one brain controlling two bodies, it was these guys.

There were a lot of amazing lines in hockey history. Lots of amazing lines at every level all the way up to the NHL. Lots of amazing lines here in the WHHL too. So how come I'd never heard of these two?

"Why would you walk away from that?" I muttered as I replayed the video again. "That right there is something that doesn't happen...ever. Why would you quit the team, Coach? What made you hate him so much?"

After watching the fights again I knew in my gut that it had been Clay who had walked away from the team, and not Nowak. Coach had quit. And I just didn't see quitting in him, not in the man he was now. He was a hockey player. He wasn't made to quit.

Unless there was another answer as to why Clay suddenly left the team he and Nowak played on so perfectly together. Another option.

And then it hit me.

"No way."

I rubbed at my eyes and blinked hard to clear the blurriness. I was tired. And hungry. We had to hit the road early to get to Bend. And before that, I had to go to meditation class.

Still, I followed my hunch and looked up one more list.

And there he was, way down on the list. Coach Clay was a Dead Man.

4

"HE WAS A DEAD Man," I yelled into the pillow.

"Get off my head," Random said. Or maybe he said "get off my bed." Hard to say since I was currently sitting on top of his bed, my mouth mashed against the pillow Random had covering his head.

He was pretending to be asleep. Wasn't that cute? He was also pretending that I was bothering him.

Brothers, right? Always joking around.

"I. Will. Kill. You."

"What's that, buddy?" I yelled into his pillow. Right over his ear this time just to make sure he really heard me. "Did you say something? I can't hear you with this pillow over your head."

That did it. Elbows and knees went flying. There was a slap and push, then a pretty decent take down move I didn't know he had in him.

"What the hell?" I asked, as my not-as-favorite-as-usual brother held my arm behind my back and shoved my face into the floor. "Where did you learn that?"

"My girlfriend. All her brothers were wrestlers. Can you hear me now, Duncan?"

"What? I'm not sure I quite heard…ow, ow, okay! Fine. I can hear you."

He stopped pinching that point on my wrist he always, always found, and relaxed the angle of my arm. Slightly.

"Stay out of my bed."

"I wasn't *in* it. I was on it."

"Nope. All I want to hear is: yes, Random. I will stay out of your bed, especially on a Friday when you are trying to catch as much sleep as you can before we take a road game."

"Do I have to repeat it back word for word, or can I sort of ad lib that one? Because it's a lot to remember and really, doesn't sound all that much like me."

He patted the side of my head. "You are such a dim dim." He shoved off and shuffled back to his bed, falling into it with a sigh before burrowing under the covers and pillows.

I rolled over and stared at the ceiling. No dead jelly fish here. The ceiling was a nice clean white I'd helped my parents paint when they decided to "freshen" up the house by way of twenty gallons of paint and way too many weekends of masking tape and Duncan sweat.

"He was a Dead Man." I folded my hands on my chest tapping my fingers in rhythm to the song in my head: "Hungry Like the Wolf."

"Who?"

"Coach Clay."

Random rolled to one side, tucked his fist against his temple and stared down at me. "He was a Dead Man? When?"

"Way back. I think that's why he left the Topeka Twisters. He got picked by the team in last place, the Sacramento Rush, so it makes sense. Kind of."

"Kind of?"

"The timing doesn't match up. He left a month before Dead Man week."

"Maybe it was a different week that year."

"Yeah. No. Maybe. I don't know."

He flipped onto his back and scratched at his head. "Okay, so coach Clay quits his team for some reason, doesn't immediately get fired for it—which, weird—and then a month later the team in last place picks him up under the Dead Man draft even though he wasn't a working player on the team."

"Something like that. Could be a loophole in there. Like his old team kept him on as a healthy scratch or something."

"Hmm."

"I watched some vids last night."

"Did you see the one with the big fight?" he asked.

Of course he'd already gone looking for this stuff. "Harsh," I said.

He hummed again.

"There was another clip," I said. "Him and Nowak working a shift."

"And?"

I got to my feet easily because my bruises were already mostly healed, and stared down at him. "They were...I don't even know how to explain it. They were amazing together. Like two parts of the same body, you know. They had this *chemistry* on the ice. Worked plays like magic, man."

Hazard wiped a hand over his forehead and left it flopped there. "Yeah, I saw it too. They...clicked."

"Yeah."

"You know who they remind me of, Dunc?"

I waited. Was pretty sure I knew the answer. Hoped I knew the answer. Hoped he saw things the way I saw things.

"You and me."

Yes! I grinned. "Aw. Did you just pay me a compliment? Did you just say we are great together? Like you can't live without me. Oh! We should move in together and date."

He threw a pillow at my head. I ducked and it crashed against the far wall. Brother had a good arm.

"We already live together," he said. "You are constantly in my room even though I never invite you, and we *are* planning to move out together."

"All we need now is that date."

"Genevieve might have something to say about that."

"Something like, 'Wow, look at those two hot hockey players together. The shorter one is sort of ugly, but that tall guy is the stuff dreams are made of.'"

"One, she does not sound like that, two, she likes the shorter, *more handsome* one just fine, thank you."

I opened my eyes wide. "Sure thing, buddy. You got nothing to worry about. You're totally tolerable."

He pointed at the door. "Out. Now. Get me breakfast."

I wanted to stay and bother him, but my stomach rumbled. Breakfast sounded good.

Even though I hadn't gotten much sleep, I was full of energy buzzing beneath my skin. I'd need a quick jog before I was trapped on the bus for hours.

I followed my nose to the kitchen: coffee, eggs, sausage, and my dad's aftershave.

"Morning, Duncan." Dad stood at his normal spot, leaning one hip against the counter right in front of the coffee pot. He held a cup out for me.

People tell me I look a lot like my dad, and I like it. I'm a little taller than him, wider at the shoulders and chest. He's got more of a runner's build now, though he used to speed skate. He also wears glasses and unironically dresses in Mr. Rogers style sweaters.

My reddish hair and freckles? Those are all from my mom.

"Mornin', Dad." I swooped in for the cup, and kept going for a one-arm-across-the-shoulder hug. He smelled good. Like pineapple and vanilla and home. His squeeze was firm and long.

"Did you sleep?" he asked near my temple.

I had no idea how he could always tell when I was up most the night.

"Not really." I sat at the table in front of a pile of eggs, toast, and turkey sausage. "Mom already at work?"

"Hours ago. Did you get Random up?"

"Yeah. I'm gonna eat then go for a run. I think he's in the shower."

"He's right here." Random strolled into the kitchen. "Morning Mr. Spark."

"Still want you to call me Sean, son. Have a seat. Eat while it's hot."

Random blushed and mumbled something that had Sean in it—which, what a dork—and then sat and helped himself to whatever I'd left behind.

Here's a thing about hockey players: we burn a shitload of calories.

Here's a thing about shifters: we burn even more than that. So it took shoveling a lot of fuel into the burner to keep us going.

Wizards were a little different in that magic wasn't constantly burning through them. It only consumed calories when they used magic. But when they cast spells, it caught like a

41

wild fire and burned the holy hell out of everything in their bodies.

Second and fourth-marked—shifters—were always on a low simmer, magic banked and burning, burning, burning.

I shoved as much protein and carbs in my face as possible. Hazard took it a little slower, but wiped out a respectable plate of food.

He might skip lunch before practice, but I wouldn't. I'd need something, even if it was a heavy bar to get me through practice, and then I'd need something right before the game to make sure I didn't run out of gas.

Food, food, food. My twenty-four hour job.

Staying fed had another side effect: it kept the beast quiet and happy. A hungry wolf was not a happy wolf. The hungrier a Canidae or Felidae shifter became, the harder it was to suppress the beast inside us. And since the beasts were already hyper-alert during a hockey game from the violence, adrenalin, and physical output, going into a game hungry was throwing out a welcome mat for trouble.

I cleaned my plate while Dad and Random talked about training, the trip, and the team we were playing against: Bend Brimstones.

They had taken some time finding their legs this season, much like our team had. But now they were burning up the standings, winning game after game, racing us for a place in the playoffs.

They played a hard, physical, rough and dirty game.

They were fun as hell.

I gulped the rest of my coffee as I carried my plate to the sink.

Winter in Oregon meant dark mornings, and lots and lots of cold rain. It was dismal running weather, but hey, what's a guy gonna do? If I didn't burn this energy now, I'd go crazy in the meditation session.

"Wanna run?" I asked Random.

"I'll do it before practice," he said. "Go."

I waved at the two of them and bolted out the back door.

I stretched on the little concrete path that led from our backyard around the house to the sidewalk.

Inhale the slick, sweet taste of rainy drizzle, exhale. Inhale the biting cold air until the lungs sting, exhale. Twisted, bent, rolled my shoulders, feeling my way through the newly healed bumps and bruises from last night, feeling my way through my body.

A hitch here, a tightness there. My calf was sore from a blocked slap shot. Not too bad, but I'd need to be easy on it. By tonight, it should be almost fully healed.

I trotted down to the sidewalk, cracked my neck both ways, bounced on the balls of my feet, then started off.

About a half mile from our house was a path that wandered between a stand of trees and circled a field. A creek ran through the woods and field. The footpath made a two mile loop.

My eyesight was sharp, even in this darkness before sunrise, with street lights and porch lights, the edge of the foothills graying up toward dawn. I couldn't see in the dark as well as an actual wolf. But even in pitch fricking blackness I could see shapes, could track movement.I jogged the next half mile, clearing my head and getting in the rhythm: feet and lungs, muscles and brain all working together.

The wolf in me responded, reaching for this, craving the run. It was the best way to tame my beast. Give it the dark of the sky, the slap of foot on solid ground, the drum of a heart beating, beating between each steady, even breath.

I loved it. This was the only other place I felt as free as I did on the ice. This was the only other place where me and the wolf snapped together and became one thing instead of two.

My shoulders relaxed, my mind calmed.

This might be what Coach was hoping I'd find by meditating. But holding still was a punishment, not a reward.

I would do it. After I ran.

The sidewalk gave way to softer ground. The cold green of mud, brown grasses, and old pine needles reached my nose, filled my lungs. I inhaled a little deeper, letting winter in, wanting it to blow me open, wanting it to howl through me until I was empty. I growled with joy I couldn't contain any longer, tipped my head down and ran.

5

"WE SUCK!" WATSON, OUR defenseman who was a Felidae, fourth-marked—tiger—groaned and collapsed onto the bench. He clunked his head on the locker wall behind him.

We were down four-one in the second. He was right. We sucked. "When did they get so fast?" I scrubbed a towel over my face and neck, sopping up sweat.

"They're the same speed as they ever were, Donut." Joelle Thorn, our goalie, sat next to our captain, a very intense Swede: Laakkonan who we just called "Lock."

Thorn's long brown hair was braided back but bits of it had pulled free and stuck down the side of her face. She was just as sweaty as the rest of us, having thrown every move she had to keep the score from plunging off an even steeper cliff. She was amazing in the net, but I knew she was angry they'd gotten four past her.

She still had on her heavy goalie pads, but had set her blocker and stick to one side so she could down a sports drink and eat a bar. She was third-marked, a sensitive, which meant she was calm as a brick wall in the net, and swift as death on skates.

Off the ice, she was loud and fun. On the ice, she was solid, fierce, and could carry our entire team across her capable shoulders.

But no matter how many times she blocked the puck, if we didn't shoot the other team's net, we were not going to win this thing.

"You're just slow, Donut," Jada Green said. She was a second-marked like me, but instead of wolf, she was a coyote shifter. She was also six two, had darker skin and curly short black hair, and was our second line center between Fisk and Yoffie.

Her hockey sense was wicked sharp. She was intense, focused, and our clutch scorer during a power play. "Maybe you should try skating instead of standing around waiting for a play to fall in your lap."

I scowled at her and she serenely showed me her teeth.

Coach Clay and Assistant Coach Beauchamp stalked into the room.

Two ex-hockey players had never looked more different. Coach Clay was blond, had an easy going vibe and body language, tended to smile and motivate with carrots instead of sticks. He gave off that California surfer dude kind of thing, and was strong in the shoulders and long in the leg.

Assistant Coach Beauchamp was a brick shithouse ex-defenseman. To put it bluntly, he looked like the butt end of a bear—an ugly bear. At just over six foot, he was wide everywhere. Big paw hands, big barrel chest, big stomach that used to be all muscle and was now muscle covered in a thick layer of fat.

He was somewhere between old and expired. We had a betting pool on when he'd retire, and the pool didn't cover more than two years.

He and Clay were our coaches and along with some rich cake shop guy who liked to invest in losing prospects, they were also owners of the team.

Clay and Beauchamp had dragged the Thunderheads out of the muck of a failing franchise and built a team that was something worth watching, something worth cheering for.

That was even before they picked up the ex-NHL rookie wizard. Bringing Hazard onto the team spiked ticket sales. There were a lot of eyes on our team right now, and advertisers were catching on and cashing in.

The Thunderheads hadn't gotten into the playoffs under Clay and Beauchamp's watch yet, but this could be our year.

This could be our year to take the Cup.

"All right, listen up," Assistant Coach Beauchamp growled. "Pay attention to the damn neutral zone. They are riding roughshod over the top of you out there. Get off your damn heels and shut them down. Hard. Grow some balls. Block those damn passes. And stay on your damn man. Or woman. You know what I mean."

He stared at me the longest. Heat prickled across my neck and face. I'd let two cringe-worthy passes slide right in front of me and hadn't been able to get a stick on them. Plus, I'd botched my coverage and was pretty much responsible for at least one of those goals they'd scored.

The Brimstones were *fast* in the neutral zone and didn't put on the brakes at the net, either. As the game had gone on, they'd somehow gotten even faster.

They had found third gear and we were stuck in first.

"Do you hear me?" Beauchamp asked.

"Yes, Coach," I said along with the other players.

"Defense," he pointed at the players. "I better see you scrambling for some offensive assists. Get in the damn dirty areas, get the puck and shoot top shelf on Yancy's ass."

"Yes, Coach," the defensemen said. Well, all except Graves.

Hawthorne Graves was tied with Bucky as the oldest man on the team. He'd played on almost every team in West Hell. I hoped he wasn't thinking about retiring because he had, somehow, been the one who had pulled us all together and made us finally "click" as a team.

My wolf and I got lots of mixed signals from him.

He gave off alpha vibes like no one else I'd ever met. He was quiet, steely-eyed, tall, strong, scarred. He was smart as hell on the ice, swore like an inmate, and talked with a Texas drawl and had the cowboy attitude to sell it.

So it made sense he felt like an alpha.

But sometimes...sometimes he was *more* and *different* and *danger*. Like the silence before a really big *boom*. I didn't even know how to describe it. I hadn't talked to anyone about how much he threw off a sense of *other*.

His record said he was second-marked, wolf shifter, and yeah, I guess if I tipped my head to one side and squinted an eye, that worked. He sometimes radiated alpha vibes and that was a wolf thing. He had pack intelligence and teamwork too, both things that wolves possessed.

And when he whistled—which he did during games, on the bus, when we took a few hours of downtime in whatever city we were visiting—it was like he cast a spell over us.

Okay, he didn't actually cast a spell. I knew what wizards could do now that Hazard had gotten over himself and used magic. Wizards manipulated reality, turned it into other things with the sheer willpower of their minds.

That was magic.

What Graves did came out of magic, just like shifting came out of magic. But his hypnotic whistle had something else behind it. Something primal. Primordial.

Hearing it drew us together, settled us, created a connection we sometimes struggled to find on the ice.

The team needed that. Needed him with us because he made us better. He made us more. Which is why I didn't want him to retire.

His head was down, eyes closed. He wasn't breathing hard, but I knew he was in some kind of pain. It was odd to see him checked out, eyes closed, not responding to the coaches.

I took a tentative sniff and didn't smell his blood, didn't smell sickness. He'd been playing physical and aggressive out there, laying out the body checks. No more than normal. I wondered if someone had gotten a dirty hit on him, and therefore was curious as to whom I'd be taking down in my next fight.

Or maybe it wasn't just pain he was dealing with. Maybe he was digging deep, doing some kind of his own meditation thing so he could do what the coaches asked.

Usually he sat loosely, staring at the coaches out of sandy-brown eyes, silent as the desert.

I glanced at Hazard. He caught my gaze, followed it to Graves and frowned.

Okay, so I wasn't the only one who thought Graves was acting weird.

Assistant Coach Beauchamp was done with his pointing-out-the-obvious speech, so Coach Clay took over.

"This team is not defeated. We've been behind before. We know how deep the damn hole is, we sure as hell know how to dig out of it. Play your damn game. The same damn game you play every practice. Every warm up. Every match. Trust your damn linemates. Trust your damn instinct. Trust your damn gut.

"Be *there* for the pass, the check, the rebound. They showed us their game, now let's shove ours down their throats.

"Shoot. Every damn time. Keep the damn pressure on. Fight for it until the last damn second. This is your damn game. Get out there and take what's yours." He raised one finger, punching it toward the ground.

We all knew what he was going to say, so we said it with him. "Dammit!"

Players yelled, hooted, whistled. Coach stepped back so our captain could have a word.

Lock stood and kept standing. The tall Swede's straw-colored hair was plastered flat to his head. He was red-faced, fire-eyed and ready to get his pillage on this village.

"They might have put us in hell, but we're not going to let them out of it."

We howled, stomped our feet, someone yelled "Thunder! Thunder! Thunder-heads!" and the room filled with the chant.

Jada turned on the music—AC/DC's "Thunderstruck," of course.

We yelled with it, clapped with it as we got on with our rituals.

We taped sticks, changed socks, retied skates, juggled tennis balls. The Terminators— Tetreault and Troiter who were making a name in the league as a hell of a defensive line—launched into their boxing/hand-slap game, fists and palms connecting faster and faster until they screwed up and punched each other in the shoulder as hard as they could.

I fed on the energy of my team, drank it down, ate it up, breathed it in. Their hope that sharpened every heartbeat, fear that made it all sweet and uncertain, lust, raw and zinging under their skin, my skin.

Life. It was life. Distilled, thickened, concentrated.

This was what I needed. This was what made me whole. Teammates, family, pack.

I retaped my stick to keep my hands busy while I soaked up the energy. I'd already downed a heavy protein bar and guzzled enough liquid to keep me going. The wolf in me was antsy, excited, chomping for movement, ready for the fight.

Hazard was over there in his own zone, meticulously retying his skates, his gaze focused inward. He needed a clear head and a lot of willpower to keep a lid on all the magic boiling around inside him. Now that he'd started using magic, he said it was harder—all the time—not to use it.

I don't know why he tried so hard not to use it. If I had magic at my fingertips, you can bet your butt I'd be ala-kazaming all over the place. Want a sandwich? *Ala-kazam!* Got bills to pay? *Ala-kazam!* Three points behind at the end of the third? *Ala-ka-frickin'-zam, baby!*

But he was all, "no, Duncan. There are rules about magic in hockey. Rules that keep players safe, you idiot." My brother was a total killjoy do-gooder.

I snorted. Chump.

He didn't even look up, but he paused in messing with his skates long enough to throw me the bird. I cackled. He'd known what I was thinking. Little brothers/linemates were like that.

"Not even a little spell?" I shouted loud enough for him to hear over the music. "Wham, bam, Ala-kazam!"

"That's what she said!" Watson chortled.

JJ threw a towel in his face.

Hazard ignored them both. He gulped down a sports drink, eyes on the ceiling. Probably going through the failed plays and botched shots. Analyzing how he was going to bring it, to turn the tide.

If anyone got a good shot, a breakaway run, a hot rebound, it would totally change the momentum of the game.

But if it was Hazard who buried the biscuit? The crowd would lose their minds.

He was the only one of us who had made it into the NHL. The coaches and the team expected big things from him. The fans expected fucking miracles.

And with Hazard, miracles weren't out of the question.

I thought he'd stand up and become the center of this team, the heart. But he hadn't done that yet. He was still learning to control magic. Learning the ways hockey and magic fit together.

First wizard to play the game came with a lot of responsibility. Or so he insisted.

Someday he'd be the captain of a team—this team, with any luck—and we'd be damn lucky to have him.

Without Hazard stepping up into that gut-solid center of us, the vacancy seemed to be filled by Graves.

It should be the team captain, Lock who held us together, but he preferred players to work out their own problems for a bit before he stepped in with advice or assistance.

I mean, not on the ice. On the ice Lock was one-hundred percent there for us. Ready for every play, digging it out against the boards, putting his sweat where his mouth was. But as the one person on the team I wanted to look up to?

Nope. That was the scarred old defenseman with a Southern drawl who was sitting across the room, still and silent.

Quiet before the *boom*.

I was about to poke him with my stick just to see what he'd do.

Right before I lifted my stick, Graves finally opened his eyes. He blinked a few times and holy crap.

Just before his eyes went back to their pale brown, they flashed red. Devil red. Monster red. I-don't-even-know-what-the-fuck red.

For a second, long enough I knew it was real and I was not seeing things, his eyes blinked *sideways*.

Like, dude. For a second, he had a second set of eyelids that worked the wrong way.

What.

The.

Hell.

I jerked my head toward Hazard, who wasn't paying any damn attention, damn it. Then I looked back at Graves.

Who was staring at me. Cold, unconcerned. He studied my face, which was probably doing things I didn't want it to do. Shock things. Surprise things.

A small, wicked smile curved his lips and he lifted his eyebrows once quickly. He blinked again, a totally normal blink with totally normal man-eyes and totally normal man eyelids.

Then he bent and retied his laces like nothing had happened.

Like he totally hadn't had monster eyes just a second ago.

Monster. Eyes.

"Airing out your tonsils, Donut?" Johan Jorgesen, or "JJ," asked. He was third-marked and the right winger to my left winger, with Hazard as our center.

He and I got along like frogs and mud. I liked him off the ice, a-fucking-dored him on the ice, because he was a sharpshooter with the long pass.

I'd played with a lot of people since I was a kid, but there was something great about JJ that made him the perfect linemate. He knew where I was going to be. Even better, he knew where my stick was going to be. The boy made me look good, even when I was on my heels.

He was a sensitive and could tell how magic was moving, who it was pushing and who was being pulled by it.

And he could follow that puck like a duckling imprinted on a mama duck's butt.

I snapped my mouth shut. He started laughing.

"You look like you just found out someone didn't really throw the ball, but hid it behind their back."

Bait and switch. Yeah. That's exactly how I felt.

"You have a stupid face," I said. It made no sense, but got him laughing again. JJ had this sort of ridiculous laugh. It was scratchy and high and had honest-to-God "yuck-yuck-yucks" in the middle of it.

Contagious. He was the kind of guy you wanted at the comedy show. The one who belly laughed so hard you couldn't help but laugh too.

I chuckled. He threw his old socks in my face, I beaned him with an ACE Bandage roll.

Other players got into the laughing and the throwing. Jada and Thorn high-fived each other and pressed foreheads together while they repeated whatever they said to each other before games. Our backup goalie, Tomas "Happy" Endler, who always seemed to have his eyes on Thorn smiled as Jada and Thorn slapped each other's shoulders.

Then Thorn stood and so did Endler. They had their own ritual: a hand slap, a shoulder slap, a stick tap.

Graves started whistling that sly, dark Decemberists song about getting revenge from inside a whale's belly, and I held my breath for a moment, just savoring being here. With my family. With my pack. With my good, good life.

Right where I belonged.

6

WE BURIED TWO PUCKS in the net in the first ten minutes of the third, got one more garbage goal two minutes later, then spent the rest of the period grinding on that four-to-four stalemate.

Thorn was the frickin' Rock of Gibraltar in net. Josky shut down every shot, stood against every rush, and held her ground like the lives of a million starving orphan kids relied on it.

She was big, fast, and smooth. Even when the game rolled right into overtime.

We were hungry, angry, and desperate to rub defeat into the Brimstones' wounds.

At speed.

We'd already played a full game. Taking it to them in overtime meant working harder than the 'Stones. They hit hard, we hit harder. They scrambled, we blocked, picked pockets. They skated, we flew on jet engine wings.

Every player out there was running on fumes. Beasts were a claw's edge away from digging free. From finishing the game off with blood instead of points.

Still, we hit overtime with everything we had. Hell, we borrowed from the future and hit it with that too.

Any play could be the one that scored. Any shot could be the one to end this.

To win this.

Hold the offensive zone and shoot and shoot and shoot.

Shift after shift we blasted off the bench. Tagged out on the fly, jumped the boards like there were drowning babies to save.

On the bench we shouted at our teammates, giving them our voice, our heart. We shouted at our foes too, giving them the finger.

"Looking tired, there, Smitty," I yelled at the defenseman who had been up my ass for most of the game. "You need a nice long nappy?"

"How old are you, kid?" he asked. "Your parents let you swear yet?"

"Oh, fuck yourself with a toad, asshole," I replied cheerily.

He grinned. Okay, so he was my enemy and fucking kept getting his damn fucking stick in between me and the fucking puck, but he was a hockey player. He loved this game just as much as I did.

A brother of the other.

Hockey, man. At the end of the day, we were one big happy, angry, funny, weird, dysfunctional family.

Some of us would never get along. Some of us would be friends for life. But all of us ate this, drank this, breathed it in and out.

Hockey was life. And we were living the hell out of it.

I shot out onto the ice for my shift.

Graves won the face-off and cleared it back to the boards. Hazard plucked it up and took off. Insanely quick. JJ and I dug hard and pushed, catching up to slide into position on either side of Hazard like the Blue frickin' Angels.

Everything burned: my muscles, my lungs, my skin.

We soared across that ice: fighter jets in tight formation arcing down for the kill.

Graves must have spit out his mouth guard. He whistled, breathy snatches of the other Decemberists song about butchers coming into town on a wicked wind to kill.

That song did more than remind me of his position on the ice. It laced us all together, all the players on the team, tight. Somehow we fit together as if we'd never been separate, as if we'd been here, practicing this split-second play a million times.

And that play was pure beauty. Perfect snap of the stick, slap of the puck, catch and return. And then Graves, big, tall, lanky Graves, who the other team had forgotten had a shot like a heat seeking missile, gripped it and ripped it.

Corner pocket.

High blocker.

Nothing but net.

The crowd did not go wild. This was an away game, and we hadn't had a lot of our hometown fans show up. The exhaled groan was loud, as was the general snarling.

But that didn't stop us from going crazy.

I shouted, JJ yelled, and Hazard threw both hands up in the air. We all piled on top of Graves, knocking him into the boards, and smacked at his helmet and shoulders and back in celebration, in gratitude, in pride.

The bench unloaded and we all broke free to go jump on Josky. It was sweaty, messy, and jubilant.

We crowded in a ragged line, touching helmets with Thorn, a tradition, a superstition, a benediction. Thanking her for holding the line. Trusting her with our home territory, and wanting all her luck to rub off on us, and whatever luck we had to rub off on her.

It was amazing.

It was a win.

And we had earned the hell out of it.

THE CELEBRATORY HIGH HADN'T worn off by the time we packed our gear and headed out of the arena for the bus. Team rules meant we dressed nice whenever entering or exiting a game, but it was late enough the press and crowds were long gone. Since we won, Coach gave us the go-ahead for sweats so we could get some sleep. It was a long drive home.

Hazard had rolled his eyes and left the locker room while Watson and I were acting out the last play for the sixth time.

But as I jogged out of the building, every instinct sharpened. Coach and Hazard stood a little to one side of the bus.

Coach's hand rested on Hazard's shoulder. My brother stood shock-straight and too fucking still. He looked like he'd just seen his own death.

I wasn't a sensitive, I couldn't feel magic worth squat.

But I knew my brother. He was about to lose his grip on that bottomless pit of magic inside of him.

I charged up into their space and dropped my hand on his other shoulder before he tried to turn the world inside out.

"What's going on?" I asked.

Random's muscles tightened under my hold as magic rolled beneath his skin. It was an earthquake in his bones. Like something big was tearing apart and rearranging everything about him.

"I got you," I said quietly. "Just breathe, okay. Just breathe. I'm here, Ran. I got you."

Hazard hadn't said a word. Hadn't even acknowledged I was there. That scared the crap out of me. But he breathed along with me, slow and shaking as more tremors rumbled through him.

"Coach. What's going on?"

Coach released Hazard's shoulder but didn't step back. I thought that was for the best. Coach radiated that Zen vibe and I could feel Hazard reaching for it, trying to breathe it in and use it to ground himself.

"It's not something I can tell you," Coach said. "But you can ask Hazard. He can tell you if he wants."

Hazard focused on Coach as soon as he said his name. My brother was pale. Much too pale. Shocky. But he nodded. "I'm f-fine," he said even though he very much was not. "Thanks, Coach."

"You remember what I told you," he said. "Think it over. We'll talk after you get some sleep."

Coach met my glower. He nodded, more cat and killer in his gaze than coach.

He wasn't sad or apologetic. He was furious.

He turned and walked to the bus, silent as only a snow cat can be.

I wrapped my arm around Random's shoulder, not quite a choke hold. Letting him know I was there. Really there. Letting him know I had his back. "What do you need? Want to walk?"

He shook his head in little jerks. His breathing was coming in and out labored now, like he was still back on the ice playing that last grueling shift.

"Want to sit? Need water? You gonna pass out? You're totally gonna pass out. Random, talk to me."

He exhaled a thin stream of air, dragged one hand back through his hair, then wiped at his mouth. His body rolled through a full shudder. All of that boiling, pressing, storming magic under his skin went still.

Hazard one, magic zero.

Boy was a badass.

"Okay," he said. "It's okay. It's going to be okay."

"Damn right it is. It's all going to be okay. We'll make it okay. What are we talking about, dude?"

Fear knocked on my brainstep. I didn't know what would shake Hazard to the bone like this. The only thing I could come up with was his mom was hurt or dead, or Gen was hurt or dead, or someone he'd done magic on was hurt or dead.

Nothing else made sense. It wouldn't be my parents were hurt or dead, because even though they were Random's parents in everything but blood, I was their actual biological kid. If they'd been hurt, Coach would have told me first.

"Who's hurt, Random?" I shifted my weight to stand in front of him. I gripped his upper arm like I was trying to keep him from blowing away in a wild wind.

"No." He swallowed. "No, it's not that, Duncan. Everyone's okay. No one's hurt."

"All right. Good. Okay. But you are sweating wounded vibes, Ran, like...like you're dying. It's starting to freak me. Talk more. You need to tell me more."

"I don't want...I n-need to think first," he said. "Just. Just give me the bus ride, okay? I'll tell you everything when we get home. I can't..." He shook his head and the magic in him rose like a tidal wave.

The wolf in me pushed.

Protect.

Hunt.

Run.

Kill.

Yeah, not helping.

Random inhaled through his nose, exhaled through his mouth. Swallowed again. The magic receded, back and back and back.

"I got this, Duncan." His eyes flashed with impossible colors. "Give me a little time."

"Dude, you should see your eyes right now."

He frowned.

"Crazy eyes. All the colors. It's like staring at two Technicolor disco balls."

He smiled. It was a weak thing, but a bloom of real color finally spread under his egg-white skin. His heartbeat steadied, and the pain-shock stiffness faded.

"We gotta talk about this obsession you have with my balls, Dunc."

I barked a laugh and pulled him into a rough hug.

The air sort of *woofed* out of him.

"You seriously need to learn boundaries, idiot," he mumbled against my shoulder. "Like, giving me a little space will not kill you. Jesus, Duncan."

I squeezed him harder. "But I'm so loooonely," I whined. "You know wolves are pack animals and I might diiiie without you, Randoms."

He squeezed back once, then leaned out of my arms.

We walked to the bus, shoulders bumping.

"Shut up," he said. "You'll be fine without me."

That stopped me dead in my tracks. Random kept walking like he hadn't just told me his secret. Like he hadn't just told me what was freaking him out.

Holy shit.

He was the Dead Man.

RANDOM CHOSE A SEAT near the back and propped his wadded up coat against the window. His eyes snapped shut before the driver had even started the engine.

I sat next to him, my legs stretched out, taking up space. I crossed my arms over my chest and stared down anyone who came near us.

They scowled or rolled their eyes, and found other places to sit.

Which left me a lot of space and time to stew on the problem.

Random could take care of himself. With or without magic, he could hold his own and come out on top. I knew that. But playing on the Tide, a team that hated him? Trying to click with a line that didn't want to have anything to do with him?

He'd spend half his time watching out for hits from his own players.

It would only take a few well-placed shots, too many minutes on the ice, a few injuries, and the first wizard in West Hell would become a footnote in hockey history.

Coach Nowak could tank Hazard's career.

I scrubbed fingers over my scalp, and chewed on the inside of my cheek.

It was hard to think when I just wanted to *bite* something.

Graves shifted in the seat behind us. He'd walked right past my glare like I didn't even exist. Something metal shifted in his bag or coat as he leaned forward, and then the metal thing tapped my armrest.

I glanced down. It was a flask.

Well, hello there.

Coach didn't let us smuggle booze on the bus. If we opened it, every wolf shifter in the place would smell it. Probably the cat shifters too.

Which meant Graves had either cleared this contraband with Coach or just didn't give a fuck.

I was betting it was the second thing. I, for one, was one-hundred percent behind his poor choices.

Hazard was really sleeping this time instead of pretend-sleeping. No one on the bus was going to bother him since I'd sort of erected a huge "fuck off" sign.

Everyone was asleep, except for the driver and Assistant Coach Beauchamp who was up in the cab with her.

I eased out of my seat and sat next to Graves.

He handed me the flask. I opened it, took a swig. It was whiskey, or maybe bourbon. I couldn't tell the difference.

It burned almost as hot as my anger and worry and fear, and that made it taste really, really good. I took a second gulp before the first one had scorched my stomach, and handed it back.

I licked my lips, chasing the burn.

Graves tipped it, just one swallow, corked the flask and tossed it in the bag at his feet.

"It's just one drink, El," Graves said.

I blinked. Coach Clay was standing in the aisle looking at us. He had a crease across his cheek, so must have been asleep. But he looked fully awake now.

Also, *El?* Graves had his own nickname for Coach?

Curious.

"Touch it again," Coach said, "I'll know, Haws."

There it was again, a first name nickname. Just how long and well had these two known each other?

Graves grunted. Coach's eyes burned ice fire in the dark, pinning me in my place. If Hazard's eyes had been disco ball lights, Coach's were the cold burning flame of stars. I swallowed and kept my mouth shut.

Coach seemed to think that was good enough answer. He melted back into the shadows of the bus.

I exhaled. "Damn, he's...quiet."

"Or you're distracted," Graves said. "Want to talk about it?"

"About what?"

He nodded toward the seat where Hazard was sleeping.

"I don't think he'd want me to."

Graves remained quiet. Waiting. Just staring at the empty air in front of us.

"I might not even be right," I said. "I think I am, but I'm going on gut. It's not like anyone has talked to me. About anything."

Graves continued to stare. Continued to wait. I leaned back in the chair, the two gulps of booze finally easing the knots in my shoulders.

"I think the Tide took him. Picked him as Dead Man."

Silence.

"If Hazard goes to that team, they'll end his career. He's good, Graves. Better than most of us. He's worked hard for this."

I didn't go into his childhood, the neglect he'd suffered, the lack of food, the lack of heat in his house, the lack of an adult who cared if he existed or not.

I had always seen him. From that moment on the playground when he lined up a bunch of little dirt clods and pebbles, and made them "race" by whacking each one in turn with a stick he'd found. It baffled the shit out of me to think that anyone could overlook someone as good and steady and...*real* as him.

And I hated, *hated* the idea of the world losing a great player who hadn't even had the chance to show what he could do yet. What he could be.

I didn't want to live in a world where I was playing hockey without him somewhere out there playing it too.

That was my great fear. That someone or something would take my brother away from me. Someone like Coach Nowak who wanted to use Hazard for revenge against Clay, the Thunderheads, or maybe just Hazard himself.

"It's not fair."

"Life isn't fair, Spark."

"I know."

"Just because you work hard doesn't mean you'll win."

"I know. I'm angry that there's nothing I can do about it."

He was my brother. My *pack*. It was my job to protect him.

The rumble of the road beneath the bus's tires blended with the snores of the sleeping team around us. It was a string of motion and clasp of sound tying us together, peaceful, safe. Like nothing was wrong. Like nothing was about to change. It made my head hurt. Made me want to punch something.

"Tide chose Thunderheads for the Dead Man," Graves said. "That won't change. Can't change. Nothing any of us can do about that."

"You knew?"

He gave half a shrug.

My stomach knotted. I clenched my fists. The wolf in me pushed, wanting to protect, to defend. I breathed and breathed.

"It's an old rule." Graves's words rolled low, softened by his southern upbringing. "You know why it's there?"

"Johnny Morton got killed on the ice."

"He was their golden boy," Graves agreed. "The Boilers' ticket into the playoffs. They were playing as good as any NHL team. They were going to take the cup that year. Everyone thought so. Just so long as they had Johnny Morton on their first line."

"August Carlisle killed him," I said.

Everyone knew about it. Hockey—even the freak leagues—wasn't supposed to be deadly.

I mean, it happened. Even in the NHL. But those deaths were accidental, mourned, regretted. This one, Johnny Morton's death, was brutally public, gruesomely bloody.

It was murder.

August Carlisle had shifted into his lion form in the third, and then he tore Johnny apart: skin, bones, lungs.

And ate him.

The cameras that were recording the game were under court order to never release the footage.

It didn't take a great imagination to picture just how a lion shifter might tear apart a sensitive.

That year, the Boilers lost.

It took five more heartbreaking years of the Boilers coming in last place in the league before they made the rule.

It was a heavy-handed attempt to try to balance the scales.

"August Carlisle murdered him," Graves agreed. "But when they made the Dead Man rule, they added an escape clause."

"What?" This was news to me. "How?"

He shifted his boot—he was wearing a pair of old, thread-worn jeans—and the things in his bag settled with a soft clank. It was almost quiet enough I didn't hear it. But what I could hear, even over the tires, even over the snoring, was Coach Clay's breathing. It changed. Then stopped. Waiting.

"The escape clause in the Dead Man contract is voluntary."

Coach Clay started breathing again. He was awake and listening. I figured Graves had kicked the bag to get his attention. So he would know Graves was telling me this.

I didn't know why.

"I volunteer," I said.

"You don't even know what you're volunteering for."

"I don't care."

He made a small noise, somewhere between a grunt and a sigh, then turned and looked at me.

I could see him clearly in the darkness. If he were a wolf shifter, he could see me as well. But I had my doubts about him being second-marked. I was beginning to wonder if he was something else entirely. A monster in wolf's clothing.

His eyes remained human enough, but he studied me as if he could see me perfectly.

"It's a volunteer clause," he said.

"You said that. What does it mean?"

"Someone on his team must volunteer to take his place."

"I can do that. Of course I can do that. I'll take his place." The relief was immense, filling me with helium and lifting away my anger.

"It's not that easy. The volunteer has to be equal to the player chosen for Dead Man."

Coach Clay stopped breathing over that too. Graves's mouth curved in a small smile though the corners of his eyes tightened as if he were in pain.

Whatever conversation was going on between Coach and him, it was between the lines. I had no idea what they were saying. I was a wolf shifter and a hockey player, but I was not stupid. That other conversation playing out in halting breaths and sad smiles had something to do with more than just the Dead Man.

"You've never played for the Tide, have you Graves?" I was going with my gut.

"That's true."

"There some reason why you've never ended up on their team? All those years, all those teams, but never them?"

"Luck, I suppose." Easy words, hard eyes.

Total lie.

"You have history with Nowak, don't you?"

Like maybe he hates you as much as he hates Coach Clay?

"Nothing comes to mind."

Lie number two. "If this "nothing" gets my brother broken? You and I are going to have a situation that ends in blood."

He blinked, once, slowly. Unimpressed with my threat. I showed him teeth.

"And if I take his place?"

I frowned. "You're not like him."

"Oh?"

"If the volunteer has to be equal to the player, I'm a better fit."

"You think?"

"Am I wrong?"

Graves's head lifted so slowly, it was like watching a cobra draw itself up.

I just plowed on. "You're a defenseman with a lot of miles on your skates. You're not a hot, fast, rookie center. Unless you have some other abilities you want to tell me about?"

"Such as?" The words were coiled lightning waiting to strike, poison dripping from a razor fang, the silence before the *boom*.

"You a wizard, Graves?"

There was a pause. Then: "No, I am not."

And that was truth wrapped up in relief, as if he'd expected me to ask something else.

"Then I don't see why they'd want you instead of me."

"That so."

"I'm faster than you, younger than you, and I gotta say my hits on goal score a fair amount more than you."

"Go on," he drawled. "You could listen to yourself talk all day."

I smiled at him, happy for a moment at that chirp. Just a moment. Because this was life or death we were talking about here. Life or death of Hazard's career.

It probably made sense to ask Random what he thought about me volunteering to take his place. Ask him if he wanted to stay with the Thunderheads where he belonged.

But he'd just go on about fighting his own fights and knowing how to take a punch and standing on his own two feet.

I knew he could do that. He'd been doing it all his life.

And me? What had I been doing? Coasting.

This was something that would be easy for me. I made friends anywhere I went. I could keep my head down and do my work. Be one more wolf shifter left winger in a league full of them.

And if it got nasty I could get nasty right back. Unlike Random, I'd enjoy using my magic—fang and claw and muscle and speed—to shut that shit right the hell down.

I had no qualms about making people bleed.

"I'm doing it," I said. "No one stands in his place but me."

"You don't know what you're saying, Spark."

"I know he's my family, Graves. *Mine.* That means something to me."

The thing in him—whatever it was—recognized the wolf in me. For several heartbeats, one full inhale and exhale, I knew without a doubt that it was wolf behind his eyes.

And then...and then it wasn't.

Which confused the hell out of me. A cold chill shuddered over my skin. What the hell was he?

"Nice speech. Now you listen to me, kid," he said evenly.

Kid? Seriously?

"Yes?" I asked sweetly, batting my eyes.

"Don't use your agreeableness on me," he grumbled. "It won't make me change my mind."

"All right, Mr. Graves, sir. You're totally right, sir. I should respect my elders, golly gee whiz."

He pressed his eyes closed and shook his head. "I'm just going to ignore how annoying you are for the moment so I can tell you this straight." He opened his eyes. All human, as far as I could tell.

"I am going to take Random's place," he said. "When they call him tomorrow, I'm going to be the one who answers. I'm going to be the one who packs up skates and gear, and I'm going to play on the Tide. You," he jabbed a finger toward me, "are going to keep your mouth shut until then."

"What if it doesn't work?"

"It will."

"What if they say no?"

"They won't."

"You think they're gonna take a graybeard like you when they can have a fresh stud with years—good solid years—and a hell of a lot of points ahead of him?"

He sucked air through his teeth. "They'll take me."

"Give me one *good* reason why you think they'd want you. One I can hang Random's career on."

Time just sort of stretched out between us.

I could read between the lines too. Volunteering was a huge risk for him. Something both he and Coach were hoping I wouldn't pick up on. But if I could smell something fishy going on, so would Coach Nowak.

What were they trying to get away with?

"I think we should all get some sleep and think on it." Coach Clay was standing there again, right in front of me. I had not heard him—not his footsteps, not his breathing.

I hadn't caught the motion of his approach.

It was frickin' unnatural, man.

Cats.

"I've decided," I said, rubbing at the back of my neck. "I'm taking his place."

Coach wrapped his arms across his chest and gave me the look. The coach look. "Get some sleep Spark. We're tabling this until tomorrow."

Graves tipped his chin up and met Coach glare for glare, but finally, even Graves looked away. "All right then," Graves said. "We'll take it up tomorrow, Coach."

No more "El" huh? It was all "Coach" now?

Coach leveled his boss-of-the-world glare at me. "You hear me, Spark?"

"Yes, Coach. We talk tomorrow." I was going to hold him to it.

Coach moved aside so I could return to my seat. Which I did.

I was suddenly so tired, I could sleep on a pile of rocks in an avalanche.

Hazard dozed curled toward the window, a frown on his face. Dreaming. Hopefully not nightmares. If he dreamed too darkly, his magic took over and threw knives around.

Having Hazard for a brother now that he was done hiding his magic was a little like having a hair-trigger bomb for a family member.

It was totally awesome.

I moved around until I could rest and still have one hand on his arm—just in case he went nuclear.

Usually, I had a pillow to hit a couple times and some sheets to thrash around in before I could even think of sleeping. Not this time. This time I just closed my eyes and fell to the bottom of a deep, deep sea.

7

I DIDN'T REMEMBER THE drive home. Didn't remember anything except stripping off my clothes and flopping onto my bed with a groan.

I woke to my phone pinging. Message from Coach.

My office Ten.

He had copied Hazard and Graves.

I blinked at the time: nine a.m.

Okay then. We had about an hour to get to the arena. I showered, then read the fine print on Dead Man picks. If things were going to go my way, I needed to know how and when I was supposed to volunteer to replace Random.

The little note propped up by the coffee carafe was Dad's artsy handwriting. GONE TO WORK. COFFEE'S HOT. PLATES IN THE FRIDGE. He'd drawn a little cup of coffee with skull and bones in the steam.

I grinned, grabbed the plates—one of eggs, one of turkey sausage—and got those reheating in the microwave.

Then I went looking for my stray brother.

He was standing on the back porch, in the same sweats he'd been in last night, staring at the horizon. Barefoot, his hair a mess like he'd given it the four pillow rub down.

He was also using magic.

I almost didn't notice at first, too focused on finding him. He was my responsibility, I'd known that from the first day I'd brought him home and promised Dad he wouldn't get into any trouble and that I'd make sure he was okay.

I'd been seven at the time, so Dad had seen right though my promises. He'd known no kid had the skills to actually take care of another kid like a lost puppy.

No matter how much I loved my dad and thought he was an amazing human being, he had gravely underestimated my words that day.

I'd meant it. Hazard was my brother and my responsibility until the day I died. Because if it came down to death, I'd go first, putting my life on the line for his.

I was made that way. It was the wolf in me.

Dad might not have understood, but Mom did. Which was kind of funny because she usually powered through heart-to-hearts and other nurturing things as quickly and efficiently as possible. But that day, she'd taken me in her arms and made me promise that I wouldn't try to take care of Hazard all on my own. That I'd let her and Dad be his parents, and I could be his brother.

I'd agreed, shoulders slumping with relief, because looking after a little guy who was only a tiny bit littler than me was a huge weight I'd been trying to carry. And I hadn't been sure I would be any good at it.

The kid in me had loved her for letting me know we were in this together. The wolf in me had finally felt right, settled, home.

Having a sibling meant that much to me.

But this wizard thing he had going? That was new for both of us. When he was happy, he sometimes made something amazing and fun happen. Like bouncy balls falling out of the sky. He'd once, very carefully, wizarded up a small ice rink here in the back yard just to see if it would be real enough, we could skate on it.

It had been real enough.

He didn't do big things very often. I think he was still spooked about not knowing his limits. There was that storm in the middle of his bedroom with razor-sharp lightning bolts.

That time when he woke up screaming and the wall caught on fire.

The moment his frustration with me got so bad, he pushed me over without ever laying a hand on me.

So I could understand why he tried to only use magic at his classes where he was learning to control it.

But when he slipped up and sometimes used it out on the ice? Well, that was when I loved him using magic the most.

Because he used it angrily. And an angry Hazard was a sight to behold.

Today's show was subtle. It was the yard. Winter meant all Dad's beloved roses were straggly prickle bushes. They wouldn't bloom until May, and until then, roses just didn't have a lot going for them.

Hazard had made them bloom. Full, heavy flowers open to the sun surrounded the yard. The sweet scent of rose and mint filled the air and I breathed deeply, suddenly hungry for spring.

The grass was greener, and Mom's favorite One Republic song, "Made for You," played through the windows, even though she wasn't home. I heard voices, too. Mom, Dad, and me trying to outsing each other on the chorus, laughing, joking.

And there was a little kid, just a little guy, standing in the middle of the yard staring back at Hazard with those too-serious eyes in that young, pale face.

Little Hazard.

He didn't look how I remembered him, too small and way too sad. Just as I was thinking that, the sadness quickly shifted into fury.

Yeah, I agreed with little Hazard. This was something to get angry about.

"You don't have to say good-bye to us," I said as I stood next to him, staring at his bitty, angry self. "We're your family, Random. No matter what happens."

He nodded and little Random nodded too. It was creepy. I loved it.

"They picked me, Duncan," he said, little Random mouthing the words, but not actually speaking. "The T-Tide. I'm the Dead Man."

"I know."

Both Randoms looked at me. "You know?"

"Do I look that stupid to you? Don't answer that. Of course I know."

He nodded and went back to staring at his sad, sad childhood.

"He needs a ball," I said.

Random flicked his fingers and a ball appeared in the little guy's hand.

"He needs a Duncan."

Hazard tipped his head to one side. "I'm not...hang on." His face creased with concentration as if he were trying to find an image of me from some dusty folder stored in his brain.

His face went smooth again and he inhaled, exhaled, and right there next to Random was a little Duncan.

"What the shit, man?" I laughed. "I did not look like that!"

Little Duncan had stubby legs and no knees and his reddish-brown hair was a wild tangle with wolf ears poking out of it. His nose was too wide, and he had a tail. Which he was wagging as he stared at the ball in little Random's hands like it was the last steak on the continent.

"I'm the wizard here, Dunc. I know what you looked like as a kid."

I shoved his shoulder. He let out an "oof," and grinned. "Aw..." he said. "Look at how ugly you were."

Little half-wolf me ran around on those stubby legs, chasing Random who was holding out the ball. Then little Random hid the ball behind his back, and wolfy-Duncan got a ridiculous confused look.

I burst out laughing. "You are hilarious. I never fell for that trick."

"Yeah, you did." Little Random repeated the same trick, and little Duncan turned a circle staring at the sky, like the ball would fall out of the air.

I bumped into his shoulder again. "You suck."

"Naw...I remember this day very clearly. Poor little wolf. Such a tiny brain."

"This day never happened, jerk. And if it had, you know what I would have done."

Random's grin was wide. "This?"

Little Duncan lifted his lip in a tiny puppy snarl and with a watery baby howl, he launched himself at little Random. They fell to the grass in a tangle, little Random getting the upper hand a lot faster than I ever remembered.

"No! No way!" I yelled. "You did not know that take-down move until last week."

He shrugged. "I know it now."

There was no way I was giving up on this fight. "Get him, little Dunc! Get that ball!"

Little Dunc rallied and wriggled out of Random's hold by biting down on his arm and not letting go. Little Random apparently felt no pain, because he just pulled his arm away and brushed it off like little Dunc's teeth weren't even sharp enough to break skin.

Which—not.

Little Random chucked the ball and little Dunc's ears perked up as he tracked its flight.

Then little Dunc took off running—on all fours.

I laughed. Little Dunc tackled the ball but hit it wrong so he high-centered and flipped over it, somersaulting into the roses.

I couldn't stop laughing. "Okay, that's just dumb."

Hazard wasn't watching little Dunc, he was watching me. "Naw. It's perfect."

I rolled my eyes. "Dude, you do not get to stand there mooning over me like this is the last time you're gonna see me laugh."

"I wasn't doing that."

He was totally doing that.

"Did you even check your phone this morning?" I asked.

"No."

I held mine out to him. He read the text. "Why did he text you? Why did he text Graves?"

"Go put on a shirt and eat breakfast or something. I'll tell you on the way."

I DID NOT TELL him on the way. I just gave him hell about that magic scene he'd dreamed up and poked a bit of fun at him being such a sad, lonely boy who, at the worst, was only going to be a few hours' drive away from home.

I didn't tell him that I would be the one moving.

I didn't tell him I wasn't going to let Graves throw himself on this bomb because it was my place to look after Random. My place to be his brother.

By the time we were walking down the hall to Coach's office, Hazard was exasperated with me, totally annoyed, but he was not giving off stress waves so strong it made my nose sting and my teeth grind.

I bounded down the hall ahead of him, smacking the back of his head as I passed, then calmed and took the last few steps to Coach's door. I ran my palm over my hair and straightened my hoodie.

Random just shoved his fists into his pockets and shook his head at me.

"Come in."

Coach Clay sat behind his desk, one of those little red-hooded rock statues he collected in his hand. He turned it over and over through his long fingers.

Graves leaned against the wall, arms crossed like he'd just been in the middle of an argument he wasn't done losing.

"Hey, Coach," I said. "Hey, Grayedigger."

"Duncan, Random," Coach said. "Take a seat."

I took the closest to the door so Random had to sort of shove his way past me, or climb over my feet to get to the other chair.

He leveled me a glare, then took the time to step squarely and hard—ouch—on my foot.

Jerk.

"You wanted to see us, Coach?" Random asked while I resisted the urge to kick him in the ankle.

"I did." Coach set the little rock dude down next to three more rock dudes.

"Random, this isn't the way I would usually handle things, but I decided we should all put our heads together and make some decisions. No matter which way we go with this, it is going to affect the team. This is about the Tide picking you as Dead Man."

Random nodded woodenly.

Graves low drawl filled the room. "This is about me taking your place."

Random's whole body twisted toward him. "You can't do that."

I was glad to hear he agreed with me. He wasn't going let Graves take the fall for him.

"I can do just that," Graves said. "And I'm going to." His gaze flicked up to me. Yeah, I heard him.

Bite me, buddy.

"How?" Random asked. "They pick one guy. One guy. Me." He redirected his question to Coach. "How?"

"There is a clause that allows one replacement. It must be entirely volunteered and must be a replacement who is equal in value."

"What value?" Random asked. "Graves and I don't even play the same position. Plus he's a lot better than I am. More experienced. He has a proven track record, I don't even have a season in the league yet."

Yep. My brother. Never saw his own value, always saw the value in others. Was it any wonder he needed someone like me to keep him from doing stupid things?

"I'm not sure that's how they're going to see it," Coach said.

"They want me because I'm a wizard," Random said. "They're not going to accept Graves as a substitute. Unless there is some other reason they picked me?"

"What kind of reason?" Coach did a stellar job of not letting Random see how hard those words hit him. Breath even, expression calm, hands resting easily on his desk.

But the animal in him was pushing. I could feel it in the way only a wolf can sense a cat. A very angry cat.

"Something…personal?" Random said. "In the past? Coach Nowak…I know I didn't tell you about all of his threats when they happened…"

"No, you did not. We talked about that. Is there something else you're not telling me?"

The cat was ready to attack. His anger made my mouth water, and I had to push my wolf away.

"No," Random said, "Nothing. If anything happens, you'll know."

"Immediately."

"Yes, sir."

Coach grunted.

"I think there are better players Coach Nowak could have picked if he wanted to improve his chance for the Cup," Random said. "I think he picked me just to mess with our team."

Left unspoken was that Nowak wanted to mess with our team because he wanted to mess with Coach Clay.

"Trades are a part of the industry," Coach said. "Part of the game. You'll have to get used to that. The harder and better you play, the more people will notice. And when they notice, they'll be gunning for you. On the ice. Off the ice. In trades and negotiation."

"So this isn't some kind of…revenge?"

Clay rocked back in his chair, folding his hands together. His knuckles were white. He was furious. Not about the conversation. He was furious Nowak was sniping Hazard to make Clay suffer.

"I don't know what Nowak is thinking, but he made this move very purposely. I do think he wants you. I do think he wants the Thunderheads to falter. He wants to win."

Oh, there was so much more he wasn't saying. Things that his elevated heartbeat and heavy scent of rage expressed.

"I don't think Graves should take my place."

"You don't get a say in it," Graves said. "I volunteer, and it's a done deal."

Random opened his mouth, but it was time for me to set this straight.

"That's not going to happen," I said. "If Graves tries to take Random's place Nowak's going to fight it. Graves isn't close enough to Random's skill level to be a one-to-one trade. I looked up the rules. If a team asks for a centerman, they'll want a centerman. Defense can't be a substitute. A wingman can under certain conditions.

"One of those conditions is if the player has an equal record. Haz and I are just about tied in points and goals. I played

Center for several teams in the juniors. So I know how to handle that position.

"Graves doesn't. The other condition of a volunteer sub is they must be of a similar age. Haz and I are almost the same age. The last condition is that they have to be of similar mark. So a sensitive for a sensitive, a human for a human, a wolf for a wolf.

"I don't know what you are, Graves, but you are not a wolf."

Everyone in the room paused. Clay's gaze fastened on Graves. Coach wasn't surprised at my announcement. He was waiting to see what Graves was going to do about it.

Random was surprised, but he didn't say anything.

Graves just looked really annoyed at me. I grinned.

He inhaled, his arms rising on his thick muscled chest. "You're full of shit, Spark."

"Sure," I agreed. "But I know a wolf when I see one. And yeah, sometimes you give off wolf vibes. Okay, most of the time. But sometimes…you aren't a wolf. At all."

That was the definition of being rude. You never just asked someone flat to their face what kind of shifter they were. It was supposed to be information willingly offered.

"Oh, I'm a wolf," Graves said. "Want to see my teeth, pup?"

Random *snicked* in a hard breath.

The wolf in me yearned for this. Finally. Finally. To stand up. To prove. To be…something. Something I wanted. Something I needed to be. I shivered as the wolf strained against my hold.

"Bring it on, old man."

"No shifts." Coach Clay slammed both hands on the desk. Not loud, but enough to break the staring contest Graves and I were about to elevate.

"Here's why you should let me volunteer," I said, still not looking away from Graves's dust colored eyes. "I am his brother. Brother means something more to wolves. I love this team, but I love that jerk a hell of a lot more than all of you together. If he goes, you'll lose me as a player, because I will follow him. Even if they don't put me on the team."

Random made an angry sound but shut up at the pointed look Coach gave him.

Graves lifted his eyes heavenward like he was asking some god up there to give him patience.

"For fuck's sake, Spark," Coach said when I finally looked at him. "You can't follow Hazard everywhere he goes in this league."

"That team wants him dead. If he were traded to the Brass or the Brimstones today, I'd miss him, but I wouldn't try to get picked up by them."

"As if I can't take care of myself," Random snarled. "You always think I'm just going to fold when things get tough. You're wrong, Duncan. I am so much stronger than you realize."

"Tell me Coach Nowak won't try to destroy your career," I countered.

Random pressed his lips together. "All right. Sure. I think he hates me. I think that's the reason he picked me instead of a better player. I think he wants to make it hard—damn hard— for me to succeed. So what? I'll put my head down and play my game. Fuck him. Like I'd let a coach tell me who I was and what I could be."

He blinked, realized where we were and then shot over his shoulder: "Sorry, Coach."

"Noted," Coach said.

"Look at me." I bent my head a little so I could look my brother straight in the eyes. "I am not going to change my mind. I can't let you play on that team. I will break your legs before I let this deal go through."

I was three thousand percent sincere about that, and he knew it.

"Jesus," he groaned.

Graves sighed. "Easy, Spark. We don't need to resort to fratricide."

"The player has to be similar to me," Random said. "You're a wolf, dumbass. I'm not."

"There aren't any other wizards in the whole league to match you with. In every other way, I fit. Am I wrong Coach?"

"Is he wrong, Graves?" Coach asked.

"In the head, maybe," Graves said. "But no, not about the fit. Just because there isn't another wizard to match Hazard, doesn't mean you're going to volunteer, kid."

"There's only one shot at this." It was time for me to put all my cards on the table. Including my ace in the hole. "We can't offer them two volunteers. Only one player can stand up and Katniss this bitch.

"We have to choose the player Nowak will have the least amount of valid arguments against. If we give him any room, he'll find a way to overthrow the volunteer and take Hazard. If I can argue that Graves isn't a good fit, so will he. We need to take a chance at our best bet. And I am that best bet."

Coach Clay tapped the pad of his finger on the edge of the desk, thinking. Graves stared at something up near the ceiling, either wishing he weren't a part of this conversation or wishing I weren't.

Probably the second thing.

Random stood. His shoulders were tipped, his chin up, gaze level like he was in the middle of a breakaway down the ice and pushing hard for the net.

"No one volunteers in my place," he said. "I'm not a child. I'm not delicate. I'm not afraid. I won't break. Tell the Tide I'll be there Monday like they asked."

Then he shouldered his way past me and stormed out of the room, not even looking my way.

I closed my eyes and rubbed fingers in my hair, pulling on the roots.

"You surprised me today, Spark," Coach said quietly. "I knew your loyalty, but I haven't ever seen you work so hard to get what you want. Would be nice if you'd show this kind of single-mindedness on the ice."

I blew out a breath, too worried that I'd fucked everything up to decide if that was a compliment or an insult. "A fat lot of good it did. Nothing's different."

"You and Hazard seem to have both forgotten that neither of you have the final say in this. Only I call the shots for this team."

"You can refuse to send him?" That was an easy solution. A simple solution. The best solution. Hope did a little pancake flip in my chest.

"No, but I choose the volunteer to stand in his place."

"Okay?" I glanced at Graves who was still staring off in the distance, except now he was scowling.

"I think it should be you, Spark."

A wash of relief hit me like a spring flood. "Oh, thank God," I exhaled. "You're making the right choice, Coach. I promise you that. And I will give the Tide one hundred percent. I know I am representing our team. I know I'm representing you."

"What you are doing, Duncan, is representing your brother. I happen to agree with you that if Nowak gets his hands on Hazard, he will make...choices that could be a detriment to Hazard's career. And I'd very much like to see Hazard succeed."

"But could this happen again? I mean, since I'm going to be a Tide now," I had to swallow the sudden dryness in my throat to continue. Just saying I was going to be a Tide felt so weird and wrong. "Since I'm going to be a Tide, you know that team is going to start winning."

Graves snorted, then sighed, his arms falling to his sides.

"But on the chance that the Tide are the losingest team next year, could they Dead Man Hazard again?" It would be better than them taking him this year. Because hopefully, I'd still be there and we'd be together again.

Even if Coach Nowak traded me by then, I planned to do a lot of damage before I left. Enough to let them know that if they messed with Hazard, I would be coming back to get them.

"Once chosen, a player can't be picked as Dead Man again," Graves said. "Random was chosen. He won't be up for Dead Man for the rest of his career."

Relief sent a chill down my spine and I exhaled quietly, a layer of stress lifted.

Hazard might be traded to another team in the future, but he wouldn't be *stolen*. Just knowing that set all sorts of things at rest in me.

"Okay," I said. "Good. This is good. This is great! I'm so glad it all worked out this way. Thank you Coach. And thank you too, Graves, for, you know, standing up for him."

Graves tucked his thumbs in his front pockets and lifted one cowboy boot to rest against the wall. "Think about this, Duncan. Think about what your career is going to look like. As you're fond of reminding me, I'm closer to the end of mine than you are."

What would my career look like? A flash of images of me playing and scoring goals and being amazing crossed my mind. I figured I could look as good doing that in one uniform as another.

But there were a lot of darker images too. Fears. Things I worried would happen to Hazard that would probably happen to me now. Fights, injuries, bad calls, abusive coaching.

Yeah, I could handle it.

I could not only handle it, I'd take over and thrive.

"It's going to be amazing," I said to Graves. "It might not be what I planned, but this isn't an ending. It's a new beginning. And I'm going to make it work."

Both men were quiet for a second. Long enough I wondered if I'd said something weird. Those expressions on their faces almost looked like respect. I had the urge to shovel some words into the silence just to bury the awkwardness.

Coach Clay stood and I followed his cue. He extended his hand over his desk and we shook. "I'll make the call. You better go deal with Hazard."

For a second I felt like a jerk. I had just made a huge decision for Hazard's life. He was going to hate me.

But he'd be alive to hate me. He'd be in the league playing hockey to hate me. He'd be a Thunderhead to hate me.

That was enough.

"Thanks Coach."

"And Duncan? It's been a real pleasure having you on the team."

His words, so final, so different than the direction I thought my life would take, hit me like a brick hammer to the gut.

"Thanks, Coach," I said faintly. "It's meant a lot to me that you took a chance on me. I'll always be proud to be a Thunderhead. Thank you for the opportunity."

I left without saying anything more to Graves because I knew he'd just try to talk me out of volunteering again.

But that ship had rowed. I was going to be a Tide.

8

THE NEWS OF THE Tide picking Hazard as Dead Man cannonballed through the league. The casual but emphatic refusal of Coach Clay to agree to that pick, and his counterplay of me taking Hazard's place, went off like a nuclear blast.

Coach Nowak was livid.

He challenged the substitution. The commissioner weighed in on it. Nowak lost. We won.

Nowak was furious.

The press wanted to know why the Tide had chosen Hazard. They assumed it was because he was a wizard and might bring a new fire and energy as the Tide dug their way out of the bottom position.

Some reporters thought it was just a marketing ploy by the Tide to sell more tickets. After all, Thunderheads' sales were up ever since Coach Clay had drafted Hazard.

Others argued maybe Hazard had hockey skills and potential coaches wanted to foster. He had been, briefly, a part of the NHL.

Only a few, a very few, floated the idea that maybe it was just because of the old bad blood between Clay and Nowak, and that Nowak was using this pick to hamstring his old rival.

But the one thing I'd always remember from those press conferences was the look on Random's face: utter betrayal.

The day after the commissioner's ruling, I checked into a hotel that had a kitchen and a living room and wasn't too far from the arena. Tacoma was only about three hours drive north of Portland. It wasn't the drive that had been bad.

I was still licking my wounds from my departure. I'd been a complete coward and hadn't told the team goodbye. I wouldn't have been able to handle it, and didn't want to put the other wolf shifters through that broken-bone feeling of losing family.

Hazard was somewhere a few planets past rage. After yelling and shoving, he'd gone stone silent.

And when the ruling had come down, he had stormed out of the house and hadn't returned. I'd left him texts. All of them apologies. Okay, a few jokes, and a few jabs.

He hadn't replied.

He was gone. I thought maybe he had holed up with Genevieve, and that was good. She'd look after him. She might even be on my side and tell him I'd done the right thing.

Or she'd write some rage metal song about setting my car on fire.

Not that she'd set my car on fire.

Yeah, I wasn't actually sure about that.

The old Vega was back at my parents' house. Dad had pulled off a miracle and gotten a friend of his to sell his used, but only two-year-old, car to me so I had something reliable on the freeway.

"So you can visit any chance you get, son," Dad had said as he handed me the keys. "Your mom and I will be up to help you find a new place. You let us know your first game as soon as you find out, okay? One of us or both of us will catch it."

He was he best person on Earth. I hugged him and told him that. He patted my back and told me he'd keep an eye on Random for me.

So everything was good.

Except everything sucked hard.

It was Monday morning. I was nervous. I drank too much coffee at the continental breakfast that came from whichever country made stale donuts and room-temperature orange juice.

I'd tossed and turned all night, so I'd splurged on a soda.

Then I'd worried about not being hydrated enough if we were going to have a hard skate and I'd guzzled down a bunch of water.

Too much coffee, too much water, I was bloated and jittery, but I looked sharp in my suit, slacks, and tie.

I knew this was just practice, but it was also the first time I would meet Coach Nowak face-to-face as the newest member of his team.

The unwanted volunteer.

The loophole.

My recent life decisions had pissed off my defenseman, my brother, probably his girlfriend, and my new coach.

So, basically everything was coming up Duncan.

Of course, I still had to meet my new teammates. I squared my shoulders and walked across the wet, dark parking lot toward the players' entrance.

I nodded to the people I passed, some of them support staff for the hockey franchise, some of them support staff for the arena and the other sports and events that used the space.

I didn't need directions to the locker room. I heard them long before I saw them, a sort of low, short muttering. No one was laughing, no one was shooting off snipes and chirps. It was Monday morning and they'd just lost out on bagging a wizard.

This was going to be a less-than-friendly welcome.

I also smelled them before I reached the locker room. I paused in the hallway.

Cat, wolf. No sensitives. There was another scent in there. Coyote? Maybe more than one strange scent.

It was rare when a shifter deviated from Felidae or Canidae. I tried to remember who was what and drew a blank.

This was not my team. I'd walked away from my entire hockey family. I was alone here.

Holy shit.

It hit me hard enough I doubled over. I needed to breathe, but the realization of what I'd done roared down like an avalanche and squeezed everything out of me.

I'd lost them. I'd walked away. They would never be my family. They would never be my pack.

A knot clogged my throat and I swallowed hard. There was no spit in my mouth and things had gone fuzzy at the edges.

How could I have been so stupid?

The image of Random, anxious when he was just a little guy, but so much stronger now, plenty strong enough to take the hits on his own, flashed behind spots peppering my vision.

Yes, he could take the hits, but I was his big brother. His protector. I'd chosen to do this because it was the one hit I could take for him.

We were both adults now. There would be so many things in his life I wouldn't be there for. So many hits he'd have to take that I wouldn't be there to catch.

I knew he was strong enough. It was just this one thing, this one particular runaway freight train, was the thing I could stop.

Nowak hated him. Hated.

I'd like to think any coach would keep it professional no matter what his personal feelings were about a player, but I wasn't stupid.

Hazard was good enough he should be in the pro leagues. Maybe in the next decade the NHL would change its policy and allow marked to join the league. If that happened, I wanted Hazard to get that chance.

Which meant he had to be developed by a coach invested in him becoming the best player he could be.

I knew that was Coach Clay.

I took a few steady breaths and pushed all those feelings to the side. Going into the locker room grieving would be like shaking a baby seal at a pool full of hungry sharks.

I straightened, adjusted the gear slung over one shoulder, and strode into the room.

"Hey boys," I called out. Not too loud, since they were all so quiet. Not too friendly, not too aggressive. I needed to get a read on the room before I gifted them with the full Spark charisma.

Silence.

A few of them stared, but most of the team didn't even look over at me.

Nice.

The All-American blond football-type Captain stepped away from his locker and held out his hand. "Spark."

Tabor Steele. Center, known for his physical play, panther shifter. I didn't like him because he'd tried to hurt Hazard at the beginning of the season.

I knew this would be part of the deal of signing up with the Tide. I'd have to make nice with a lot of guys for whom I had no nice left.

I shook his hand, and gritted my teeth around a smile. "Captain. Where do you want me?"

He bit the inside of his lip and narrowed his eyes, trying to keep this professional, pushing down the cat in him that sensed the wolf in me.

We let go of the handshake almost as quickly as it started and squared off like we were ready to drop gloves and grab sweaters.

He gave me a nod. "Empty stall right there. Next to Slade."

I flicked a quick glance at Slade, got the basics: red hair, sharp features, all attitude, then looked back to my captain. "Just so you know, I'm not here to be a problem. I'm here to play hockey."

He blinked, all cool cat and disbelief on a face that didn't look like it was used to hosting many expressions. He didn't believe my bullshit for a second.

Too bad. This time the bullshit was true.

The silence of the other players lacquered the air and made every breath heavy and thick.

"Sure, Spark," he said. "The game is all this is about."

A player sniffed, another made noise taping his stick, someone in the back got busy slamming things around in a locker.

Steele turned his back on me like I wasn't his problem. Like I wasn't enough to be worried about in the first place.

Neat.

I waded through the hostility and indifference and dropped my duffle where I'd been pointed. "Spark." I stuck my hand out at the ginger.

His skin was pale as a diner coffee cup, and dusted with freckles like someone had held a cinnamon shaker over his face when he'd been made. He rubbed a finger under his nose and sniffed. "You stink like wolf."

"I should." I let my hand drop. "You got a problem, butterpup?"

His chin jerked, tipping his head so quickly his expression would be comical if it wasn't so...sharp.

Those eyes, too. So hazel they were more yellow than brown.

That wasn't cat behind his eyes. It wasn't wolf either.

I took another quick sniff and finally placed it.

Fox.

Right. He'd been brought up to cover for one of their injured guys. Ginger was Icarus Slade. Weird name. Wondered if he was a weird guy. I hoped so.

"If you live long enough," he said, "I'll let you know if I have a problem." Those yellow eyes slid to the side and I followed his gaze.

Sergei Drozdov, the Big Dog, the Big D. He was a defenseman, brutal, old school, fast and hard. He was also a wolf shifter.

Okay, not *just* a wolf shifter, there were five wolves on the team, four men and one woman. Six wolves in all, including me. He was pretty much *the* wolf shifter on the team. The big boy to whom everyone exposed belly and bared throat.

Yeah, this might be a problem.

I refused to go belly up for him. I also didn't want to be torn apart by him. Literally.

This guy had accidentally-on-purpose killed a couple players on his way to dominating the field.

Oops. So sorry you're dead.

Welcome to West Hell, folks. Hockey with a heaping side of blood and guts.

Last year someone had accidentally-on-purpose given him a lower body injury that had him out for the season. There were even rumors that this would be his last year. That he was going to retire.

Looked like his healing ability outstripped the doctor's doom and gloom. The cold dead look in his eyes told me it wasn't the end of his playing days.

When I was a kid, my dad told me to make friends before I assumed someone was my enemy.

My mom had told me that was good advice, but that I shouldn't be afraid to hit first and ask questions later when needed.

My parents. Like, how lucky was I?

This first wolf-meet-wolf could go either way.

I nodded to the Big D and slid my gaze to the side. I was not challenging his authority or position on the team. I was not starting a fight. But I was not tipping my neck to offer him any of my squishy bits either.

This was an offer to live and let live. To ignore each other. I knew I was just passing through.

Coach Nowak would drop me the first chance he got.

There was no need for me to get tangled up here. No need for me to stake claim to anything.

Someone snarled. One of the other wolves.

Big D sniffed derisively. "Leave it alone," he said in his low, heavy accent. "It is nothing."

It. He wasn't even going to acknowledge I was a wolf.

I stared at the floor, clenching my teeth and my fists. Like hell I was nothing. But if I argued that here, if I proved myself to the other second-marked on the team, there would be bloodshed. His. Mine.

I could give as good as I got, but it would be stupid to think I wouldn't end up broken and bloody on a stretcher. He was a proven killer.

I inhaled through my teeth, exhaled the same way, trying to keep a hard hand on the beast inside me. Trying to ignore the howling in me to *fight, fight, fight*.

Big D slammed his stick against the bench, a gavel making his word law, then heaved up and lumbered out of the room.

The wolves—three men and one woman named Sava who played second line defense—close behind him.

I took another deep breath, the wolf in me twisting, simultaneously wanting to be in that pack, and wanting to tear it apart, teeth, gristle, bone.

"Looks like my problem's solved," Slade said. "'Cause you're gonna be dead before the day's over, Sparkle."

Strangely, that was good. That was normal, him giving me shit for how spectacularly bad that had gone.

It was almost like being home.

"You love me, Slade. I can see it in your eyes. You like what you see. And who wouldn't?" I held my arms out wide, displaying myself with a bright smile. "I'm just so very lovable."

He held up his middle finger and twisted his wrist back and forth like he was screwing in an obscene lightbulb. His mouth tightened against a grin trying to knife its way out.

Yeah, he liked this shit too.

Good enough.

"Get on with it, Spark," Steele said from where he was acting like he hadn't seen all that go down.

"Yes, Captain."

I dropped down onto the bench next to Slade and got busy keeping to myself.

No one else said anything. No shit-talk, no jokes, no bad metal music. An ice age slowly rolled through the room crushing everything in its path.

I hadn't seen so many cold shoulders since I walked through a butcher's freezer.

But there was more to the silence than everyone hating the new guy—because if nothing else, that came through loud and clear.

I was not welcome here.

They didn't ask for me, they didn't need me, they didn't want me.

I didn't belong.

I could understand that, but the silence got my hackles up. A locker room was never silent. Someone was always mouthing off, playing music, even if it was just overly loud through a pair of Earbuds.

The only sounds among these teammates who spent more time together than they did with their own families, was the tug of laces through skates, the shush of clothing being pulled on, the clack and rattle of equipment checked and shuffled as it was made ready for practice.

If not for those sounds, those very normal, familiar sounds of hockey about to happen, I wouldn't even know where I was.

Weird. As. Hell.

I shucked out of my street clothes and kitted up. Everyone was gearing up for a skate, I did the same.

Head down. Play my position. Play my game. Work hard. No matter where Coach threw me. Mouth shut. Sealed. Silent.

I snuck glances at the other players as they suited up. None of them were wolves. Cats though. A lot of cats. Remembering Big D writing me off as nothing made me flush with heat. What had I wanted him to do? Fight?

Yes, I realized. Just the idea of teeth and claw and blood showing what I was, proving I was stronger than him, plucked at the inside of my chest, a dull pain like a heavy wire snapping somewhere between my lungs and my heart.

I wasn't here to fight anyone for alpha status.

I'd never wanted to do that before.

And no matter the weird urges, I wasn't alpha of any team. Especially not this team. I didn't want that.

The dull pain plucked against my ribs again. The idea of being alpha turned a hard circle in me, pacing, wanting. Something I'd been trying to ignore for the last couple years pressed, stretched. Something I had no hesitation pushing away.

Nope. No. No way.

So we had five wolves on the team plus me.

The cats were pretty obvious. Anyone with eyes could tell who was a cat shifter. They moved a little like they were more tendon than bone, all fluid and dancer-like.

I counted ten cats. The husband-wife lion shifters were sort of a fascination in the league. She played left wing, he played center, both on the third line. I'd expected them to look alike, but he had dark, almost black hair, a strong hooked nose, and a hard face that was too wide at the cheek. She was tall, long-armed and thin, her hair straw colored and chopped shaggy on one side, buzzed up the other.

They sat next to each other as they got ready. They might not look alike, but they moved alike, in sync, each piece of gear going on in tandem, as if they were two bodies operated by the same puppet strings.

When they glanced up to meet my stare, they were mirror-twins, eyes burning with challenge.

I looked away. All the wolves were ignoring me, and all the cats hated me.

Terrific.

Ginger next to me was a fox, which explained that scent I hadn't recognized. I knew one of the other D-men was a coyote, he'd been the one who had sent the refs on a chase during the first game Hazard and I had ever played against the Tide. I couldn't smell any sensitives on the team.

No humans either. It wasn't strange to have more Felidae or Canidae on a team, but all the teams had at least one sensitive, and most had a few humans.

Humans didn't have physical advantages over the marked, but that didn't mean they couldn't out-hockey the marked.

Plus, some humans liked playing down in the Hell leagues where shit got the realest of the real. More blood and bruises than any of the other leagues, it was still hockey.

Hard, competitive, fierce, and rewarding.

For a certain kind of player, for a certain kind of person, this league was everything they could want and more.

I knew there were no wizards on the team since my man Haz was the one-and-only.

A wash of sadness threatened to overflow the banks of my brain, so I sandbagged that shit before it got anywhere near my tear ducts.

I pulled out my phone and texted Random.

I miss your smell, jerk.

It was dumb. It would be embarrassing if anyone read it. But it made me smile, so hey, win.

"Gonna be last on the ice first day, Sparkle?"

Slade stood, helmet in his hand, stick in the other, ready to go. Only two or three other players lingered, silent and sour.

"Jesus," I muttered. "This place."

Slade glanced over his shoulder, checking who was in the room, then leaned a little toward me. "Keep your head down. Don't do cute. Show what you got on the ice, and keep your damn mouth shut."

The last two players walked past us, acting as if they couldn't hear us, which was a load of crap. They were marked, and had enhanced hearing.

Slade took a couple steps as if to follow them, and I stood.

He slowed his pace to give us a little more privacy from the guys in front of us.

"No talking at all? No yelling? Can we grunt? Growl? If we bleed do we have to make sure the drops of blood aren't too loud?"

He huffed a short, small laugh. I thought maybe it was only a tiny portion of his usual laugh and I found myself wanting to know what the rest of it sounded like.

Did he laugh like a rusty wheel? Like a donkey? Did he have that stupid "yuck, yuck, yuck" we all gave JJ shit for while also doing everything we could to keep him laughing?

"Go ahead. Be an ass," he said.

"I don't want to make waves."

He tipped his chin real quick and the tip of his tongue flicked the corner of his mouth then disappeared. "Yeah, you do. I've seen you play. I know what you've got in you."

"What do I have in me?" I hadn't meant it to come out as a challenge, but I was off my footing here. Unmoored.

"So much bullshit."

My grin made my jaw hurt. I would have laughed but he closed the distance to the ice with a few strides that should not have gotten him that far that fast, then darted across it like an arrow, a flash of red swallowed up as he fastened his helmet mid-stride.

The rink was quiet, no music, no people in the seats. Just the team moving, the timpani and snare of our sport. The slap of pucks popping the boards, the punch of pucks smacking goalie blocker and pads. Skates scraped and sliced fresh ice, hissed in quick stops, sprayed snow in gusty exhales.

Hung between all that was the breathing of the players, the grunts, the calls.

Compared to the noise of a normal Thunderheads practice, this was grave-side silent.

I would lose my mind if my teammates never talked to each other. I could keep my mouth shut. But not forever, and not on the ice. Never on the ice.

It was a Pavlovian response: skates touch ice, mouth starts running.

I pressed my lips hard together and studied my teammates.

Thirty-one was slower on the ice than off it. Twenty was pulling a pre-game Crosby, tracing every line, every advertisement, every graphic under the ice with a puck, and doing it so well I was a little hypnotized.

Eleven and Seventy-one liked bashing the puck against the glass at about head-height. Repeatedly.

Our goalie... Holy mountain. No, holy entire mountain range.

Playing against the six foot six Paul Johnson, was one thing: he was fast, limber, and didn't give up on a puck until he had it in his fist.

He also liked to break his stick and throw his blocker at his players when he was mad at them.

He was mad a lot.

That had played to my advantage when we were opponents. Get the goalie worked up, wait for the flying glove, then snap every damn shot as hard and fast as you could at his bare hand.

Here on his own ice, he came off as even more intimidating.

I scuffed a puck around just skating, limbering up, getting a feel for the team, how they moved, how they clicked, but I couldn't get a read on it.

Even in practice, maybe especially in practice, the team seemed disjointed.

The wolves circled the boards, passing pucks tape to tape. But only to each other. The cats lined up to take shots on goal.

It was like there were two different teams on the ice.

No, three. The outcasts, which apparently included me, Slade and the coyote, Nadreau.

I had thought Nowak forced his team to throw those last few games so he could take his shot at Hazard. But after looking at this non-functional, non-integrated, non-team team trying to get through practice made me think I'd overestimated Nowak's evil.

The players didn't want anything to do with each other. From the shit effort they were putting into warm-ups, they didn't want anything to do with the game either. And the assistant coach and special coaches weren't much better.

What the hell had I gotten myself into?

A whistle broke the silence and players gathered at the bench where Coach Nowak stood glaring out at his domain. I followed along at the back of the pack.

Coach Nowak was a hard-faced man with a puckered scar down one side of his craggy face. He had dark hair and angry eyes and was in combat shape. Everything about him waved the militant flag. The black pants and jacket, cut tight enough to show he had all the muscle he needed to take us down if he wanted.

To top off his asshole ensemble, he carried a stun rod at his hip.

A fucking stun rod.

Okay, I knew they were part of the league. I knew they were necessary. Sometimes shifters got out of control. Hockey players lost their cool. Claws were bared. Bones broke. Shit happened.

But this was fucking practice. This was where we put in the time and work to become a team that gelled. A team that clicked.

There was no conversation or play that would justify the use of a weapon. We were all on the same side here.

Either he wore it because he was a crappy coach and let things get out of hand, or he wore it because he wanted to look tough.

Ass. Hole.

He waited while we all stood there, muscles getting cold and stiff. He glared at each player in turn until they looked away.

And hey, if that's how this game was played, deal me in.

When his gaze met mine, I held it with as much respect as I could muster, then slid my gaze sideways so he could be the big alpha asshole he thought he was.

Still, the silence. Sweat trailed from my pits to my waistband, itching.

I wanted to wipe my face, but no one else was moving.

Someone skated on the ice behind us. I squashed the desire to turn and look.

The rattle of pucks meant the new skater was one of the assistant coaches setting things up for drills.

"Break into teams," Coach barked.

"Fucking finally," I exhaled a little louder than I wanted to. Coach's Mt. Doom stare swiveled my way.

Slade tapped his stick almost silently against my skate.

I took the hint, ducked my head, and avoided eye contact.

I was not going to bare my neck. I didn't bare my neck to anyone.

"You'll remain, Mr. Spark."

Everyone quickly and silently skated off, no comments, no "yes, Coach." They formed mixed groups on either side of the ice, and finally made some real noise.

The assistant coaches weren't silent, and within moments, there was conversation, shouts, and unbelievably, quick chuckles.

"What are you doing on my ice?" Coach Nowak asked.

"Standing, Coach." So much for not being a smart ass.

I thought I heard a snicker, but didn't dare take my eyes away from staring over Coach's shoulder.

"I didn't want you on my ice, Mr. Spark. I haven't invited you to my locker room. I sure as hell don't need you in my arena. But you are here. Right here. In my house. You think you have any power? You think you are worth a gnat's ass to me? You are nothing. And the sooner you understand that, the better."

"Line-to-line, Mr. Spark," he ordered. "You don't stop until I tell you to stop."

Bag skate. Fuck me. He was going to push me through drills until I puked.

God damn.

But all I said was, "Yes, Coach."

And for the rest of the day I didn't pay any damn attention to the other players, or the other coaches, or the silence, or the conversations or the shit cohesion of the team or anything else.

All I heard was my own heartbeat, my pounding pulse, my hard breathing. All I heard was Coach's whistle breaking me into one grueling drill after another.

Hard work became painful work. Painful work became agony. Somewhere beyond agony was this fork in the road. A place where either I chose to hold on to being human and pass out from exhaustion, or go down that other fork in the road where the wolf waited.

Waited with burning eyes, hungry for a chance to chew its way out of the chains of my weakened will. Waiting for its chance to turn on my tormentor and make him pay.

Yeah, that couldn't happen.

I held the wolf back, fought against the rushing, primal survival need to give in to it. To give in to the magic it shaped within me.

Coach knew what he was doing. Knew he was pushing me to the edge of my limit. Knew he was going to find out just how good, or bad, my control over the beast really was.

The whistle blew again. Coach yelled at me to move, to skate, to do it faster and do it now. The *bang bang bang* of that fucking prod slammed against the boards, punctuating his orders.

To remind me he could hurt me at any moment.

To remind me he had full control over me.

To remind me he liked me in pain and would make sure I remained in pain.

Pissed. Me. Off.

I wanted to bite, to break, to tear.

My breath came out in short, hard growls. The beast was so close to the surface, I could taste the metallic tang of blood in my mouth.

No, wait, there shouldn't be blood in my mouth.

I blinked hard and pulled up short. Had I hurt someone?

I pressed my glove against my mouth. It was my blood. I'd bitten through my lip. I hadn't felt it, but a dizzy wave of relief rocked the world under my feet.

"I did not tell you to stop."

Coach was suddenly in front of me. I hadn't seen him move. Or maybe he hadn't moved. He'd probably just told the ice to slide to the side until he was standing in front of me, and I bet the whole arena, the city, and the tectonic plates beneath the continent had shifted to his wishes.

"Skate, Mr. Spark. Now."

I held up my bloody hand, because words just weren't making it through my brain anymore. I was hot. Really hot. But also really cold. I'd puked so many times, my stomach had crawled around behind my spine and tied itself in a knot. I wasn't sure I was breathing hard enough for oxygen to stick. My heartbeat was a hummingbird.

Blood ran down my chin fast enough to *click, click, click* as it hit the ice at my feet.

I remembered that, the blood falling.

"You're not done until I tell you you're done."

I did not remember seeing him pull the stun prod off his belt.

I did not remember him swinging it at my head.

I remembered the look in his eyes right before I blacked out though. It was not the look of an animal. It was something much, much worse.

9

FIGHT. RUN.

"Easy," a woman's voice said. "You need to stay still. You're hooked up to an IV so we can push some fluids, but you're okay. Can you hear me, Duncan?"

The voice got distant and watery while I drifted. The wolf in me struggled, wanting out, wanting free, wanting away.

Run. Runrunrun.

The voice came back. A hand pressed my forehead, my cheek, my shoulder. "Duncan? Can you open your eyes for me? Can you let me know you're awake?"

Yes, the wolf agreed. *Eyes wide. Eyes open. To see. To bite. To run.*

I tried to move my eyelids, but someone had replaced them with three hundred ton weights. The wolf in me began to panic.

I worked harder to move my eyelids, and finally did it.

Oh, said the wolf. *Oh.*

"Hey, there," the woman said. "Wow, look at those green eyes of yours."

Her blond hair was crinkly and pulled back in a clip thing. Her eyebrows were almost black and arched above liquid brown eyes that went extra wide at the edges.

Her skin was browner than mine, and she had a smattering of darker freckles across her round nose and cheeks. Cheeks that dimpled when she smiled.

Talk about wow. She was breathtaking.

I inhaled, the need to smell her, know her, to make her lilac and strawberry scent a part of me, overwhelming and sudden.

Yes, the wolf breathed her in with me. *Her. Yes. Mine.*

"I'm Bernadette, you can call me Netti. How are you feeling?"

I opened my mouth.

Mine. Mine. Mine.

Closed it again, stunned at the push of longing pouring under my skin. The wolf stretched, wanting, reaching.

"You still with me, Duncan?"

I nodded.

"Good. I'm the team's new assistant trainer, which means I'm the boss right now and you need to listen to me. Got that?"

"Team?"

"The Tide? Hockey? Forecheck, backcheck, paycheck?"

Hell. I was flat on my back in the trainer's office in the arena. Not a safe place for me to be.

I pushed up on one elbow.

"Every time," Netti sighed. "I tell a player to lie there and rest for a second and they ignore me and start messing with the lines. Cool your jets and lie down."

She punctuated that with a little push at my shoulder. Not hard enough to hurt or move me.

But she pressed her other hand against my chest. Right over my heart.

Everything in me stopped. All I could see was her.

Second-marked are tactile. Wolf shifters more so than other Canidae. We need family, friends. Pack.

But that hand on my chest, over my heart was more. So much more.

Mine.

She added a little pressure and I did what she wanted and lay back on the bed.

Her eyebrows quirked up. "Well, look at that. He listens. Good job. Do you remember how you got here?"

I shook my head, didn't look away from her eyes. Couldn't. How could brown be so deep, so rich, so warm? I wanted to lose myself in them, curled in that heat, that fire.

"You were doing drills for Coach Nowak. Do you remember that?" She held up a cup with a straw in it.

I sucked the straw into my mouth. Water, clean and cool. I swallowed, but I was drowning in her.

She took the cup away and I made a small protesting sound. She pressed a little harder on my chest, which made me happy, so I quieted. She had my total focus.

"You can have more if you keep that down. So when you were skating drills, you lost control of your shift."

"The hell I did." My voice came out scratched and raspy. Like I'd been screaming.

A cascade of memories tumbled through my head. The prod to my head, my neck, my heart, my spine. Over and over.

I had not shifted. Even though Nowak had shot me full of electricity. I had a very clear memory of sprawling face down on the ice and staring at my hand. My bare hand had not shifted into claws, had not shifted into fur, had not gone wolf no matter how hard the beast inside me bashed against the iron of my will.

Coach repeated the shock treatment until I blacked out. He could have killed me. I was second-marked, which made me a fast healer, but I was not invincible. Even through black out, the wolf had remained under my bloody, stubborn grip.

"Coach brought you in here unconscious and told me what happened. You overheated and passed out in drills. It's... I don't like his methods." Those warm eyes glittered with fire for a moment. I inhaled again, savoring the sweet pepper scent of her anger. "He always tests the new players to see where their control breaks. Lots of coaches do it so they can make sure something catastrophic doesn't happen during a game."

Lots of coaches did that without a stun prod. Usually they used a hard skate and some well-placed insults.

What Coach Nowak had done was abuse, just a hair short of torture.

Netti removed her hand, and I whimpered a little from the loss of it.

She turned to her tablet on the desk against the wall, her back to me.

Missing her touch, I turned my attention to the small, clean room. A desk, the table thing I was lying on, medical equipment including a defibrillator, and restraints mounted on the wall.

The framed certificates were for a Gerald Waite, who had a bunch of other initials behind his name, most of them having to do with physical therapy and sports medicine both for human and marked.

"Where's Dr. Waite?" I asked.

"He's been let go."

And left all his certificates on the wall? "Today?"

"Last week."

That was about the time Nowak would have decided to Dead Man Hazard. Had the doctor not seen eye-to-eye with him on that decision?

Or was I just making up conspiracy theories because I hated the bastard?

"Why'd he get fired?" I slid feet from under the covers. If I was sneaky, I could find my shoes and put them on before she noticed.

"I can hear you moving back there. Just don't unplug your lines yet. And forget about the shoes. I have a couple other things I need to fill out before I can release you, okay?"

"Since you asked so nice." I leaned back and stared at the back of her head. I liked the scrub top she was wearing: black with unicorns and planets and skulls scribbled on it. The jeans that hugged her ass were even better, and the knee high boots were a big plus in my book.

"Stop staring at my ass."

My gaze snapped up. She hadn't moved, but somehow, even without seeing her face, I knew she was smiling. I could *feel* the happiness in her.

Mine.

"Sorry." I pushed down the wolf's demand to run to her, hold her, keep her. "It's just…you're so…I'm just…I want…"

Home.

"Want?" she asked.

"Can I have some more water?"

"Since you asked so nice." She glanced over her shoulder with a smile. "Cup's right there. Drink it slowly."

I drank it slowly. My heart skipped every few beats, which was fine with me. Blood, oxygen, none of that mattered as long as I was the target of Netti's smile.

Because, damn, that girl had a stunner.

"So did you really volunteer to take the Dead Man fall for the wizard or did the wizard talk you into it?"

"I volunteered."

She flashed another smile. "Sexy. Okay Starpower. Let's get you good to go." She took a step, then stopped, her eyes shifting to the door. Two seconds later a man stepped into the small space.

I instantly hated him.

He had to be in his fifties or sixties, his once-blond hair going gray, and built solid like he'd played a sport all his life and hadn't given up his conditioning. His face was arranged a little too close together, eyes just slightly too near his nose, lips just a little too near his pointed chin that was shaded with stubble.

"Spark," he said, thrusting his hand toward my solar plexus. "I am Doctor Sheridan."

I took the hand, shook. He did that crushing squeeze and hard eye-contact thing I'd seen a million times before from unmarked who thought they had to establish dominance with a shifter, as they would an animal.

I lifted one corner of my mouth and stared him down.

Because. Fuck. Him.

It took every damn ounce of my control to draw my hand away and not slam a fist in his face.

"That's good," he said. "We need to understand who's in charge here. Who is in charge here, Mr. Spark?"

Inhale. Exhale. Try not to punch. "Bernadette?"

She snorted and that did everything to put me at ease.

I gave her a wink.

Well, well. Didn't she look cute when she rolled her eyes? And was that a blush? I grinned. She lowered her eyebrows, judging me silently, then turned to the doctor who stood with fists planted on both hips, legs spread, like a total jerkwad.

Wrestling. I was gonna guess he'd been a wrestler.

"I am in charge here," Doctor Jerkwad said. "I will be signing off on all your medical needs. You only play in this game if I say you play in this game. Do you understand me, Mr. Spark?"

What I understood was that Doctor Jerkwad and Coach Asshole were cut from the same cloth.

"Oh, I understand you," I said.

"Would you like to see his vitals?" Netti said, saving me from the glaring I was getting.

Dr. Jerkwad leaned against the desk, which put us at roughly the same height since the exam table I was sitting on was tall. He took the screen from Netti and looked over the info there.

"You're slow, Mr. Spark."

Not what I expected.

"You weigh one eighty. I want you down to one sixty."

I blinked. I hadn't weighed that since middle school. I was six foot three inches tall, and carried the extra muscle mass common to wolf shifters. One sixty would take me down to bones and sinews.

"Yeah, that's not going to happen," I said bluntly. "I might be able to drop down to one seventy, but losing twenty pounds is going to rob me of strength out there."

"You're second-marked. You're plenty strong out there."

"I burn hot. I burn hard. I need a lot of calories to be an effective player. One seventy is my bottom healthy weight."

"Who's in charge here? Do we need to go over it again?" He set the screen down on his desk. I could smell the anger and testosterone rolling off him in bitter waves.

The muscles in his arms tightened. He was all-in for me to take a swing at him. Looked like he'd be happy if I did.

I was not about to give him the satisfaction, or an excuse to bench me.

"You," I ground out.

"Correct. I am in charge. I say you drop weight, you drop weight."

When I didn't argue, he pushed off the desk and crossed the room to a locked cabinet.

Bernadette chewed on the corner of her mouth, her eyes narrowed at Doctor Jerkwad.

She was lovely. She had this sort of soft grace about her that came through even when she was angry. She held herself with the kind of poise I'd seen in hardcore dancers.

I sniffed the air to see if I could catch more of her scent.

She stopped chewing on the corner of her mouth and turned to me, a curious light shining from her face.

Are you sniffing me? she mouthed.

I nodded in short little shakes.

What marked are you? I asked silently.

She puckered her lips in a little smile and flashed her eyes wide for a second. She didn't want to tell me. Saucy. I liked that.

Hell, I liked everything about her.

"You will take one of these every morning with a glass of water." Dr. Jerkwad tossed a bottle of pills at me, and I caught them easily.

The white bottle didn't have a label on it.

That was not normal.

"What is it?" I asked.

"It is a diet aid specially formulated for second-marked physiology."

"So why doesn't it have a label?"

"We remove the label because we don't want other teams to know our health strategies."

He was lying. It drifted off each word like the stink of sulfur.

"Not dangerous?" I asked.

"No."

Lie.

"Not addictive?"

"No."

Lie.

"If I get pulled for a random blood test, am I going to pass it?"

"You let me worry about that."

Which meant no.

I licked my swollen bottom lip and ran my thumb across it. "Drop weight. Take pills. That it?"

"That's it."

"We aren't going to go through any concussion protocol?"

"For what?"

"For making sure Coach Nowak shocking the shit out of me didn't scramble my brains?"

"Coach Nowak only used the stun prod on you once. Briefly."

Lie, lie, lie.

"I blacked out."

"Briefly."

Did he think I couldn't smell the lie? Couldn't see it in the dilation of his pupils, the tightening of the thin skin around his eyes, near his mouth, beneath his jaw?

"So I imagined all this." I pointed a wide circle at my face, which I knew was bruised. I could feel it.

"A couple bruises is nothing to write home about. This is hockey, Mr. Spark. Not a daycare." He walked out of the room like he couldn't wait to be anywhere else.

So. Much. Bull. Shit.

I tugged at the IV tube in my arm and just like that, Netti rushed over, her hands gripping my arm, my hand.

I was wholly her captive.

"Do not pull that out, idiot."

My stomach did a little flip at her using a pet name for me.

Which, okay, yeah, idiot wasn't the best pet name, but I loved anything that she said that involved me.

I grinned at her. What was I going to do, argue? Not if that meant her hands stayed on me. I shifted the hold she had on my hand so that my fingers were threaded with hers, palm to palm.

I couldn't remember being happier.

She shook her head a little and her eyes filled with fondness or curiosity, or amusement.

"You should drink plenty of water," she said. "You're dehydrated. You lost a lot of fluids out there."

"Sure," I said. "Sure." I didn't want to look away from her. Ever.

Mine.

Yeah, I thought to the wolf in me. Mine.

I inhaled, hoping she wouldn't notice. The sweet scent of lilac and strawberry and something else that reminded me of cookies, maybe ginger, filled my senses.

She shook her head again, just enough to jostle her hair and send a little more of that intriguing fragrance my way. "You and the sniffing."

I almost held my breath, but instead I took a huge, noisy inhale. And I mean I pulled a big, big lungful.

"Oh, for real?" She glanced up. Our gazes locked. Held.

Bam. Just like that.

Something clicked between us.

It was recognition, a shared knowledge, like hearing the first halting chords of a favorite song long forgotten. Like smelling the faintest fragrance that brought back a happier time, a bright memory.

It was summer and sunshine and warm, drowsy starlit nights.

It thrummed in my chest, telling me this, *this* was someone I needed. Someone I could not turn away from.

I wanted to stay here, by her side, forever.

Mine, the wolf whispered. *Ours.*

And as that truth hit me, all the bits of who I was, how I was, settled and fell into place.

I never knew I was a puzzle until I was staring right there at the one piece that would make me whole.

And wasn't she something? Wasn't she beautiful? Wasn't she brightness, and sass, and grace, and caring?

Wasn't she the most amazing person I'd ever seen?

A sharp pain raced down my nerves as all my arm hairs were pulled out in one strong yank.

"Ouch!" I yelped.

"This might hurt," she said blandly about a minute too late. She held up the tape that had kept the tube in place. Red hair prickled from the edges of it like some kind of hairy caterpillar.

"Sorry," she added.

She didn't look sorry at all.

"A little warning next time?" I asked, even though I was still grinning. I probably looked drunk. I didn't care.

"What did you think was going to happen, genius? You were pulling on the tubes."

"I thought I was going to walk out of here with less injuries than I came in with."

She stared at me for a second and something shifted on her face. It was a subtle thing, just the slightest twitch of her nose, and something soft about her mouth.

"Oh, my Gretzky," I said. "You're a cat." I knew it was true. Could see it in the arch of her throat, could see it in the tip of her head and the glitter of her gaze.

She blinked once, slowly. Very slowly. As if I'd gone from something to be ignored, to prey.

"Am I now?"

"Yes. Yes, you are. A cat."

I didn't know if I was more shocked or more...no, it was shock. I was shocked.

I'd dated lots of girls. Marked, unmarked. But I'd only dated one fourth-marked, a Felidae shifter, and I swore I'd never date a cat again.

What had started as fun and teasing, dissolved into something borderline vicious. Neither of us had been able to resist the instincts of our inner beasts. Our relationship wasn't the only thing that had been damaged.

A flush of heat smacked at my neck, cheeks and ears, and the old scars on my back suddenly itched and pulled.

"Now, now, Starpower. You make it sound like being around a sweet little kitty is a bad thing."

I swallowed hard and licked my lip.

"I...we can't."

"We can't what?" She taped a cotton ball to the inside of my arm, not that I needed one. I was a wolf and whatever hole that needle had left in me was already closing.

"Hey," she said. "Are you okay, Duncan? I was just kidding around with the kitty thing. Maybe you should stay here until you feel up to going? There's no rush."

"I can't." It came out mostly wheeze.

"Sure you can. It's okay. I got you."

And didn't I want to hear those words? Didn't those words wrap gently around the jagged, frightened corners of my mind?

But she was a cat. And I knew how this would end. I couldn't do that to her. Couldn't let her do that to me.

Mine, the wolf insisted.

But the fear was as real as my racing heart.

"No," I said. "Wait."

To her credit, she stopped and went still. The kind of still that only a marked could pull off. Nothing in her was at motion, but somehow everything in her seemed hyperaware, fully alert.

And my heart caught at how quickly she responded to me. I didn't want her to step away and become someone who would hurt me.

Who would leave me.

Whoa. Hold on. This was all too…it was confusing.

No one had left me. I was the one who had walked away from my team. I'd left my brother, my family, my friends behind. I'd lost them.

Pack. The wolf keened.

Yeah, that too. I'd left all of that. And one person, even if she was the best, shiniest person I had ever seen, was not going to fill that gap inside me. It was unfair to even ask that of her.

"What do you need?" she asked. Even that was perfect. The concern I could hear beneath the words, the warmth that reminded me of sunshine in spring.

"To…" I cleared my throat, worked to get rid of the sourness that coated it and threatened to bury me like a sandstorm in the Mojave.

Her fingers tightened gently where we were still joined, hand in hand.

I could lose myself to this. Her hand, her touch, grounding me, making me more than I was, making me all that I was.

Reminding me I was not alone.

"You are dismissed, Mr. Spark," Doctor Jerkwad said from just outside the room. I wondered how long he'd been there, watching us.

"Bernadette, stop throwing yourself at him and let him go."

She pulled her hand away like someone had sprinkled fire ants on it. Her face did this most amazing thing. She was pissed off, and that put a crease between her eyebrows, which I found adorable.

I opened my mouth to tell Dr. Jackoff exactly what I thought about him trying to whore-shame Netti, when she turned toward him.

"Dr. Sheridan, I know we haven't been working together for very long, but I can assure you I do not throw myself at patients, and I do not date hockey players. I take my professional behavior very seriously and if you accuse me of anything like that again, I will not just consider it demeaning, I will take it to higher ups."

Holy, shit. So much for riding to the rescue. This girl could handle herself. A warm surge of pride filled my chest. I leveled a lazy glare over her shoulder at the doctor.

Dr. Sheridan flushed an ugly bluish red, but he pressed his mouth into a thin line and refused to meet my eyes, or Netti's.

"I said you are dismissed, Mr. Spark," he said, striding into the room and taking over the desk like it had personally offended him and he was going to teach it a lesson.

"Remember to hydrate, Mr. Spark," Netti said.

"Got it." I started toward the door. She walked with me, showing me the way out. I wanted to ask her to stay beside me, her presence so needed, it knocked me off my feet.

It wasn't love at first sight. It couldn't be.

That kind of thing only happened in movies.

And comic books.

And probably novels.

But not in real life.

Not in my life.

And not now of all times. Being here, a part of the Tide, was no place to fall in love.

If I were going to survive this team, however long I was here, with the hope that there would be a home to return to, people to return to, I had to remember one thing.

This wouldn't last forever.

10

I DROVE TO A grocery store, picked up a few things, remembered Dr. Jerkwad saying I needed to drop a few, so I threw back some bags and boxes and picked up green leafies, lean meats, and the lowest calorie protein mix I could find.

It wouldn't hurt me to lose some weight. It might even make my game faster. But twenty pounds was too damn much. I was second-marked. Keeping the beast settled under my skin took energy.

That beast had to be fed.

I'd just try to do it with smarter choices.

I thought about Coach Nowak, and then just…didn't.

It was better that way. Now that I knew what he was capable of, I'd walk off the damn ice before he'd have another chance of using that stun prod on me again.

I was here to play hockey, and that's what I'd do. I just had to keep my eyes open, my head down, and my mouth shut.

I winced at that last thing. I was shit at keeping my opinions to myself, but I would try. Not only for Random, but also for my real team—the Thunderheads. I didn't want to rock the boat so hard Clay regretted tagging me in as Dead Man. I'd do anything else before letting him down.

On the way back to the hotel, my phone vibrated and I pulled it out of my pocket.

I'm still mad at you, asshole.

It was from Hazard. What an angst lord. But at least he'd texted back.

I replied with the kissy emoji and a dog and a donkey and a cake, because I was hungry, and waited for his response.

Nothing.

Yeah, he was angry. He just needed a little more time to get used to me throwing myself on this bomb for him. I knew taking the Dead Man hit was absolutely one hundred percent the right decision.

Because I was his big brother. And there was nothing he could do to stop me from looking out for him.

I let myself into the hotel room and unpacked the food.

The suite was dead silent. I couldn't hear neighbors or even traffic beyond the walls. The silence swallowed me whole, drenching me in aloneness, crowding in on me with weighted emptiness.

I hated it. It made me restless. Jumpy. My life had always been filled with noise, activity, people. Standing here was like being gagged and bound, trying to breathe under deep cold water.

When I'd gone to college, I'd shared a tiny dorm room with two other guys. The dorm was full of activity, songs, arguments, basketballs being thrown at walls, hockey pucks skated down halls.

It had been the first time I had lived on my own. But I hadn't been alone. Not really. Not like this.

I shivered and rolled my shoulders trying to shake off the instinct to put my back to a corner for safety. I'd get used to my new normal eventually.

Maybe I needed something to make me feel better. Yep, I knew just the thing to do it.

I dug the white bottle of pills out of my duffle, strolled into the bathroom and dumped them into the toilet. Watching them swirl as I flushed them down was satisfying as hell.

I whistled my way back to the kitchen, then put on some music and cranked it up as high as I thought I could get away with, filling the place with sound. Next up: grill chicken to fill the place with good smells. Put together a salad with fresh cucumbers and cherry tomatoes and pretend I enjoyed cooking for one.

I didn't bother setting the tiny table. Being the only person sitting at it was too depressing.

So I ate on the couch and watched recaps of the day's games.

Things were good. Fine. And they'd only get better.

BUT IN THE NIGHT, with the darkness of my room broken only by the digital numbers on the clock beside my bed, not even the hum of the refrigerator interrupting the silence, I was still awake.

Random hadn't texted. I couldn't stop staring at my phone, waiting. Almost dialed him a dozen times, but didn't think I could take his anger.

Or worse, his rejection.

I wanted to move. Needed to hear someone else breathing, moving, living.

I wanted to walk down the short hall and check on Hazard, wanted to smell Mom's perfume she always sprayed in the bathroom before she went to bed after she'd pulled a long late shift.

I wanted to hear Dad's soft snores that started with a little hum as if he'd just found something interesting in his dreams.

I sighed and sat up, rubbing my face. Nothing felt right. It was like my skin no longer fit, my own body knotted and itchy.

The clock ticked over to three a.m.

It wasn't like I was going to sleep.

I stood, stretched until things popped, then walked outside the room, leaving the key beneath the fake moss of the fake potted plant just down the hallway.

I walked, barefoot, in nothing but a loose pair of pajama pants, to the side door, opened it and stepped out into the cold and damp.

I inhaled, exhaled, breathing the city into me.

Tacoma swirled with scents and tastes that Portland lacked. Deep, weirdly oceanic kinds of smells: swampy greens, salty browns, rot and wood pulp and diesel and tar surrounded me along with the cabbage stink of something rotting.

But there was more just past all that. The clean scent of wind and rain and a cold that hinted at crisp, pure snow and traces of warmed sugar and coffee from the bakery at the end of the block.

I stripped, shivering from the smack of wind on bare skin. I folded my pants and tucked them beneath the stairs where I hoped they'd stay hidden and dry until I returned.

The short burst of a police siren whooped down an ally several blocks away, and the clanging of industrial trash bins being upended into a garbage truck replied. Late night or far-too-early traffic breathed an infrequent growl as commuters droned toward their destinations.

I rolled my shoulders, tipped my head from side-to-side loosening cramped muscles.

Now, the beast within me urged. *Now move. Now breathe. Now run.*

I exhaled gratefully, closed my eyes, and just...dove.

The gut-clenching pleasure of *more* sucked me down.

One moment I stood on the edge of a diving board, a cliff, a mountain, miles and miles of open air below me, with the sure sense that something thrilling waited for me way, way down there at the bottom.

All that open air, all that freedom, all that thrilling speed and falling tore through me like ice and peppermint, hard winters and shattered diamonds.

And then I landed.

Hard enough to sting.

Hard enough to shudder with the pleasure of it as I surrendered to the wolf.

Hard enough to forget what I had been before this, before the beast.

I needed it, to feel...to connect...to be...*more.*

Here, I didn't have to think.

Here, I didn't have to feel.

I was muscle and blood and movement and scent and *heartbeat, heartbeat, heartbeat.*

I ran, leaped, howled.

This power, this speed, this freedom, I craved it like clean air, shuddered for it like water after a fever.

Yes, the wolf around me snarled. *Yes*.

The city took on the shape of smells. Sidewalks and roads built out of the scent of dirt and oil and piss and food and rodents. Air and sky, mountains and holes carved from the odors of wild and domestic animals. The heady perfume of humans, old, young, sick, addicted, virile, clean, dying, tumbled out in a brickwork of bridges, buildings, bars.

And the magic, oh, the magic.

It was everywhere, seeping through cracks in walls, dripping from stones and trees, slick and thick and so, so rich.

Magic poured in jewel colors, vibrant and shining. Dull pastels caught against windows, wrapped around flower stalks. Sharp white, silver, gold, purple, hot as fireworks glittered against metal railings and light poles, making every sign neon, every car glisten.

But it was the people, oh, the people. The unmarked vibrated with energy that sang, a hundred, thousand different strings plucked and humming. The entire city a chorus of notes, a wave of sound, stretching thin, then rumbling deep before rushing up, up, sliding high and sharp. The unmarked were a song made of a thousand songs.

They were chaos, racket, life.

Always, always, though, I was drawn to those changed by magic, the marked, their magic easy to see, clear, *familiar*.

Wizards: cool sparkling stars and silver shine, steady, explosive, light.

Canidae: hot burning, blood-red, dark and deep.

Sensitives: flowing greens and branching, reaching rivers.

Felidae: silk and muscle, tawny golden slash and speed.

Others: broken edged, brilliant, discord of beauty, of terror.

My people. All of them. And yet...

...and yet I was alone.

I ran streets, hunted shadows, chasing the night as dawn drew gray and soggy across a cloud-heavy sky.

Without laughing brother.

Without loving father.

Without strong mother.

Miles away, my pack, miles away, my home.

I was sorrow, my heart upon the wind, a long and lonely howl.

11

THE NEW CAR STARTED on the first try, because it had no personality at all. I made it in to practice right on time. I heard the voices from a long way off and half expected them to go silent as soon as someone sensed me coming.

But when I stepped into the locker room, they all just kept right on talking. Not the buzz of jokes and jibes like the Thunderheads, but at least they weren't silent.

Thank Gretzky.

I strolled over to my spot on the bench next to Slade who was messing with the laces on his left skate.

My name, written on masking tape, had been added above the bench. It wasn't permanent, but it was there. When I looked up, Steele, who sat across the room, nodded at me.

That was a start. It would take time to prove to the captain I could be an important part of this team. I wanted the win just as badly as they did and would give everything I had to get it.

"Coach know you're here?" Slade asked as he worked his other skate.

I shrugged off my shirt. "He should. I'm his Dead Man."

"Not you, asshole," some guy across the room said. "He wanted the wizard, not your broke ass."

I shot a look over at the mouth.

Dark hair fell down to his shoulders and then some. That had to be a pain in the ass under a helmet. I mean there was flow, and there was flow, but this was more like the damned Mississippi, just waves after waves of hair.

His eyes were the lightest green I'd ever seen, but everything else about him skewed dark. His features hollowed at the cheek and black eyebrows cut a hard V across his forehead, dipped in a permanent scowl.

Resting asshole face.

He waited, all kinds of interested in my response. Like he was looking to start a fight. Like he was begging for it.

I squinted and sniffed to get a read on what kind of marked he was. Came up short until he tipped his head reacting to a movement behind him, and I *knew*.

Coyote.

Philippe Nadreau, the only coyote on the team, and he wanted to make trouble with the one wolf everyone hated.

I took a breath, thought about how to play this. I could not be bothered to second-guess every damn interaction on this team.

"Kiss my broke ass, Wile E." I flipped him off and went back to putting on my gear.

A few muffled snickers followed that. Maybe some of the players had room for a sense of humor wedged in beside those ponderosa pines shoved up their furry asses.

And if not?

Let them come at me. Coyote first. I could hold my own.

Slade shook his head. "Make friends a lot, do you, Spark?"

"I'm here for the hockey, dude. Don't care about anything else."

"Your mouth says hockey, but your eyes say fight me." He gathered his gloves and stick. "No win on that play," he shot over his shoulder as he left the room.

The rest of the players strode out of the room in a steady stream, leaving only a couple of us stragglers behind. I sat to tie my skates.

"We don't like you."

I looked up. Coyote and two other guys crowded close, glowering.

One of the guys was none other than Kremlin Kitty, the D-man by the name of Paski. He was a fourth-marked tiger and it had been hate at first sight between him and me since the first game we'd played against each other this year.

The guy on the other side, Roman Zima, stank of mountain lion. He was a fourth line center who was making a name for himself by fighting his way up the league.

Hadn't killed anyone yet.

That they could prove.

"I don't care," I said. Calm. Peaceful, even. Coach Clay would be impressed with all this Zen I was omming. "I'm here to work hard and snag some W's."

I went back to ignoring them. Nadreau closed in, breathed on me. I didn't know if he was going for intimidation or if he just had zero personal space boundaries.

"I got no issue with you, Nadreau," I said, not looking up from adjusting my skates. "Maybe you want to keep it that way."

One heartbeat, two. He snorted. "Big talk, pigeon," he said. "You think you can take me? Think you're a big hero? Bring it, Dead Man."

My heartbeat kicked up a pace. I inhaled and exhaled, counting down by threes. Hell, yes, I wanted a fight. It would feel fantastic to punch his smug face.

What was stopping me?

Bite, tear, break, the beast in me snarled.

Still, I didn't rise to the bait. I was here for hockey. And I would damn well prove it.

Nadreau sucked air through his teeth. "Pathetic." He turned and stormed off.

And then there were two. Cats.

Wolves and cats did not get along.

I knew what was coming. They were going to rough me up. Give me a couple bruises to remind me of exactly where I belonged in this club. I healed fast. If they were careful about where they landed blows, no one would need to know. This could be just our little secret.

It wouldn't be the first time this had happened.

My shoulders tightened and my stomach clenched. The wolf growled, wanting to turn, fight, kill. Wanting to take them down and piss on them. That was not going to happen.

This was all a part of being on a new team. Being the new guy. A test of sorts to see what I was made of. I could take it.

A meaty fist slammed the back of my shoulder, hard enough I grunted.

Bad. The cats liked hearing prey make sounds.

I turned, squared off. There was no human reason in those heated, glittering eyes.

"Take your shot, then get the fuck out of my face," I snarled.

I didn't have to ask twice.

Paski pounded his fist into the side of my head.

I'd been expecting a body shot—easier to hide, but this asshole was not fucking around.

Everything went buzzy as he followed that blow with a jackhammer to my collarbone, which popped as it broke, and a punch to my side that cracked a rib.

I clenched my fists and swung. But he was fast for such a big guy.

He laughed and spit in my face.

"Fuck you—"

Before I could get anything else out, the mountain lion grabbed the back of my neck and threw elbow shots to my face that I could not duck.

The wolf *howled* with rage. What had been buzzy went black, and sparks of furious pain snapped through me.

My vision went red hot. Caught fire.

I could feel the shift. The edge, the fall beckoning me to leap.

Kill. Maim.

Visions of tearing my tormentors apart flashed through my brain with gruesome detail. Flesh pierced, shredded, wet and thick, stretched until it snapped. Bone crushed, blood bursting.

I swung, missed, swung again, blind with fury.

"Paski, Nadreau! Get your asses on the ice."

I couldn't place the voice. Was having a hard enough time standing against the storm of the beast's rage.

The beating hearts I wanted to—

—*bite, tear, devour*—

—end, moved away. Distant, distant, gone.

A new heart stood alone with me, not too close, steady, beating, beating.

"Spark?"

I blinked, but saw only blackness. I thought I was standing. Slowly I became aware of the cold hard floor against my legs, the wall against my back, the taste of blood sliding down my throat.

I was on my ass. Aching.

The heart crouched. Foe? No. But not friend.

"Get that out of your system?" Tabor Steele asked. Captain. The one who should be holding this team together, the one who should make us click. Belong.

But he was not alpha. He couldn't be. Because I...

"No one wants you here, Spark. You don't even want to be here. But I didn't think you were this stupid."

It took a hell of a lot of concentration just to breathe. So I focused on that and let his words roll over me like slow water. I was still in man form. I was vaguely impressed with my control not to go full beast and tear their throats out.

It would have been—

—*easy*—

—wrong.

"Anything broken?"

I shook my head.

"You need the trainer?"

Dr. Jerkwad? I shook my head again. "I'm fine. Winded."

"Take a minute. Pull yourself together. Then get the hell out on the ice before Coach comes back here and finishes the job those two goons started. Like I need your shit in this shit show."

I blinked and Steele came into focus, crouching. I hated how perfect and golden all-American he looked. Wanker.

"Jesus, they hate your face." Steele frowned. His eyes skipped as he took in the blood and bruises. He shook his head just slightly, his lips pressing a frown. "Grow a brain, dumbass. There's no wizard to save you here."

He rose, and walked out of the locker room.

I sat there for a full minute just breathing. I wasn't wallowing in pity, wasn't nursing pain or plotting revenge. I was burying everything as quickly and deeply as I could. My hurt, my sorrow, and my anger.

Oh, so much anger.

I piled everything I had on top of that. All the denial and disinterest I could muster. What happened to me didn't matter. What happened to my body didn't matter.

All that mattered was hockey.

And hockey was out there, on that ice.

The wolf snarled and strained under the chains of my numbed emotions, snapped at the bars of my detachment.

Because Steele was wrong. I didn't think there was anyone on my side.

It had been years since Steele had been the new guy. Years since he hadn't been the captain of a team.

He'd forgotten how much of an enemy a player was when they first joined a team. He'd forgotten how much anger, hatred, maybe even frustration and fear a player could throw on the new guy. Just to have a place to hang it. Just to have a way to make sure it wasn't rotting in their own head.

I inhaled, grunted at the bite in my lungs. Those ribs were a mess.

I rubbed my shaking hand over my eyes, pressing away the moisture there, then wiped the blood off my cheek and from under my nose. I heaved up to my feet and breathed, breathed, breathed until the pain notched down to bearable.

One eye was fuzzy, but the other was clear. My teeth weren't too loose. I couldn't breathe out of my nose yet.

But I was standing.

I grabbed my gear, keeping my left hand out of action as much as possible to guard the broken collarbone, and walked out to the ice.

Because I was here for hockey, damn it.

And nothing they did to me would change that.

12

COACH DIDN'T SAY ANYTHING as I took to the ice. Didn't even look at me.

I did a slow once-around the boards just to get my stride and breathing in order and figure out how bad the broken collarbone was going to limit my puck handling.

Answer: pretty bad. The shoulder was swelling. Under that swelling it was also healing a lot faster than any unmarked could heal.

If I didn't move it too much, the bones would set. The fracture would mend. I'd be fine in a few days, a week at most.

I scooped up a puck and did a bit of careful work, keeping my left arm involvement to a minimum. From the corner of my eyes—well, *eye*—I kept track of the goalie coach running the big Iowa boy and the extra-bendy backup goalie through drills.

The wolves all kept to themselves on the other side of the ice. The cats were all over the place, taking up all the room they wanted, fast, unpredictable.

I gave an involuntary shiver. I wanted to fight them. I wanted to avoid them.

I was a mess.

The coach and assistant coaches got drills running. Pucks banged the boards, slapped the open net, pinged posts and smacked goalie pads. Passes, shoves, shouts and chirps filled the air. It sounded like a hockey club. Better, it *felt* like a hockey club.

About damn time. And it was about damn time I took my place in that.

I angled across the ice, caught a back pass that had gone astray, gave it forward to one of our wingers.

Who completely ignored it, and me, like I wasn't even there. Like I was nothing.

Okay. Whatever.

I got in line for the drill, dug in hard and sprinted to the goal, ready for the pass.

The pass never came. The guy running the drill with me never looked my way. When he got near enough to shoot the net, he hucked it at the boards instead.

"Nice shot, asshole," I snapped.

He skated back in line as if I were invisible.

And that was just the beginning. I talked, yelled, bumped shoulders, tapped sticks, picked pockets, hustled. Nothing.

Like I wasn't there.

They made their point painfully clear. I was a ghost. I was not a part of the team. And not even their captain telling them to knock that shit off and fucking play did anything to change it.

Normally, I'd just bullshit my way through this kind of thing. But the broken bones, the hitching pain, the lack of vision in one eye made everything around me too sharp. Too hot.

The lack of physical contact, audible contact, visual contact twisted my guts. I didn't step away from the drills, didn't sulk my way out of practice. I was there, giving a hundred and fifteen percent. I passed, rushed, took the shot. I threaded the puck through pucks scattered on the ice at speed.

But I did it alone.

When Coach Nowak blew the whistle I was sweating, shaking, and sick to my stomach.

I also had a hell of a headache.

I missed half of Coach Nowak's rant, but tuned back in for the finale: "So get the fuck off the ice and show up to win tomorrow," he said. "You give me anything less than a W, there will be cuts. None of you are safe."

The team tromped off the ice, and I stood there, partly in the way on purpose, waiting for one of them to slam a shoulder into mine as they walked by. Waiting for any sign that they saw me at all.

Nothing.

It did...weird things to my head. As a man, a logical thinking being, I knew what they were doing was bullshit meant to put me down. But being shut out so hard right on the heels of losing my family, my brother, my team—

—*pack*—

—sent all kinds of mixed signals to the beast. They were my team, my pack now. And they wanted me dead.

I wanted to yell, lash out. Make contact. Violent contact.

That might be the migraine talking.

I really needed to get my shit together.

I might have made a sound.

Coach Nowak stopped in front of me, darkness and challenge in his eyes. There was cat behind his gaze and a cruelty that cut to the bone.

I wanted to fight him too. Maybe him most of all.

It took everything I had to drop my gaze and look away.

"That's what I thought." He spit at my feet and walked down the corridor that led to his office.

I closed my eyes. Breathed. Ignored the burning shoulder, chest, ribs, face. Ignored the howling, raging beast. Ignored the heavy darkness that felt like shame and made me want to find a hole in which to bury the world.

I would not start a fight just to know I was seen.

Just to know I was a part of something.

I breathed. Breathed. Was the last off the ice. I'd held still long enough my joints had rusted stiff.

The locker room was empty when I got there. I pulled off my gear, teeth clamped hard as I grunted and hissed through each painful catch of bone and tendon.

I needed a shower, but couldn't face going into that open space with my back turned. Didn't want to be naked—

—*vulnerable*—

—here longer than absolutely necessary.

So I shucked everything into my bags and headed for the parking lot.

But before I even left the locker room, my phone pinged.

Hey Starpower. Stole your # from records. Didn't see you after practice. You good?

I stared at the message and unfamiliar number for a long minute.

Who?? I texted.

Netti. From PT?

The memory of her smile, her perfume, her hand warm and strong pressed on my chest poured over me like sunlight through rain.

"Get your ass in here, Spark," Coach Nowak yelled from his office.

I thought about ignoring him. Like he and the entire team had ignored me. Just savored that tiny rebellion for a full, long beat. Then I walked to his office, paused at the door.

"Yes?" My voice was dust and grit.

Coach Nowak leaned against the edge of his desk, arms crossed over his chest, a scowl stamped into his face.

His sharp features were stone-edged, a lot of snow leopard prowling behind his eyes.

"What the fuck was that out there today?"

I had no idea how to respond to that. I was supposed to be a part of his team. That's why I was here. That was the *only* reason I was here.

"I'm here for every practice." I gazed steadily over his shoulder. "I'm here to play the game any way you want me to." I kept my tone neutral, for the same reason my body language was relaxed.

He waited until I was sweating. With the pain spearing me on every breath, it really didn't take that long.

"Let me make this clear." His voice rose just above a snarl. "You are garbage. A poor excuse for a player and a worse replacement for Dead Man. You are nothing, Mr. Spark. The moment you fuck up—and you will—I will burn your career to the ground."

I breathed through my nose as evenly as I could. "Can't fuck up if no one will pass me the puck."

Groan. Why couldn't I keep my mouth shut?

"What did you say?"

And now that I'd said something, there was no way in hell I was going to stop.

I slid my gaze to meet his. Straight on stare with none of that bullshit meekness.

"No one wants me here. I don't give a damn. I'll play the game just as hard for you, Coach Nowak, as I would for any team whose jersey I wore. I'll play my ass off for you. But I can't do jack if the entire team ghosts me. I don't care if they hate me. You need to tell them—"

He moved faster than I thought he could. One second I was standing in front of him, the next I was slammed up against the wall, his arm pressed against my throat.

I groaned, from pain, yes. But to my shame, also with relief.

This was contact. This was someone else in my space. Someone else in my world.

Here I was seen. A part of something, even if it was just violence and anger.

"You tell me what I should do with *my* team, boy, and I will feed you to a chipper, you understand?" He pressed hard enough he could cut off my air, maybe even kill me if he were in the mood.

Everything in my brain screamed at me to say yes. Tell him I understood. Tell him I wouldn't speak up again.

But he was touching me. It was pain, but it wasn't more pain than I could handle. His anger fell like a blanket weighting the air around us.

I could feel that. The air, his anger, the clench of his muscles and twitch of his pulse as he fought to keep the beast inside him from breaking free.

As he fought not to kill me.

There was something in that, some kind of acknowledgment I was alive, here, right *here*. He could see me. See I was solid, real.

The wolf in me shivered for it.

I nearly threw up. I didn't need other people's attention to know I was real and alive. I wasn't that needy.

But I had spent all of my life belonging, knowing where I fit into a family, a brotherhood, a school, a friendship, a sport.

And now I was so adrift, so suddenly unanchored, I couldn't find my equilibrium.

I might be a creature who needed contact, but I was also a hell of a contrary dude. "Just do your fucking job and play me."

His smile was sharp and cruel.

"You are a stupid son of a bitch." He leaned harder, cut off my air, landed a punch to my ribs that eliminated the question of if they were broken or not.

The pain was hot and clean and shone like a wicked, twisted sun.

I turned toward it, held it, let it rattle the last of the air out of me.

Before I could push him off, before I could fight back, something pounded the side of my head and everything went deeply, gently, black.

I WOKE IN THE corridor, just a few steps from the exit door. I was on my knees. I didn't know if I'd crawled, or if Nowak had dragged me here.

It was dark outside.

Hours had passed and I didn't remember any of them. I reached out for the wall to steady and brace as I pushed up to my feet.

"Shit," I exhaled. Pain rolled foot to head like a freight train grinding over broken rails.

It hurt. And by "it" I meant everything. I blinked pain sweat out of my eyes and spit on the concrete floor, hoping that would be enough to keep me from losing my lunch.

Not that I'd had lunch.

I didn't move, taking time to decide if I was going to barf. Nope.

My legs weren't broken, my arms both worked. Breathing sort of sucked, but that was the broken ribs, so not a surprise.

One eye wouldn't open all the way and my jaw had swollen so that even the thought of biting down made me shudder.

All-in-all, not the worst I'd come out of a hockey practice.

"Winner," I muttered. Then I huffed a laugh because if I couldn't laugh at my own stupid ass and the situation I'd gotten into all on my own, then what was the point?

I turned a slow circle searching for my gear bag, found it to one side, still packed, which was something at least. Picked it up with a moan, and staggered out the door.

It took several steps and a lot of cursing before I figured out how to walk and breathe at the same time, but I finally got it. I made it all the way to my car and leaned there on the trunk, one arm braced straight against the metal, head hanging, gear bag somewhere by my feet.

It was raining. It took me a while to figure that out, but when I shivered from the wind licking my T-shirt against my skin, I realized I was soaking wet.

So it was either raining hard, or I'd lost some time again.

I tipped my face skyward. It was coming down like Niagara.

Fantastic. I opened the trunk and hefted my bag. My hands were shaking from the cold and pain. Maybe shock. Still, I got in the car, ready to drive even though it took three tries to buckle the seatbelt.

I am nothing if not determined.

"Yeah," I muttered as the engine turned over and I flipped on the windshield wipers, hoping it was rain blurring my vision and not damage to my eye. "You're a real Stanley Cup champion, Spark."

My voice sounded as bad as the rest of me felt.

I wiped water off my face, shucking my longer bangs back out of the way so I could drive. Then I found my way home.

I SHOWERED, RINSING OFF the sweat and blood. I didn't look over the damage in the mirror. Hopefully my marked DNA would do enough healing overnight I wouldn't have to worry about it by morning.

But if the stab in my ribs and the weird hitching pain somewhere between my lungs and heart meant anything, one night's sleep wasn't going to put me back together. Or at least not in top playing condition.

Tomorrow was going to be hell.

I fell into bed and pulled the covers over my hips. My phone on the side table next to the bed buzzed. I stared at the caller: Dad.

I knew he wanted to talk. Everything in me wanted to hear his voice.

But I knew, I *knew*, if I answered that call, if I heard him say anything at all, even one word, I would beg him to let me quit. I would beg him to let me come home.

I couldn't do that. If I backed out this early into the Dead Man deal, they'd send Hazard here in my place.

I refused to let Hazard go through this crap. I was already here, already hated by the team. It had to get better. Eventually.

So I lay there and watched my phone buzz. Watched the last lifeline to home slip away.

He called back two more times. Then it was late enough I knew he wouldn't try again until morning. Maybe later than that.

The phone went dark and stayed that way.

Hazard didn't call.

But then, I didn't expect him to.

THE NEXT DAY I got the same silent treatment.

But I came in with a brand new attitude. I didn't need these jerkknuckles to tell me how to play hockey.

They didn't want to pass the puck? I stole it.

They didn't want to run drills with me? I tripped them, hooked them, boarded them full speed no matter how hard it knocked the wind out of my lungs and made my bones scream.

They didn't want to play hockey with me? Who the ever-lovin' fuck cared?

I was there to compete, fight against an adversary.

If they didn't want me to play with them, I was more than happy to play against them.

So I did. Hard and loud.

I threw insults, laughed at botched plays, gave them hell.

The more irritated they grew, the happier it made me. It wouldn't do a damn thing to forge bonds, but I was having fun.

Sweet revenge.

I took a break when the others did, gulped water while coach gave them shit. He wasn't looking at me, and since I'd had a good hard stare at my injuries this morning, he was smart not to make eye contact.

I could walk into any police station in the country with these bruises, explain what he'd done and there would be a pile of lawyers ready to take him to the mats.

If I had proof. As it was, I was stuck in a he-says/he-says situation.

West Hell was a shit league for safety measures.

We played hard—no, we played deadly.

But one rule remained steadfast: coaches did not touch their players in violence. The stun prod was only to be used in self-defense, and then only when a player was shifted.

The taste of copper and ash clung to the back of my throat as I swallowed the last of the water.

No proof he'd beaten me. No proof he'd electrocuted me pre-shift until I blacked out.

He could get rid of me. I'd looked into that too. It was called a grace clause. The coach had until the trade deadline right before the push for the Broughton Cup to release the Dead Man as barter for a higher standing in the trade.

So there was a way out, but I couldn't be the one to pull the trigger.

"Spark."

Hearing my name for the first time that day startled me enough I jumped.

Hugo Kudrar, fourth line left wing and fourth-marked leopard if I smelled him right, had skated over to me.

His mop of yellow hair fell almost to his shoulders and his brownish eyes were just a little close on either side of his straight nose. His mouth was wide and expressive, softening the harder lines of his cheekbones and eyebrows.

He smiled, and transformed a face that seemed easy to scowl into one shining with light and friendliness. I had heard he was a serial dater, and yeah, when he put on the grin, I could see what the women saw in him.

"Kudrar," I replied warily.

"Someone's gotta cross the street right?" He held out his hand. "Sorry I was a dick yesterday."

"Just yesterday?"

The smile cranked up to a grin. "You got hustle. Keep it up. Coach Nowak isn't what I'd call friendly, but he's not stupid. He'll play you."

"Eventually."

"Lotta season left. So you got ribs that match that face?"

I pulled my shoulders back, ready for a fight.

"Why? You like it?"

"Naw. Black and blue aren't your colors, dude." He glanced over at the team, considering what he was going to say next.

Lots of guys and a few women on the team stared over at us. No humans, no sensitives.

It was weird. All the misfits of hockey sifted down to these rocky depths. There were plenty of sensitives who wanted a shot the league and more than enough humans who liked the pure violence in this kind of play.

But somehow none of them had ended up on Nowak's team.

"He hate everyone except second and fourth-marked?" I asked casually.

"Naw. He just hates second and fourth-marked the most." He turned to me, his back to the team. With all the cats and wolves on the ice, there was no way he'd be able to speak quietly enough they wouldn't hear.

"Let's go out for beer some time. Me and you. Build team spirit. Mend the rip between cat and dog, eh?"

I had no idea why he hadn't tried that with any of the other wolves on the team, but hell, maybe he had. He was risking a lot by reaching out, so I reached right back.

"Why me?"

That surprised him. He gave me a full, considering look, lot of beast shining through his gaze. Not like he was sizing me up for a kill, but like he was confused.

"You got that thing. That wolf thing. It's. You know. And I think the team could use..." He shook his shaggy head. "You know what I mean, Ace?"

131

I had no idea what he was talking about. "Probably not, but you can tell me over food. Name the time and place, I'll buy the beer."

"Attaboy, Sparky. Like I said, good hustle." He slapped my ankle and skated back to join the team. Most of them were glaring at me. I just waved and smiled.

Practice wrapped up like it had yesterday. Everyone left the ice and I stayed behind, skating, messing with the pucks, banking shots to slither to a stop closer to the equipment handler.

Talking to Kudrar had set off a little fizz of hope in my head. The need to play, to prove what I could do and who I could be built in my blood like a soda that had been shaken too hard.

When I left the ice and stripped to shower in the empty locker room, I knew either Coach Nowak would play me like Kudrar had said, or he would cut me free.

At least I wouldn't be stuck here in neutral.

I grunted as hot water sluiced my skin. The bruise from my neck to ass was magnificent shades of purple and black with weird red spots.

The bruise across my swollen ribs was even more colorful.

But hey, I'd stopped pissing blood. Things were looking up.

"Nice ass, Spark. You get the number of the truck that ran you over?"

I threw a quick look over my shoulder. Netti leaned on the doorway to the showers, the grin at odds with the concern in her eyes.

"You should see the truck." I wiped my hair back and resisted the temptation to cover my neck with my hand, or turn all the way around. Just because she was a trainer and had probably seen every player naked, didn't mean she needed a Full Monty in her face.

I was a classy guy. I liked to go on at least one date before I bared all.

"After the shower, come see me." She didn't wait for me to answer, just walked away.

I turned off the water, dried, and dressed, all the while talking myself into and out of going to see her. I didn't need her questions about my injuries, and sure as hell didn't want her pity.

Also, I was sort of ducking Dr. Jerkwad of the diet-pill scam. What a loser.

The idea that maybe she wanted to see me for a personal, not professional reason flapped through my brain. But she'd told Dr. Jerkwad she didn't date hockey players.

I almost left the building, but curiosity steered me to the exam room door. I peeked in. No Dr. Jerkwad.

"You wanted to see me?"

She stood at the desk, tablet in hand. "You haven't been in here after practices. So I decided to come to you. I was going to ask why you haven't come by, but after seeing those bruises, I'm gonna change my question to who did you get in a fight with?"

Would she believe me if I said two guys on the team jumped me? Would she believe me if I told her Nowak got in a couple cheap shots too?

Maybe.

Would she be in any danger of losing her job if I told her those things?

Also maybe.

But the big question, the one that kept my mouth shut was, would she go to the press and get me pulled so that Hazard had to replace me?

That seemed possible. But it wasn't like I could say I'd fallen down a flight of stairs.

"New neighborhood," I lied with all the charm I had. "New bars. Got a little too opinionated about the Seahawks."

"Is that right?" Her eyes were searching, flicking across my face and down the rest of my body, watching my breathing, my movements as if she could see the injuries through my clothes.

"Were these people at the bar members of the team?"

I shrugged. "I've been wanting to ask you something too. What do you say we have coffee sometime?"

That had the effect I wanted. She stopped cataloging my injuries and stared me straight in the eyes. "I don't date hockey players."

"I'm not really playing right now, so…"

133

"Neither am I."

Well, that was crystal clear. She wanted none of me.

"All right then." I tapped the doorframe. "See ya, Netti. I'll come by after next practice."

"Spark," she started. "I need to see you for—you have to come in, or you could get cut. I know you can hear me."

But I was already down the hallway and heading out into the cold Tacoma air.

I DROPPED DOWN INTO an open seat up in the nosebleed section. Healthy scratch meant I wasn't playing. No surprise. But Nowak couldn't keep me from showing up to watch the game if I felt like it.

The crowd was totally into it, howling and shouting and waving blue flags that were supposed to make it look like the entire audience was made of water.

After a few songs, and the audience shouting: "*goat eyes*"—well, probably "*go tides*,"—the Tacoma Tide and the Redding Rumblers came out, spinning tight laps on their sides of the blue lines. Goalies dropped to the ice, stretching and contorting.

Lights flashed, blue and green washing across the arena. It was hype, but nothing like the big leagues. No holographic projections, no explosions or cannons, no fucking Vegas Knights medieval LARPing in the middle of the ice.

A local woman in a tuxedo belted out the National Anthem, and then it was time for puck drop.

I leaned forward, elbows digging into knees. I grunted as pain lanced my ribs, then sat back so I could breathe and scowled down at the ice.

The Tide were off to a slow start. The Rumblers were already in third gear out of the blocks pushing hard, working together with quick passes as they rushed the neutral zone to keep the game in their offensive zone.

It wasn't a hard-hitting physical opening, but they had speed.

Watching the Tide stand around blinking stupidly while the Rumblers outskated and outshot them made me crazy.

I yelled with the crowd at a missed drop pass that ended in a turnover, groaned at the breakaway rush on the net which our goalie managed to hold off alone because our D-men were still halfway across the ice.

Good thing Johnson was the size of a Zamboni.

Good thing he moved fast.

Goalies were beautiful freaks of nature.

I muttered and swore at every shot we took on goal that was nowhere near the damn goal, and the sloppy offensive pressure.

It was a hard game to watch. Each period was worse than the last. We got slower, sloppier, and angrier.

Which was exactly what the crowd wanted. Well, violence and a winning game would probably be their preference, but this was West Hell. Fans wanted a little blood, a little fang, and a little pain.

Heading into the third period, something snapped.

My shoulders hunched, my vision went sharp and clear, every instinct in me narrowed and fastened onto one player on the ice.

Kudrar, our fourth line left winger, the leopard who had wanted a beer with me was positioned for the puck as four players trapped against the boards fought for it.

The Rumbler covering Kudrar had had some kind of hair up his chute all game. He'd made a point to hit and check and target Kudrar no matter what was happening on the ice.

These two must have history. Part of game play was getting under the other player's skin, getting in their head. That, and dirty hits and slashes the refs never caught.

One minute Kudrar and the Rumbler were jabbing at each other while jockeying for position by the scrum on the boards, then their gloves hit the deck and fists went flying.

The crowd broke into a thunderous roar for blood, for pain, for payback. The entire arena surged to its feet to watch two guys beat the crap out of each other.

And then the chant started.

Shift, shift, shift, shift.

The players lost it. Jerseys tore, helmets scattered, breakaway straps on skates popped as muscles heaved and stretched and twisted.

A leopard and a tiger faced each other and snarled.

The crowd lost its bloody mind.

The other players put their backs to the boards and dropped to their knees. They weren't facing away from the cats, because good damn luck if anyone tried to get a bunch of marked to turn away from predators in their midst.

The two unmarked Rumblers and their sensitive cleared off the ice completely.

All four of the refs had stun prods in their hands, ready to put a very quick end to this if they had to.

Or they could let the cats fight it out.

The crowd was a huge, living thing. A single-minded entity that wanted pain, that craved it, swaying forward with grasping hands like an addict begging for a hit.

The snarl and growl of the cats pricked up the hair on my arms and knuckled chills down my spine. I palmed the back of my neck reflectively guarding the old scar there.

I didn't care how stupid I looked. I was not going to get bit by some rando in the crowd who couldn't keep it in check.

The fight should have been stopped about ten seconds into it, but the refs let it run a full minute.

Sixty full seconds of battle between two huge, feral beasts was a hell of a long time.

And there was blood.

Restless teammates already pushed to the edge of exhaustion lost control of the magic churning inside. They gave way to their beasts, though they did it with practiced moves, like someone who was sick but didn't want to get barf on their shoes.

Players stripped out of as much gear as possible, then dropped to their knees and shifted, still near the boards. Two players on the bench hopped the board and stripped before falling to their knees.

Extra security flooded out onto the ice, and then, at that sixty second marker, something went *crunch*.

The entire crowd moaned, one huge hollow, "oooooooh."

Silence crashed down, plunging us in ice water.

There was stillness. Everywhere. The players on the ice. The refs and enforcement. The teams behind the benches. The coaches.

The crowd, that massive, living thing, held its breath.

Because they knew, we knew. We *felt* that break as if it were our bones, our flesh smashed and torn.

The cats were the first to break the silence. Players on both teams who had shifted gave out a gut-deep wail, the yowl acrid with shared pain. Felidae shifters in the crowd joined the cry.

The Canidae shifters picked it up, on the ice, off the ice, howling, howling, howling.

Knowing one of ours was wounded could result in an attack, the beasts within sensing weakness, prey. Or it could trigger the instinct to protect. To stand between one of our own and the threat.

But it was more than just base instinct and magic that drew us together. It was loss.

We mourned the pain of one of ours who had fallen and might not rise to fight again.

I didn't have to see it to know what had happened, it was there in our voices, it was there in the magic that tied us all together on a level we could not ignore.

Still, I could not tear my gaze away from the ice. Could not look away from Kudrar, my teammate. The pain had snapped him back into human form, and he did not look good. His gaze stuttered and jagged across the crowd, up and up until he saw me.

There was something in his wild look. Maybe an apology. Maybe just pain. But he was looking at me, and me alone. I wasn't going to let him down. If he needed me, I'd be there for him, a rock in this ocean of crazy.

I nodded. "You're gonna be fine. We got you. I've got you."

His eyes glittered with relief and then they rolled back into his head, showing nothing but white as he passed the hell out.

I looked away from him, and every Canidae gaze on the ice, on the bench, was fastened on me. They stared as if I were suddenly unveiled, as if they saw the whole of me in a way no one ever had before.

I couldn't take it. Couldn't take the unspoken language they shouted at me, yelled silently, asking, wanting.

What the hell was going on? I shook my head trying to clear the noise.

The beast in me pushed, paced, wanting that noise, wanting those gazes. The wolf knew exactly why all the wolves were looking my way.

Alpha.

No. Chills shuddered across my skin, tightened my stomach. The beast in me wanted out, wanted to go down to that ice where I didn't belong so it could force each of those wolves to recognize me.

To see me.

To submit.

And then everything changed. The crowd was suddenly restless, murmuring, shouting, whistling as paramedics rushed onto the ice to Kudrar. The trainers from both teams were out there too, including Dr. Jerkwad and Netti, who was a step ahead of all the others.

Now that it made no difference whatsoever, the refs finally used the stun prod on the tiger, who dropped to the ice, shaking his head as he shifted back to man. He didn't appear to be badly injured.

But Kudrar still wasn't moving. There were plenty of skilled professionals there to make sure that heavy injuries...

...crushed pelvis, broken femur, shattered vertebra...

...were taken care of quickly as possible.

Shifting from cat to man would have mended some things, but not all of it. And not always in the way it should be mended.

I stayed standing while Kudrar was loaded onto a gurney, strapped in, and put on an IV line. I stayed standing while the shifted players were led off the ice so they could change back into their human forms in the rooms set aside for that sort of thing.

I stayed standing while the audience applauded the medics taking Kudrar away, and while the remaining players tapped sticks on the ice or boards in solidarity.

I stayed standing while the announcer gave a bland recrimination of the violence, recited the level of fighting that was not allowed in the WHHL and as an afterthought, gave a wish of a speedy recovery to Kudrar.

All that time, every second, every heartbeat, the wolves stared hungrily at me.

And then, just like that, the music queued back up, everyone took their place, and it was time to play the rest of the period.

Hockey must go on.

The rest of the game was strange and strained. The blood had been scraped away, new water poured to ice up the spot where a player had bled so hard and fast. The repair was so good, nothing about that piece of ice looked any different than the rest of the ice.

Except the players avoided it as if it were a pool of blood, as if it were still fouled by magic that had gone too far.

We, of course, lost.

13

I WAITED FOR THE crowd to leave then walked down to the locker room. I'd never been welcome there, not really, but the atmosphere in the room shifted when I walked in. Not exactly anger, just a tension I couldn't name.

"Looking slow as shit." All eyes were on me. "But good control on magic. That could have been a madhouse out there. Glad no one else dropped gloves. I'm gonna go check on Kudrar. Anyone with me?"

No one said anything. Slade tipped his head so far to one side he looked like a sweaty little orange owl. He was frowning at me like I'd just spoken in tongues.

Finally, "I'll come with you." Quiet but firm.

Big D grunted.

"Anyone else?" I scanned the room, holding eye contact until each player found something else to look at.

And the second strangest thing happened. Every Canidae head swiveled toward Big D.

So I squared off from him and held his gaze. "You with me?"

His gaze was iron and ice. He did not look away. "No."

And just like that, everyone went back to ignoring me.

Except Slade. "I'll drive," he said. "I'm going with you. I'm taking you."

That was fine with me because my wolf was howling, begging for a fight. It was better I didn't get behind the wheel. We left the arena behind us and piled into Slade's Toyota Camry.

Keeping the wolf locked down was taking all of my concentration and some deep breathing exercises.

Slade didn't say anything, and I left him to it until he almost drove into the median separating oncoming traffic.

"What the hell, Slade?" I gripped the chicken bar above the door and leaned as he rocked the damn car up on two wheels.

We tipped one way, tipped the other, before skidding back down to smooth pavement.

Slade didn't even break a sweat. "What?"

I opened my mouth, closed it. Pointed out the window. "Watch the damn road."

"Grow a pair."

I sputtered and stared at him. Which turned out to be a mistake. He had this weird thing of staring out his side window for several dozen seconds too long before he returned his attention to the traffic in front of him. He was more interested in the signs and businesses and people and trees and trash cans than actually driving.

It wouldn't be so bad if he didn't also constantly fiddle with the buttons and screens inside his car. Heat, cold, up, down, volume, windows, seat settings.

I was horrified.

"If you kill us, I'm dragging you down to hell with me."

He snorted and went on twitching, as if he couldn't get his hands on the world around him fast enough. He constantly moved hands, feet, face, head, shoulders, elbows and knees. It was hypnotic, just this side of spastic, but didn't seem out of control.

Maybe he was doing it to see if I'd crack.

In case that was his deal, I sat back and did everything to appear like I was there to enjoy the show.

By the time we reached the hospital, he had settled down, though if that was because he'd run out of interesting sights and things to fiddle with, or because he was done screwing with me, I had no idea.

The woman at the desk wouldn't let us see Kudrar since we were friends, not family.

But it was a busy place and we were two determined hockey players. We found an Employees Only door or two, shoved through and took a few out-of-the-way stairwells, following our noses.

Kudrar's room was big enough to hold several beds, all separated by curtains.

We sniffed our way to his curtain and slipped behind it. Kudrar was still in man form, pale as hell, but he breathed steadily, which was good. His heartbeat sounded good too, both on the machine and the low dull thud my wolf senses picked up.

Slade stood stock still for a moment, as if he were listening with every sense he owned, and then he sort of relaxed. He strolled over to mess with a machine and watched me from the corner of his eye.

I walked to the head of the bed and put my hand carefully on Kudrar's shoulder that wasn't bandaged. From the wrappings on his head, his shoulder, his arm, and the cast on his left leg and sling under his hips, he was a mess.

"Hey, Hugo, it's Duncan. Just came by to say you're going to be fine. And everyone on the team wants you to get better. You need to take some time and heal up the right way, okay? We can't be down a good winger for too long. You were the only one out there with hustle tonight, buddy."

I didn't know if he heard me. His heartbeat seemed to even out a little more, like maybe some of his pain had lifted. I kept my hand on his shoulder. Contact always made me feel better when I was sick.

Slade made his way around the small space, brushing fingers across everything. He turned away from the machine he shouldn't even think about messing with.

"Good?" he asked.

No, not good. Nothing was good. A teammate, *my* teammate, was broken. Even if none of them liked me, now that I was on the team, I wanted to protect them. On the ice, and off.

Which was fucked up, since they'd made it pretty clear they hated me.

"Not really good, no," I admitted. "But good enough for now."

Slade stood on the other side of Kudrar and bent to study his face. I didn't know a lot about fox shifters, didn't know if he had senses I didn't possess as a wolf.

He pressed his forehead to Kudrar's, just a brief moment. His lips moved silently. Maybe a prayer.

Then he straightened and shoved his hands into his back pockets, as if by locking them there he would remember not to touch anything.

"Done getting your germs on everything?" I asked.

He pivoted, and walked toward the opening in the curtain.

"Yes, Spark," I said in a snotty tone, following him. "I'm done being gross, thanks for asking."

He threw me a quick grin, an even quicker finger and strode more quietly than I expected from a hockey player in work boots.

We left the hospital the same way we came in—quietly and unnoticed—and then were across the rainy parking lot.

He unlocked his car and we both climbed in.

"Why'd you come to see him?" he asked. He started the car, backed out of the parking lot, rolling his window up, down, up, down, a quarter of an inch.

It was annoying as all hell.

I was starting to like the guy.

"You mean why tonight?"

"Why at all?"

"Because he's my teammate and he got mauled within an inch of his life. Why? There gotta be another reason?"

He slid a look my way. "Could be another reason."

I had no idea what he was talking about.

He stopped messing with his window and started messing with mine, rolling it down a half inch, to let in rain and a slap of cold air, then up again.

Jerk.

I jabbed at the button and held it so he couldn't mess with the window anymore.

He chuffed a laugh and got busy changing the rate of the windshield wipers.

"Kudrar got hurt," he said, like that was news.

"You are the most annoying person I've ever met."

143

"He looked for you. When he got hurt."

I thought I was the only one who saw that.

"So?"

"So. That's what I mean. He knew where you were...he knew you would see him and...look, that isn't a little injury. He'll be out of the game for the rest of the year."

"Yeah." Even being fourth-marked and very quick to heal, it was enough to lay him out. "We're gonna be down a winger."

He gave me a weird look like he expected something different. Something better.

"It was a shit fight and the coaches should have been out there to de-escalate the situation," I said. "If not the coaches, the captains. And if not the captains, then...someone."

The alphas. That's who should have stepped in. The alphas of the teams should have helped their teammates keep the beast instinct in line. Should have tipped the scales toward fight, not kill.

But this wasn't my team, not really. I didn't have a say in what happened or didn't happen on the ice.

You could. The wolf deep in my brain said. *You should.*

I ignored it.

"Don't be stupid, Spark. You might be a loser, but you know."

"Know what?"

"He looked for you. Out of everyone in that arena, you were the one he needed to see."

"Because he was hurt."

"Because he thought he was dying or crippled."

"Okay?"

He stopped messing with the speaker balance: front, back, right, left, middle. Front, back...his hand stilling on the steering wheel. "How long have you been playing hockey?"

"Since I was five."

"You ever play on a team that was only second and fourth-marked?"

Only shifters. Only Canidae and Felidae.

Every team I'd been on had included a mix of people. There'd always been sensitives and non-magic people too since all the teams below the WHHL were mixed.

"No."

He stabbed through the preset stations, then hit something that let the radio just wander through whatever station it could get reception for. I turned the volume down because I didn't care if we were listening to trombones or talk shows, but I didn't need to hear any of it at full blast.

"It's a…" He paused for a second and focused on just driving. He glanced at me, then away again.

"It's a thing," he said. "When someone is hurt. I mean really hurt. Not just a fracture or break or bruise. When it's a big thing, a hard thing, when instinct is telling you it's not just bad, it's passing horrible and it might even be the…ending of…something. You…you look for the person you know has your back. You look for the person you…trust. The one who will stand over you and…stand against others for you. You look for your…"

Alpha, the voice in my head supplied.

"…leader," Slade finished.

Yeah, I knew exactly what he was implying. But I also knew how team dynamics worked.

Big D should be alpha.

Even as I thought it, I knew that wasn't right. The wolves fell into line and did exactly what he wanted, but the cats stayed to themselves and ignored him.

An alpha was the touchstone for all the shifters, not just half of them. An alpha had to be a friend to all, even the unmarked. An alpha had to be a protector of all.

Big D was there for the wolves, but he didn't give a damn about the cats.

And that was the thing about an alpha, wasn't it? It was more than being the big guy, the tough guy like Big D. It was more than being a leader who could get everyone moving together like a captain. It was about being a person other people could be vulnerable with.

Being the one who could be trusted to take care of shit they couldn't deal with, take care of them if they were injured, not the little hurts, but the big stuff.

The world-ending stuff.

Holy shit. Me? Slade thought I was that guy?

No. There was no way anyone would rely on me like that. Sure, I'd always been there for Random. But he was my brother. There was nothing I wouldn't do for him.

Including throwing my life away so he could live. Including coming here.

Alpha, the beast in me insisted, smug.

No. I would do anything to keep Hazard safe. And yes, okay, I would to anything to keep my parents safe, and my friends, and Random's girlfriend, and her band mates, and all the guys and gals on the Thunderheads.

But that didn't make me a big ole protective alpha.

"Nothing?" Slade asked. "You got nothing to say to that?"

"Nothing to say to you."

"I wasn't the one who looked for you in the crowd."

"You were the one who volunteered to take me to the hospital."

"Not my fault you've made yourself what you are."

"Like shit I have."

"Sure. You've totally backed down, not gotten in our faces, not practiced *against us* which, you know, only makes us play harder and better as a team. You haven't stood up to those assholes Paski and Zima, taken their hits—yes, I was watching—and refused to give them what they wanted, which was you fighting them.

"You stood up to Coach Nowak first day. Fuck, Spark. I saw him stun you. I saw you take fifteen jolts from that sadistic ass."

"That's...you're...that's nothing to do with...you don't get it," I said. "No one on this team gives one fuck about me. And honestly, I do not care. I came here to..."

"...play hockey," he mouthed along with me because he was a jerk like that.

I scowled. He laughed.

"Play the game," I insisted. "And no one has let me do that one thing. That one thing I came here for."

"Yeah? You think that's the one thing you came here for?"

"What the hell else would I come here for? Tacoma's kind of a dump, dude."

"Are you in love with him?"

"Who? Kudrar?"

"The wizard. Hazard."

This time I laughed. "Hard no. He's my brother. Like I basically adopted him when he was six. And if I were going to fall for a guy it'd be one who wasn't so mopey."

"Yeah, you like a guy who's full of laughs?" He batted his eyes at me.

"Probably. But since I'm not into guys, it doesn't matter. What the hell does Hazard have to do with anything?"

"Everything."

"Explain that, or I'll set the station on static and lock it there."

He tapped his fingers against his thigh, thinking. "We all know why you came here, Spark."

"Really? Fill me in, buddy."

"You took the fall for Hazard. He was Coach Nowak's pick, not you."

"So?"

The fingers tapped, tapped, tapped. "You threw your life down the crapper for him, for your brother. That got all of us asking why.

"If you're just here to play hockey, you would have been better off down with the Dunderheads. But you volunteered to take the fall. Not to move your career forward. Maybe not even just to keep the wizard from playing on our team."

"I liked it better when you made no sense in smaller sentences."

"Bored?"

"So very."

He stopped tapping his fingers and stared straight at me. For a long time. Too damn long for a guy who was navigating traffic. It was late and there weren't many people on the street, but still.

"Hey, I know a fun game," I said. "It's called keep your eyes on the damn road before I push you out the door."

The smile on him was wicked.

He turned his attention to the street again. "So you're telling me you put yourself in danger and possibly tanked your

147

rookie year for funsies? Because you're shitting yourself if you think Coach Nowak wanted the wizard for his game play.

"All Nowak wanted was to break him, ruin him. I don't know why. But I...understand men like Nowak. If there's something shiny someone else has that they can't have, then they'll make sure it's crushed and destroyed so no one else can have it."

"Hazard's strong on the ice," I argued. "Drafted by the Avalanche."

"I know, Spark," he said like I was completely missing his point. "I played against him. I know he works. You know it too. But you volunteered. Took his place. 'Cause you knew Nowak would break him."

I made a noise of protest and he held up one hand. "Maybe not break. Maybe just injure. Change."

It was true. If Random had joined this team, I would have lost my brother. It wasn't like I could always stand in the way of the hits that would come at him.

But this...this had grabbed me deep in my gut. If I let him go to the Tide, he'd never be the same.

And I couldn't let that happen. Not when he had just come out of hiding and been honest with himself and other people about what he was. A wizard. And a damn strong one. One who should be playing in the NHL, not down here in the Hell leagues.

One who could use magic to crack open the world if he wanted to. If he lost control.

A magic ability still untested gave him a vulnerability, like a fault line threading a tectonic plate. Hazard could handle a few personal earthquakes, but if a big one hit at his most vulnerable place, if say, some kind of sadistic coach did everything in his power to harm him, I thought Hazard might blow.

And test the lengths of what a rogue wizard could do to the world.

None of us wanted to see what that looked like.

So I'd thrown myself into the ring. But that's what buddies did, right? That's what—

—*Alphas*—

—brothers did?

"Hey, wolf." Slade snapped fingers in my face. "Do you understand what I said, or should I draw pictures for you?"

"Fuck off, Slade, I'm thinking."

He laughed and it was a good, genuine sound. He messed with the radio, and wonder of wonders, settled on hard rock before turning it up loud.

He pulled up alongside my hotel. As I reached for the car door, he cleared his throat.

"What?" I asked.

He stared straight ahead, more focused on the road now we weren't moving. Idiot.

I followed his gaze. The street was empty and wet.

"Okay, then. G'night."

"Wait."

I paused. "Dude, spit it out, or I'm gone."

His focus, his weird stillness felt like anger. Then he muttered something and nodded.

"I saw what coach did to you. The stun prod."

My shoulders clenched, my spine straightened. "I know. You said."

"I recorded it."

"The hell?"

Slade pulled out his phone, thumb and fingers tapping. "I recorded it. I was there. In the stands. I recorded it."

"Why?"

"Because he's an asshole. And you're not the first." He tipped his chin up. "I just sent it to you."

"Dude, you don't have my phone number."

He scoffed. "Your locker is *right* next to mine." He said it like it was impossible to think he *wouldn't* break into my locker and go through my private belongings.

My phone vibrated. One message.

"Put me in your contacts under Waxwings."

"Waxwings?"

He raised one eyebrow. "My first name is Icarus."

"Yeah?"

"The myth? The guy who flew too close to the sun?" He paused.

I nodded, then shook my head.

149

"Read a book, Spark."

"I'll wait for the movie."

"Get out of my car. You're stinking it up with stupid."

I opened the door, but didn't get out. "What do you think I'm going to do with this?"

"That's on you."

I waited, because, seriously, I didn't have any idea what I should do with the thing.

It felt like I had my thumb pressed into a grenade, trying to keep it from blowing.

He sighed. "I'd use it to keep Coach Nowak off Hazard's ass."

"Hazard's fine. Nowak can't touch him." Coach Clay and Beaumont, and Graves, would make sure Hazard was safely far away from Coach Nowak and his stun rods and death threats.

"You think Nowak will let anything stop him from getting what he wants? What is it about his personality or actions that makes you think he's not a competitive, toxic, overbearing asshole?"

I inhaled, exhaled hard. "Fuck."

"Yes, fuck. He's gone after your boy once. He isn't going to let one bad shot keep him from rushing the net."

And there it was. Coach Nowak was not going to lose. Not when coaching his team however the hell he wanted. Not when abusing his power in any way he wanted. And not in taking out the only wizard in the league.

This video might put a stop to that. To him. If I could convince someone in power that this wasn't an isolated incident.

Because as much as I knew it was bullshit for Coach Nowak to do this to me, I was just as sure he had connections that could make sure this never saw the light of day. I needed more evidence. A lot more.

"Spark?" Slade's voice brought me out of my whirlwind thoughts.

I stepped out of the car. "Thanks, Waxy."

"Screw you, Sparkles."

I grinned and slammed the door. He rolled down his window far enough to stick both middle fingers out, while gunning the gas and squealing down the road.

Ginger had a death wish.

The suite was quiet, and I didn't bother turning on lights since there wasn't anything to see anyway. Dad called and I almost answered, the phone cradled in my hand, fingers curled around the edges.

But I wasn't ready to hear his answers. Wasn't even ready to ask the questions yet.

What should I do about the video? What was the right play? Go wide with it and hope it took Coach Nowak down? Take it to the big wigs in the league? Wait until I got more dirt?

Those questions warred with the whole alpha thing.

Did Dad think I was a guy who could lead…

…*people, a pack, a team*…

…like Slade said? Or would he tell me Slade was just screwing with my head?

Come to think of it, if I were an alpha I wouldn't have so much self-doubt about it. Alphas swaggered. They heroed around like gods. Made themselves big via fear and domination.

So not me. I'd rather annoy someone until they couldn't ignore me.

Slade was right about one thing though: Hazard. I'd stepped up for my brother because I had to. There was love behind that decision, but even more, there was instinct.

Hazard was mine, my pack. I would do anything to make sure he survived and thrived.

The phone stopped ringing and Dad's message came through a minute later.

Are you okay, son? We didn't see you at the game. Call me. Text. Your mother and I are coming up there soon. Sorry about your teammate, Kudrar. We sent flowers.

My parents were the greatest. Dad always knew how to help me make sense of the world.

But I wasn't ready to ask him to stand up for me yet. If I was an alpha, then it was time to start acting like one. To get through this on my own strength.

Dig in, push hard, win.

I could make myself a part of the team. Make my own stand on my own two feet against Nowak. Make things right for my brothers. For myself.

Also, if Dad saw the bruises I still sported, my mild-mannered father would tear the league apart, tear the team apart. I'd never play again.

Time to make an adult decision. A calm decision.

I texted back. *Working hard. Team still not used to me. I'm okay. Got this. Love you. Miss you & Mom. Tell Ran he's a jerk & smells funny.*

A long minute, two ticked by. I read over my text multiple times. Had I tipped him off? What was my father reading between the lines? Did I sound needy? Weak?

Call us, Duncan. You don't have to do this alone.

My eyes and chest tightened with tears. Because, dammit, that was my Dad. Always knew when I was flicking shit to hide pain.

I will. Just need little time.

Promise.

X my <3

Love you, son. Proud of you.

I gasped at the little sob that choked up my throat, then I lay back on the couch and slung my arm over my eyes, not caring if it made my ribs hurt.

I set the phone face down on my chest and closed my eyes. I didn't need to cry. I just needed to sleep. I wiped at the moisture on my face, and threw myself toward oblivion with everything I had.

14

BACK-TO-BACK GAMES meant no one was going to push it very hard in practice today.

I kept my mind on my own game, and no one paid attention to me.

Except Slade, who broke free from his drill and did the strangest thing. He passed me the puck. I was so surprised, I almost missed it.

"Lame," he chirped. "You suck, Sparkle."

His smile was a challenge. He bared his teeth at anyone who came near us, anyone who even looked like they wanted to come at him for talking to me, playing with me. It was a clear message that he'd be more than happy to take down all comers.

It was…weirdly humbling. I had never had a problem making friends. I wasn't the popular guy, but I was fun and funny, easy to hang out with. In school, I'd made my way into every group and club I was interested in, and had kept most of the friends I'd made in those places.

But to have this one guy choose to stand beside me, stand against the team *with* me, meant more than all those easy friendships.

I whistled and hucked the puck back at him. He caught it, smooth and easy, then took off down the ice. I dug it out after him, on the chase, hassling for possession of the puck.

He won the race—damn fox—took a shot at the backup goalie who caught it easy as waving a yawn down off his face.

"Gotta work harder, boys," he said.

And then there was the next puck, the next pass, and the next drill, just Slade and me running plays. Coach Nowak ignored us. So did the assistant coach. But I caught players watching us, watching me.

So I showed them what I could do. All bullshit aside, I was a fine hockey player. Not the best, but I hadn't been given my place in the league being lazy or slow.

I was good. Fast. I had power and good ice sense. My puck handling was solid, and I didn't hog the play. I was too good to be scratched.

With a winger down, they needed me on the roster.

Not that coach would play me.

Their loss.

Literally.

I was marked as a healthy scratch again, and sat through another game, up in the nose-bleeds watching my team choke a two-point lead and go down for the count three under.

At least there were no fights this time.

At the end of the game, when the last buzzer went off and the overly silent crowd put a little gumption into *boo*ing both the Tide and the Rumblers, something happened.

Slade took off his helmet, red hair flame-bright. He turned to where I was watching in the stands, looked straight at me, and tapped his stick against the ice.

It was short, just a moment that could be misread as him applauding the audience, or being a good sport and cheering for the visiting team.

But that's not what it was.

That was a teammate recognizing another teammate.

That was—

—*pack*—

—a second-marked recognizing a second-marked, that was—

—*beta*—

—something no one had ever done to me before.

I was so going to make fun of him for it.

"You know that player?" the guy next to me asked.

"Yeah."

"Icarus Slade, innit?" The guy's words were slippery and smelled of beer.

"Yep."

"He's up for a trade, right?"

Cold shot through me. I hadn't heard about it. Maybe it was just a rumor going around? After all, not every drunk guy got his facts straight.

"Don't know," I said easily. "Maybe."

He frowned then blinked to clear his vision. "Hey, you're that guy. That dead guy. The wolf, right?"

Busted.

I smiled and nodded. "I am."

He thrust his hand at me and I took it even though it smelled like hot dogs and grease. "You ever gonna get your ass on the ice and earn your keep?" He said it with a smile.

"Plan on it. When Coach says I should."

"We wanted the wizard. No offense, but at least the wizard would have been entertaining. Coulda cast a spell or something. All this bullshit team does is lose."

I didn't reply. I might be a nice guy but even I had a limit.

SLADE WAITED FOR ME and we walked out to the parking lot together.

"That stick thing? You're fond of me, buddy. Real fond. Wanna wear friendship bracelets? Wanna braid my hair?"

He punched my shoulder. Hard.

I couldn't stop grinning. We didn't speak after that, but we didn't have to.

More than one player watched us as we made our way to our separate cars.

Maybe Slade accepting me would make other players accept me. But at this pace, it was going to take me approximately three point eight lifetimes before anyone wanted to play with me on a line.

I did not have time for this shit.

MY HOTEL SUITE WAS quiet, dark, and empty. I paced until the street sound disappeared and passing headlights became more and more infrequent. I paced until night went deep and silent. I hadn't eaten since…a vague memory of breakfast and a meal bar flickered through my head. It didn't matter. My stomach was a knot of stress. Just the idea of food made me want to barf.

What I needed was a run, a shift. I needed to get away from the anger and guilt and worry churning in my brain. Being a wolf was easier in some ways. When I went wolf, all the tangled emotions and stress softened and smoothed out, replaced by clear, easy instinct.

I needed that break. I needed not to be Duncan for a few hours.

But shifting had its drawbacks. Using magic messed up my coordination when I changed back to man form. If I shifted too often, it was going to screw with my game.

Maybe I should try meditating. I closed my eyes, shook out my arms, inhaled, exhaled. My nose itched. My feet hurt. My stomach growled. This was boring and annoying.

Nope. Still didn't understand meditation.

I carried a pair of sweats outside and stashed them beneath the stairs then stripped off my T-shirt and boxers. Deep breath, standing naked in the dark and drizzly rain.

My lungs hurt, but not as bad as they had a few days ago. Exhale, dropping my arms and closing my eyes. Let go of worry and pain. Inhale, coil up on the balls of my feet, muscles stretching.
Then….

Push. Dive. Leap off the top of that great cliff and soar out, out, out…

…and down.

I WOKE UP NAKED in the middle of my bed. I didn't remember finding my way back.

My phone screen lit up. I tapped it with the pad of my thumb.

Don't do anything stupid. I miss you, asshole.

Hazard.

Goddamn him.

I huffed out a laugh, more relieved than I thought I'd be at one stupid text.

You're stupid, I tapped back.

Yeah, it was poetry between my boy Ran and me.

If they healthy scratch U on the road, I'm gonna yell at the walls.

I shook my head and texted, *Yeah, that won't look like crazy. Healthy scratch is easy street, bro. No worry.*

Minutes ticked by. He was typing things, changing his mind and typing new things. I waited. I didn't care what he said. Just the fact that he was texting me was a huge relief. A knot of darkness in me unwound. Some of the noise in my head quieted.

Hearing from him made the world feel stable, solid.

Your dad's worried.

I waited. I knew that. He knew I knew that.

I hate U not being here. Then: *We were supposed 2 do this together, dammit. I hate what U did. But…I'm not as mad.*

I typed quickly. *U loooove me.*

How many hits to the head have you taken? Of course I love you, jerk.

Asshole, I replied. *Stop trying to drop pass to JJ. He's never in the right place at the right time.*

JJ's not my problem. Vargas took left wing. He's not even half as good as U.

Awww…

But at least he's playing.

I sent him middle finger emoji, the devil and a rooster.

Srsly, he texted, *don't get dead.*

And just like that, we were back to the real world, the real problem. Being on the Tide was a dangerous thing.

You too, bro, I replied. Not that he had to worry. The Thunderheads had his back.

So did I.

EARLY THE NEXT MORNING, I showed up at the arena with all my gear and got on the bus with the rest of the team.

No lingering eye contact, but a couple quick glances up at me, a nod, before looking away. At least they acknowledged I existed. That was more than yesterday.

Slowest progress ever.

A foot shot out into the aisle blocking my progress.

"Where you going, Sparky?"

I hated that nickname. I'd beat up a kid in second grade for calling me that. Dad hadn't approved of my actions, but mom laughed so hard when she heard why I got detention, she had to leave the room. Later, she smuggled me a huge cupcake with gold stars sprinkled on it.

I looked down at the foot, leg, and player blocking my way. Philippe Nadreau, the coyote who had left me at the mercy of his thug friends, Paski and Zima.

"Move your leg, or I break it," I said. "I ain't got nothing to lose."

I stared him down. Instead of looking away, one corner of his mouth rose. He looked devilish and mean, but there was something else behind that look I recognized. I'd seen it in the mirror plenty of times.

A sense of humor. He liked pushing his luck and messing with people.

He dropped his foot, but didn't move it out of the aisle, which meant I had to step over it and hope he didn't try to kick me in the nuts.

"Break it straight in half, Wile E." I stepped on his foot, which made him grunt, then headed down the aisle.

Paski and Zima lounged on either side of the next row, both with headphones hanging around their necks and jackets rolled up for pillows. They ignored me as I passed.

"Here." Something flew at me. I caught it out of reflex, turned it over in my hands. It was one of the cheap blankets busses like this kept stocked for overnight runs.

"That seat's open." Slade pointed at the row across the aisle from him.

"Yeah, I'm not going to sit there," I said.

He scowled, gaze dipping to the blanket in my arms as if trying to decide if he'd already offered it to me, then flicking back to my face.

"Why not?" That scowl was going full pissed off. Like he was ready to fight me.

"Because you probably touched everything over there with your ass."

The scowl flattened, eyebrows creeped upward, eyes widened, then blinked, blinked, blinked.

And then he laughed. It was a hissy, high giggle.

"Oh, my god," I breathed.

He clapped his hand over his mouth.

"You laugh like a baby!"

"Fuck you." He relaxed back into his seat, taking up the row even though he wasn't a big guy. "Like I care where the hell you sit." He crossed his arms over his chest and looked away from me, staring out the window.

"You probably licked the rest of the bus." I dropped down into the seat he had pointed me toward. "Totally gross. At least this one only smells like fox butt. I'd hate to find out what body part you touched the rest of the seats with."

He worked on not smiling while I bitched some more and settled in with the blanket.

We were headed down to Bend, Oregon to play the Brimstones. They were a hard-hitting physical team that could handle a puck from their knees. They never gave up on a goal, even a total garbage scrum in front of the net.

The best way to shut them down was either speed or just smothering their plays. A lot of man-on-man work out there, closing off shot angles, forcing turnovers.

I loved that kind of game. Loved it fast, loved it physical, and loved it when the other team gave as hard as they got.

I knew Nowak wouldn't play me, even though he'd insisted I travel with the team. The push-pull of being ignored, with only a dangling thread of hope was doing weird things to my head.

I wasn't sleeping well, wasn't eating well, didn't like being in my own skin. All I wanted to do was shift to wolf and kill something.

I rubbed my eyes, put in my headphones. Somewhere between Tacoma and Bend, I drifted off into that half-asleep/half-conscious state.

Someone was staring at me. I opened my eyes.

Turned out it was a fox, half curled in his seat, back to the window, eyes steady like he'd never seen me before. I yawned, scratched my pits, and flipped him off before turning my back on him.

A wadded up candy wrapper hit me in the head. I looked over my shoulder and jerked back.

He was sitting *right there* in the seat next to me, all curled up as much as a guy his size could curl leaning forward enough that his eyes looked huge.

"Jesus, asshole," I yelped. "What the hell are you doing there?"

"Sleeping beauty is a sleeping beast."

"What are you talking about?"

"You snore."

"I do not."

"Like an old busted car."

"Go away, you're creepy."

"I thought you wanted to be friends." He gave me a dead-eyed serial killer smile.

I snorted and shoved his face.

He unfolded out of the seat and popped back over to his own row just as the bus rumbled to a stop outside a hotel.

"All right," Coach Nowak said from the front of the bus. "Double up. Get your bags, leave your gear on the bus. Go to your rooms, shower, change. We meet in the lobby in forty-five minutes.

"You will be on the bus at exactly fifteen after the hour for pre-game skate. Puck drop is at seven. There will be local news, but this will not be broadcast nationally. Osler has your room assignments. Move!"

He strode off the bus while the team muttered and gathered their shit.

I was one of the last to leave my seat. Paski and Zima were just ahead of me in the aisle. Slade fell into place behind me. The friendship with him might be new, but having him at my back was a hell of a lot better than having ass one and hole two behind me.

I stepped out into the freezing air. Jesus. I shivered in my hoodie. The ground was covered in a thin layer of snow and the blacktop sparkled with ice.

"Fuckall," I exhaled in a plume of winter. Some of the guys already had their room assignments and were fast-walking to the door.

"Mr. Spark," Coach barked.

"Present," I said, trying not to sound like a smart ass.

"You bunk with Paski."

I froze for a moment, all the blood rushing out of my head. Paski twitched like he'd been slapped. I half expected him to lick his lips. Instead, he cracked his knuckles.

Real subtle, asshole.

I must have made some kind of sound, though I was just silently working through how not to be in the obituary section tomorrow.

Coach blinked slowly, cold as a snake. "Do you have a problem bunking with Mr. Paski, Spark?"

I shrugged one shoulder. "Not unless he hogs the covers."

Paski snarled under his breath and cracked his hands into fists.

Coach held out an envelope with two key cards in it. I took it from him without looking away from his reptilian gaze.

"Thank you."

The fire of death blazed in his eyes but his face remained impassive.

And it was that—that contrast of hot and cold—that finally got to me.

This guy didn't just hate. He didn't just yell and get angry. This guy had a taste for murder, and he was ravenous for blood.

Mine.

Probably Hazard's.

Probably anyone who got in his way.

But right this minute, he was imagining he was dining on my liver.

And just like that, I made it my life's goal to take him down.

I pivoted to the hotel, damn well planning to reach the room before Paski so I could land the first punch. I'd taken it from him once, but I refused to be his personal knuckle duster.

He rolled quietly behind me. Even in snow the big guy moved like smoke and shadow.

But I heard his breathing. I heard his heartbeat running higher, faster. Hungry.

He knew this was going to go down. Tiger versus wolf.

The room was first floor, down a hall, to the left.

I pressed the key card to the door, then stepped inside.

He was right there, *right there* behind me. My pulse drummed fast, faster. If I paused, if I turned, there'd be a fist in my face.

Naw, he was the one who should worry. I was going to pound the crap out of him.

Three more steps and we'd be far enough into the room no one would hear us. At least not if I made this short.

Just a little more. And…

…*now.*

I twisted, pulled from my core, loading my entire body like a spring coiling up and releasing in one hard, precision punch…

…that whiffed through thin air.

Ducking and dancing out of my reach was not Paski.

"Asshole," Slade said. "I cash in favors and this is how you repay me? We don't have an understanding, Sparkle? I thought we had an understanding."

I blinked. Opened my mouth, closed it. Looked at the door that was still slightly open. Paski was not there.

This wasn't…this didn't… I walked past Slade and surveyed the hall.

Paski strolled into a room about six doors down. He must have sensed me because he lifted a middle finger behind his back, then slammed the door shut.

"That was…" I said. "He was right behind me."

"Yeah. I told him to take a hike."

Slade was a creature in constant motion. He combed fingers down curtains and across the window sill. He ducked behind the pull shades so that just his legs were visible. I heard the squeak of palms petting frozen glass.

Such a weirdo.

"Stop humping the window and talk," I demanded in my "dad" voice.

He muttered, "stupid" and "obvious" but finally came out from behind the drapes. "I switched rooms."

"With Paski?"

Slade wandered over to the dresser and proceeded to open every drawer. Twice. He even stood in the bottom drawer, and looked like he was going to try walking up the next drawer level before he shrugged. "Who else was your roomie?"

He gave up on the drawer, which was good. I didn't care how short he was, and he wasn't that much shorter than Hazard, which is to say he was a lot shorter than me, but he was at least five-seven. He was too big to bounce around in hotel room dresser drawers.

I rubbed my hand over my face, and took a deep breath so I didn't growl. "Why did you switch rooms? How can you even do that? We had assignments."

With a happy little grunt, he claimed the TV remote and pressed the controller against the screen, then flipped through every button in order. Top of the remote to the bottom, then bottom of the remote to the top.

I was going to throttle him.

The TV made a lot of noise and blinked through a lot of color. Slade looked like he was in heaven.

He still hadn't answered me. "Why, Slade," I repeated. Why did you trade rooms with Tony the Tiger?"

"He hates you. You want to break his spleen. And I told you already, I follow you." He turned and gave me a dead-serious nod. "Me. *I* follow you. He just wants you dead so he can mount your teeth on the wall."

"Specific," I allowed. "Why would he trade with you?"

"He owed me."

"For what?"

"No. That's private." He tossed the controller back into a drawer, then dragged his fingers across the crappy dead-flower wallpaper and around a framed picture of an apple. Like, just one lone, sad yellow apple picked sometime back in the sixties.

He made it to the corner with the closet. He palmed the doors like he was about to bash his head into the middle of them, and then he dusted his fingertips down to the handle.

He twisted slightly. There was a delicate "click" as he tugged the doors open. Then he disappeared inside.

I could hear the slide of hangers moving across the bar.

Forget throttling him. I was going to smother him in his sleep.

"What am I going to owe you for taking Paski off my ass?"

The hangers clanged hard.

Slade walked out of the closet, annoyed. "Look. You're. That. So I'm…this." He pointed down to himself.

"A jerk?"

He raised an eyebrow. "If you're going to be the alpha of the team, I'm going to be a part of that. Because I choose it." He bared his teeth at me. "I choose." He was anger and challenge. I didn't think that had anything to do with me.

He'd only been with the Tide for the last few months. Big D wasn't the kind of alpha—if he was even an alpha, which I doubted—to accept anyone into the pack. Not me. Not, apparently, a wayward fox.

Instinct told me there had been an alpha in Slade's past that had turned him away, made him feel disposable.

And that, well, it was terrifying that he had put all his bets in my square.

"Okay," I said slowly, trying to figure out how to break this to him. He had to get the idea of me being an alpha out of his head.

"Look," I scratched my forehead, then moved my hand to cover the back of my neck.

"You do that when you're uncomfortable," he said.

"What?"

"You…" He lifted his hand and put it on the back of his neck. "You get bitten there?"

I opened my mouth to tell him no. But there was something about his voice, a vulnerability.

This was a test. Would I tell him something about myself that I hadn't told the others? Would him changing rooms with Paski add up to me accepting him? Would I allow him to know me better?

Or maybe he just wanted to know if I would trust him with a personal thing.

And the weird thing was, I did trust him.

I'd pretty much liked him on first sight. I knew we could be friends. And maybe that's what this was really about.

Maybe being the only fox on a team rife with assholes was hell. Maybe all Slade wanted was a friend. *That*, I understood.

"Yeah," I said. "Ex-girlfriend."

"Oh? You into the rough stuff?"

"No. I broke up with her and she bit me. Like…who even does that? She snuck into my room while I was asleep and sank her fangs into my spine. Freaked me the hell out."

Slade nodded, watching my body language, which was uncomfortable and defensive. Listening to my heartbeat as it echoed the panicked beat of that night.

"Was she a cat?"

"Yes."

"What kind of cat was she?"

"No, that's private." I dropped my hand. "You need to give up on this alpha idea, Slade. Seriously. The Tide aren't going to follow me. No one likes me, no one wants me here, no one is going to trust me as an alpha, which I'm not even convinced I am.

Liar.

"So get that out of your head," I went on. "If you want to be my teammate, if you want to be my friend, I'm all for that."

He scoffed and gave me a judgy look like I was the slowest bus in Slowville. "You are just dumber than a bag of rocks made of rocks, Sparkle."

"Okay, stop right there. Sparkle? Yeah, no. Call me Donuts."

"Why?"

"Because all my friends do."

He gave me that head tilt that I was starting to think meant he was dealing with so many thoughts, his neck couldn't hold up the weight of them.

Then, like a wind-up doll whose switch had flipped, he was moving again. "Which bed do you want?"

"Door."

He huffed and took a few giant steps backwards, just like in a game of Mother May I, and took a running leap at the bed.

Landed like a 747 that had lost both wings, and blown the engines.

Which is to say he landed hard. And loud.

I threw my extra pillows at him, followed it up with the comforter because those things were never washed and nasty. He snarled and complained, gathering the pillows like spoils of war, and kicking the comforter onto the floor.

I stripped to my boxers and crawled under my sheets. I flipped my pillow one way, the other, folded it a couple times and settled facing the door, Slade in his bed at my back.

The beast in me trusted him. I knew he wasn't going to take a shot at me.

At least not off the ice.

I hadn't slept well or much since I'd come to Tacoma. Maybe with Slade here in the room, I could let down my defenses long enough to get some much-needed REM.

"Good night, Slade."

"We're not sleeping, stupid. We have to change and eat. And play hockey."

I groaned. "Fifteen minutes. Then I'll do anything you want."

There was a long pause. I twisted toward him. He lay horizontally across his bed, staring at me.

"Wake me up in fifteen, okay?"

I closed my eyes, turned my back again, and took a couple deep breaths. Just as I felt the feather numb fingers of sleep reaching out to cradle me, I heard Slade's voice.

"Okay, Donuts."

I smiled.

And got whacked in the back of the head with a balled up, dirty comforter.

15

WE HAD A PROBLEM. Since Kudrar was still in a hospital bed, we were down a winger. Coach had exactly four players he could call to cover Kudrar's shifts tonight.

A guy named Busk, a guy named Keller, a woman named Lundqvist. And me.

Busk was wheeling on a knee he'd strained a few games before I'd joined the team. Doctors didn't want him playing on it, not for a full hockey game.

Busk was a hell of a player and would be one of those superstars who made a mediocre team a winning team. He'd be first line, captain and leader one of these days. The smart move would be to let Busk cool his heels and literally heal.

Keller was a fourth-marked, cheetah. He carried the second line and was the second highest scorer on the team. Lindqvist was also fourth-marked but she was a lion. She played third line with her lion husband. Breaking up that powerful combination would be suicide.

Tonight's game was basic. It might put us in better standing for the Broughton Cup run, but it wasn't the last chance we had to get there. Risking any of the other left wingers on a low-level game seemed like a pretty dumb move.

Especially since I was uninjured and ready to gear up just like all the other players.

I might not have Busk's potential, Keller's speed, or Lindqvist's line chemistry, but I could play.

And I wanted to play tonight. I had something to prove. Coach Nowak didn't think I could hold my own.

Well, there was only one way to find out.

Nowak walked into the locker room and stood with his hands on his hips, which pulled his suit jacket back and made him look bigger.

"Take this win or I'm cutting. I can build a better team, a hungrier team pulling out of the damn beer leagues. Either you win, or you're out. Not one of you are safe." He paused to make eye contact with Tabor Steele, then Big D, then Paski.

"Don't make me prove exactly how many of you I can replace. I don't care what your contracts say. If you don't bring back a win, you better start looking for another club."

He waited for comments, or arguments. Got none of either. "Read the lineup."

He strode out of the room.

Tabor Steele stood. "All right, men and women. You heard Coach. We're bringing the win home. No matter what it takes. Give it everything you have tonight. Like it's the last damn time you're ever gonna be on the ice. Because it might be. Leave it all out there. This night is our night to win!"

Players tapped sticks on the floor, slapped shoulders. At least the captain could get a reaction out of them.

As Steele read off names, I was startled to hear mine, right there on the fourth line.

Everyone else was startled too because they all stopped what they were doing to stare at me.

"Fuck to the yes," I said. "About damn time, boys."

Slade gave me a slight nod. Everyone else went back to pregame prep.

I got busy with prep too.

I had a game to win.

I WAS READY, PRACTICALLY out-of-my-skin crazy for a chance to get on the ice. But if I'd thought Nowak putting me on the fourth line meant he was going to play me, I was so very wrong.

Line change after line change, he sent out the other wingers and left me on the bench, fresh, plenty of air, plenty of gas in the tank, while my teammates came back sweating, bruised, and tired.

I looked like a fresh-faced noob, a total loser, made all the more clear by the battle-worn players around me. The longer the game went on the more obvious it became that I wasn't out there to help the team win. I was there as a punishment to the team for losing.

Coach was delivering a very clear message to the players: I was a liability. With me on the team, they'd have to work three times as hard to hold their own and five times as hard to win.

It was a dick move.

By the start of the third period it was physically painful to watch my team going through this. To feel their exhaustion and pain as a ghost pain I couldn't squirm away from.

The only reason I hadn't barfed was because I hadn't eaten anything but a heavy protein and vitamin shake. Those things went down and stayed down.

I opened my mouth to tell Nowak to just fucking cut me from the team and put anyone on the bench instead of me. Hell, put in the equipment manager.

Before I could say anything, Slade hit my ankle with his stick. Hard.

He wanted me to shut up.

I wanted us to win. I stood, but Slade grabbed my arm and forced me to stay still.

He was a lot stronger than he looked. He pressed his lips together and shook his head, bright eyes on nothing else but the battle on the ice.

God dammit.

I sat on the bench for nineteen excruciating minutes.

And then, finally, Nowak yelled my name. Told me to go in.

We were down by three. One minute left.

Here's the thing about hockey: it wasn't over, it wasn't a win or a loss until the final second ticked off the clock.

I'd seen teams score two goals in ten seconds. Seen them tie it up, and pull the win in overtime.

But a team as tired as ours, as angry and frustrated and demoralized as ours, had almost no damn chance to get the puck to the back of the net three times in sixty seconds.

I took my place at the face-off. I got into position for a drill I'd watched them run, but of which I'd never been a part.

I was there. I was ready.

So was my team.

We lost the face-off. The puck got caught in a four guy scrum along the boards.

Seconds plummeted off the clock like hail in a windstorm.

The puck squirted free and Steele snagged it up. He flew across the ice to the net, took the shot. A heavy *ping* rang out as the puck ricocheted off the post.

The horn blared, signaling the end of the game. The Brimstones's home crowd went wild.

We left the ice, one more loss on the board.

I DREAMED HARD DREAMS full of fire and pain and bones breaking.

I dreamed of teeth and clever fox fingers and piercing fox eyes.

I dreamed of Hazard's laugh, of Dad's pancakes, of Mom's horror novels with the dog-eared pages. I was a piece of all of those things. I was me, and I was all the people I loved. I was myself and I was my pack.

I dreamed of Hazard's broken wrist when he was twelve. And it was my broken wrist.

I dreamed of Slade's bared teeth. And his anger filled my mouth.

I dreamed I stood in front of the darkness, the thing that wanted to hurt and destroy those who I cared for. I stood in front of the darkness, and would not let it pass.

Coach Nowak's arm pressed across my throat, his hatred hissed like acid through my brain. He melted into a monster made of coils and scales, muscles and fang and pain. And when he rose up to strike, I lunged for his throat. Not to injure. To kill.

I startled awake. The drone of the bus engine hadn't changed, but something had brought me out of restless sleep.

No hotel beds for us. Not after that loss. Exhausted, the players had fallen asleep almost as soon as we'd packed everything onto the bus. If the highway signs were correct, we were still in Oregon.

I shifted so I could see up the dark aisles. Coach Nowak sat in the front row.

Slade stood spine-straight next to him. His face was even paler than normal, red slapped across cheeks and down what I could see of his neck.

He was furious. That was what had woken me—his hard, clear emotion clanging out like a bell in my head. An emotion I could feel as if it were mine.

I was out of my seat before I knew I was moving. I stopped next to Slade.

"This doesn't concern you, Mr. Spark," Nowak said. He was both angry and happy that the target of his anger was holding still enough he could eviscerate him and watch him squirm.

Slade was not squirming though. He was holding unnaturally still.

I'd been around the guy for long enough I knew his natural state was constant motion. I'd never seen him so motionless.

I took a couple steps closer and crowded Slade out from in front of Nowak, standing in front of him instead.

"This does concern me. What's going on?" My voice was low, demanding. I saw Nowak's pupils dilate in recognition. He glanced over my shoulder at Slade, then back to me and scowled.

"If I wanted to speak to you, you'd know," Nowak growled. "Go back to your seat, Spark. You don't belong here."

A surge of *hot* and *righteous* and *powerful* rose up my spine and filled my head, stretching, owning. A part of the wolf in me, a part of it I'd never known, suddenly woke and became something stronger. Something surer.

"What did you tell Slade?"

It was strange to be calm and enraged at the same time. A rush of determination to protect Slade—

—pack—

—filled me and it was powerful. Nowak had done something to hurt him. I wanted to smack that smug look off Nowak's face and break his arms.

Slade made a sound behind me. Just a whisper.

I pushed my way forward another step, made myself bigger, blocking Slade from Nowak's view. "What. Did. You. Do."

"I don't negotiate with gutter trash. You don't have the balls to fight me, boy? Do you? Want to come at me right here? Think you can take me down? Go ahead. Take a shot. Let's see if you've got a spine under that worthless skin."

He was baiting me. I knew that.

But for a glorious full few seconds, I calculated how many fines and jail time I could rack up if I beat the living crap out of my coach.

Too many.

Plus, Hazard would probably visit me in jail every day just so he could sit on the other side of the glass and stare at me judgmentally.

I missed him.

I turned slightly to demand Slade tell me what had happened but he was no longer there.

"That's what I thought," Nowak spit. "Get out of my sight, Spark. Before I make you regret every choice in your pitiful life."

I rubbed my hand over my head and cupped the back of my neck. This wasn't the time or place for a fight. This wasn't the time or place to lose control on my wolf.

I strode down the aisle. The thing I hadn't told Slade was that my ex-girlfriend had done more damage than I'd ever admit. She'd been in half shift with no control over her beast.

Huge mountain lion fangs nicked something important at the base of my skull when she bit down hard and shook me.

If my dad hadn't come home for lunch and knocked on my door to find out why I was not at school, I could have bled out, paralyzed and unable to call for help.

It was why I never got into a fight without a tight hold on the wolf. It was why I didn't let something like a hot-headed hockey player force my shift on the ice, why I laughed off other people's anger.

Slade sat next to the window, stiff, staring at the dark and nothing ahead of him.

Only his fingers moved. He had woven them together on his lap. But his pinkies, hidden mostly from view, rubbed at the sides of his hands.

Something told me this was an old habit for comfort. A way to be moving that no one would see. That no one would complain about.

It about broke my heart to see him so closed down.

Maybe because he reminded me a little of Hazard, and this friendship could someday make him a—

—*pack*—

—brother to me.

"Go away, Spark."

"Tell me what he said."

"Go away."

"Slade…" I reached over and touched his elbow. You'd have thought I'd just set him on fire. He jerked and scrambled to put his back against the wall, his knees up in the seat between us.

"Go away," he snarled through bright teeth. And then, in almost a whisper, "Please, Donut."

Hurt, confusion, and anger rolled off him. The wolf in me wanted to *comfort, protect, guard*. But his need to have me step back and give him room to process was a bright scent of crushed pine around him.

If he were Hazard, I would have bugged him until he spilled the beans.

But Hazard and I had been brothers for a long time. I understood him. I knew when to push and when to back off.

Slade was new to me.

So I followed my gut and gave him space. I sat right across the aisle and I leaned against the window, turned so I could keep an eye on who was coming down the aisle, and also on Slade.

I stayed vigilant. And for the rest of the trip, he did not move away from his defensive posture, hands clasped, only the slightest movement of his pinkies giving away that he was alive.

"GOTTA GET MOVING, SLADE." It was five in the morning, still dark and wet out. We'd just reached Tacoma.

He nodded, the motion jerky as if his whole body had gone temporarily numb. He didn't look at me.

Players stretched up out of seats, rolling out kinks in shoulders, testing bruises. I couldn't hold up the line for Slade, so I started forward.

Paski was the first guy in front of me. He looked back at me, his gaze flicking to Slade. He smiled and stared straight at me, as if to say, *"I did that. Do you see what I did?"*

I didn't want him looking at Slade. I didn't want anyone looking at him. So I pointed forward. "Front of the bus is that way, dumb nuts. Need a map?"

Someone behind me snickered. Paski made a kissy face and marched out the door. I strolled along behind him like nothing was wrong.

Everyone scattered across the dark parking lot, headed to their cars.

The defensive coach was yelling: "No skate today. Tomorrow at five o'clock show up ready to lose your balls. No skate today. Tomorrow at five o'clock…"

Coach Nowak was gone.

I couldn't confront him and make him talk. The only person who had the information I needed was Slade.

I waited for him to get off the bus. And waited. And waited.

I cursed and climbed back on the bus. Dawn hadn't brought much light into the darkness yet, so if I didn't have good night vision, it might have been easy to miss him.

He sat in shadows, in the same seat. He slumped, head turned toward the window, eyes squeezed shut.

He wasn't asleep—his breathing was too shallow and short. His body was hunched up as if he were in pain.

"Everyone's gone," I said quietly. "You need to get off the bus now, buddy."

He didn't move. I thought about shaking him, but instead, I settled in the seat next to him, my hands motionless on my thighs.

It took some time before he spoke.

"He cut me."

For a wild moment, I thought he meant someone had physically injured him. A wall of rage slammed into me. Then my brain caught up with what his words meant.

Nowak cut him from the team.

"When?"

Another long pause. "As of today."

That wall of rage turned concrete, became a house of rage, a fortress of rage and I was standing in the center of it all. "What about your contract?"

Slight huff of air.

"Can you go back to the minors?"

"That's…" He rubbed his fingertips over his forehead. "I'd commit manslaughter. So. No."

Even though it was only a brief motion, it was good to see him moving. A still Slade was an unnatural phenomenon.

"Really?" I asked. "You found some way to piss off every player on every team in the minors? What do you know? You do have talent."

He rolled his head to the center of the seat and rearranged legs that had to be numb from being crunched up for so long.

"Fine," he said. "It might only be involuntary manslaughter for most of them."

His eyes opened and he licked his lips like he was coming back to fill his bones and skin in stages. "Going back is not." Short shake of his head. "No."

"So what are the options here?" He didn't have to tell me why he wouldn't return to an entire league. But I wanted to know where he was going so I could find him.

He was too stubborn and strong not to land on his feet, but it could take time. A lot of time.

"I've been kicked out of hell," he said. "Who the fuck cares?"

"I care," I growled.

He stared at me, his eyes glittering in the dark. "I'm not your brother, Spark. I'm not your teammate. I'm not your friend." Each statement was colder than the last.

The wolf in me would argue every point, but I swallowed down my words. Convincing him that he was somehow mine, a part of the group of people—

—*pack*—

—that I refused to let go of, people who were my friends, my family whether they liked it or not, wasn't something he could hear buried in this fresh pain.

"You're full of shit," I said lightly. "I happen to like people who are full of shit."

"We're not friends."

"Yes, we are."

"I hate you."

"Too bad."

That got a tiny mean smile out of him. "I finally figured out why your coach let you volunteer for this team. He hates you."

A sharp stab hit my heart. I missed the hell out of the Thunderheads. My need for that family was a physical ache that made it hard to breathe.

"Talk to me," I said.

"I've got nothing to say."

"I'll drive you home."

"Why? I'm off the team."

I stood in the aisle and scowled down at him. "Like this team means shit-all to me? To our friendship? Get your head out of your ass."

All the shadows of him darkened, his eyes hardened. He didn't like hearing that. I knew he'd come back swinging.

"We are *not* friends. You know why? Huh, Duncan? You know why we're not friends? You know why Nowak cut me?"

"No."

"You. You're why. You showed up here like some kind of martyr hero and you fucked up my career." He said it like it didn't mean anything, like those words weren't a cracked lid on a pot of lava about to explode.

He said it like it didn't matter because I didn't matter.

That stab in my heart twisted, bled.

"I fucking hate you. You want me to talk? You think you're so noble coming here to save your poor pansy orphan brother's life? Fuck you. You ruined mine. You fucked up the most fucked-up team in the league. There are twenty-four people on this team, and you dropped into their lives like a steaming pile of shit.

"You're poison Spark. Everything you touch rots. You think that wizard couldn't cut it without you? Told yourself he was too weak to handle it so you swooped to the rescue?

"Bullshit. You jumped in to save the day because *you* need *him* to be a victim so you can be a hero. You like that he's weaker than you. You like taking away the power he has over his own life. You like making decisions for him and making yourself look good. Fuck you, for making me a victim so you can feel big. Fuck. You."

My heart was too heavy to beat, the knot in my throat choked off my breath.

How dare he tell me who I was, who I loved. How dare he tell me it was wrong. How dare he try to make me into his enemy.

A part of me screamed and screamed. Was he right? Was that all I did? Had I tried to make myself bigger and better because I could help people? Because I could jump in and save them instead of letting them save themselves?

Had I been taking away Random's choices for all these years? Had I been forcing him to be smaller than me, weaker then me so I could feel important?

Had I been doing that to everyone I knew, my teammates, my friends, all my life?

The idea of it, the shape of that concept that almost, so very *nearly* fit into my life shook me to my damn core.

I wanted to run from the idea of it, from the *almost* truth of it, but it sank teeth into my head, gave life to my deep, cold fears, and would not let go.

Slade stood and slapped the side of my shoulder hard enough I'd bruise.

"Shove your unwanted help up your unwanted alpha ass."

I moved so he could push by me, hands clenched into fists at his side, touching nothing as he passed.

I stood there for a long, long time.

16

SLADE DIDN'T SHOW UP for practice the next day. No one asked where he went. Coach Nowak didn't say anything about it. Just ignored that he'd been there, a part of the team for most of the season.

The bench in the locker room next to me was empty.

No one looked at it. No one looked at me. It wasn't just that there was no eye contact—there was no contact at all. No one spoke to me. No one touched me. No one touched my equipment.

When I hit the ice, there was no hole for me in the drills, no room for me in the lines.

If I thought I'd gotten the cold shoulder before, I was getting the cold everything now.

I was a ghost to them. No matter how much I chirped, taunted, yelled, or bothered the players, to a person they refused to acknowledge me in any way.

Even when I broke down and shoved Big D out of pure frustration, hoping for a fight, *needing* a fight, he stared blankly over my head like I wasn't even there and kept moving.

The only person who met my eyes was Coach Nowak. As I left the ice near the end of practice, fuming, sweating, exhausted with bitter rage, his gaze clicked to mine.

There was an unholy joy there.

I clenched my jaw to keep from just lunging at him.

I'd been up all night, Slade's words rolling like barbed wire bundles through my head. I could accept there had to be at least some truth to them. Otherwise they wouldn't have hit me so hard, right?

If I wanted to change how I helped, why I helped people, I had to back away from other people's problems and deal with my own shit. I wasn't an alpha, born to protect. I was delusional, selfish.

Which meant I didn't ask Coach why he had cut Slade.

I didn't ask why he wasn't playing me.

I didn't try to become a part of the team.

I just...didn't do any of the things I naturally did.

But, damn it all. The one thing I wanted, the one thing I couldn't give up was the *need* to play hockey.

So I dropped my gaze from Nowak's and left to the locker room to change, shower, and go back to my hotel to wait for tomorrow's game.

I TEXTED MY DAD and told him and Mom not to come up. I told them I'd be down there for back-to-back games in a couple weeks. I'd see them then.

I read it four times to make sure it sounded happy. Added a bunch of hearts and smiley faces. Hit send.

Another text popped up. This one from Netti.

Come by my office before you leave for the road game. I need to see you.

I read it over and over. Why did she want to see me? I was nothing here. A phantom. A ghost.

Please, Duncan. I'm concerned about your health.

I only read that text once. I was fine. Didn't need her telling me what to do. I'd been a hockey player for a long time. I could look after myself.

I turned off my phone, shed all my clothes in the dark. I dove down into my wolf shape as fast as I could, so I could run.

And forget.

EAT, SLEEP, PRACTICE. SPEAK to no one. Touch no one.

Repeat.

Suit up for the game. Sit in the crowd, sit in the locker room, sit on the bench.

Repeat.

Maybe forget to eat. Maybe shift into wolf and run, run, run instead of sleep.

Repeat.

My alarm blared a heavy metal song by a group whose name I couldn't remember. Didn't care. I thumbed it off. I could crush my phone if I squeezed hard enough. Maybe the broken pieces would cut. I'd feel that, wouldn't I? Feel that pain?

I licked my lips, my mouth stiff as if I hadn't moved it in hours, days. I was keeping water down. But that was about it.

Maybe I was sick. Maybe I should go see Netti.

I pushed that thought away. I didn't have a fever. Didn't have a headache. It was just…numbness. I was numb. And that was fine. Better than the alternative.

This was a good place to be. Quiet. Alone. No one touched me. I didn't need touch.

No one spoke to me. I didn't need words.

No one needed me. I didn't need anyone either.

There was hockey. Snips of it. Minutes at the end of games. Minutes, sometimes, when someone was injured and pulled off the ice.

Those minutes didn't even add up to one period of play in a regular game but they were enough to make me want, and not enough to satisfy.

I felt like I was crossing a desert with only a teaspoon of water cupped in my palm.

The moments on the ice lit a fire in me. Made my blood pump. For those spare minutes, I was alive. Breathing. Real. And I knew something was wrong, but I didn't have time to think of what it could be.

Then the moment was gone and I went back to my hotel room, stripped, and shifted into wolf. To run.

The alarm blared out the metal song again and I stared at the phone in my hand for a moment before turning the alarm off instead of just on snooze.

I rubbed my face with one hand. Beard had grown past the itchy stage, but I scratched at it anyway. My hair was longer than I usually kept it, falling well below my collar.

It didn't seem to matter.

I turned the shower on hot and got in. When the water ran cold, I rubbed soap over my body, rinsed, and got out.

I dressed, my hands shaking as I knotted my tie. We were on the road again today. Just like we'd been on the road for most of the month. I'd forgotten where we were headed, and I didn't care. My job was to dress, drink a shit ton of water, and show up so I could be ignored.

I could do that. I'd been doing it for weeks.

COACH NOWAK STOOD AT the front of the bus, and snapped his fingers.

I hunched farther down in my seat, eyes closed, listening, but otherwise not engaging.

"There is media on site," he said. "National broadcast. So button your jackets, keep your mouths shut, smile, and represent the dignity of your team."

No one argued. No one ever argued with him. Not even me. Not now. I'd gotten good at not caring.

I stood and grunted at the cramp in my back. Had I pulled something? Broken something?

No. For whatever reason, maybe vibes I was throwing off, no one on the teams we'd played had made any significant contact with me.

Maybe I really had turned invisible.

In those rare lucid moments when I could think clearly, I knew that was weird. But I'd made a habit of not thinking too hard and just kept my head down and did as I was told.

I pulled my duffle over my shoulder, made sure my headphones were stashed inside my suit jacket and took my turn down the aisle, like the last man going to the gallows.

The light, the noise, slammed into me like a physical thing. I shuddered and had to wrestle the wolf in me down and back, pushing the instant fight or flight reaction away.

A reporter was talking into a microphone and bright lights shone on her even though it was sunny at three o'clock in the afternoon. The cameraman behind her slowly panned across the players exiting the bus.

"First game between the rivals since the Dead Man draft, in which Tide coach Don Nowak chose the only wizard in the WHHL, and instead got his adopted brother, Duncan Spark," the reporter said. "That very controversial substitution has this league, and many others, questioning how to value a first-marked wizard in sports."

My heart was pounding wrong. Like it was shoved up too high against my collarbones and stuck there. I blinked sweat out of my eyes, then wiped it away. I was almost to the door of the bus. I had a feeling the camera wanted a good long look at the volunteer Dead Man.

Shit.

I smiled, but it felt fake as all hell.

"Mr. Spark! Duncan!" the reporter shouted. "How does it feel being back home, playing against your old team for the first time?"

Coach Nowak stood by the arena door, watching. I knew he had good hearing. He'd just told us all to keep our mouths shut.

So I should keep my mouth shut.

I locked gazes with him across the distance. That man was an asshole. I might not be the person I thought I was, but there was no doubting he was a monster.

I bent so my mouth was near the microphone she held.

"It's gonna be a fun game. I hope I play." My voice was shot. Too low, too rough, as if it hadn't been used in weeks. And really, it hadn't. Still, I threw the camera a steady look and smiled for the audience.

The reporter sucked in a short breath and started in on the rapid-fire questions.

I tuned her out and strode to the arena. Nowak couldn't do anything to me in public. So I was surprised when he slapped my shoulder.

That contact *hurt*. I growled and jerked away. After weeks of zero physical contact, that slap was like a gunshot at close range.

He watched me, all the muscles in him tensed, ready to go to physical blows.

And…I thought about it.

I actually *considered* getting into a fight with him. One, because he was an abusive asshole and I'd wanted to punch him in the face since I met him. Two, because I would feel something.

It would be touch, even if it was pain. I would feel my flesh, even if it was bruising.

I would be in someone's space and I would no longer be invisible.

"Told you to keep your mouth shut, Spark."

I breathed hard, shaky breaths as my body trembled with the need for contact, the need for violence, the need for acceptance, and praise.

I hated it. Hated that the lines were blurring in my head.

If he hit me, at least he was paying attention to me. At least I was part of the world, and by proxy a part of the team.

But no. That sounded wrong. I knew it was wrong.

Still, the need was a deep, instinctive yearning and I huffed out a breath trying to push away the sudden rise of tears in my eyes.

Fuck these emotions. And fuck him for playing me.

"Screw you," I growled. "You're lucky I didn't throw you to the media dogs."

His eyebrows pinched and I could see the moment he realized we were on my old turf, my hometown, my people. That here, I could trash his reputation if I wanted to and people would listen to me.

"You've got balls," he admitted. "Let's see you show some on the ice."

"You'd have to fucking play me first."

His face lit up bright with a manic smile that made me take one step backward, watching his hands, expecting a gun or a knife.

183

We weren't the only ones who had good hearing. The reporter, the cameraman, maybe even the scatter of people who were hanging around to watch the team unload, also could have sharp hearing, could be marked.

He had a reason for being outside the door, in the sunlight. He wanted to be seen and heard.

I set my stance and squared my shoulders. Preparing for whatever he was going to hit me with.

"You're playing full shift tonight, Spark," he said with that snakebite smile. "Fourth line. Don't let me down."

The breath just shot out of me like I'd been punched in the chest. That was the last thing I'd expected, and a part of me, okay, all of me, didn't believe him.

It was like he'd pushed me into deep, deep water, the sand shifting beneath my feet. I didn't know what to say. Didn't want to ruin this opportunity, but knew there had to be a razor buried in this apple.

I clenched my teeth and nodded.

He grunted then dipped his head toward the interior of the arena.

It went against every instinct in me, both man and wolf, to have him at my back, but I walked into the building.

If I brushed my hair away from my neck and left my hand there, covering my spine while I walked, well, no one but one ex-girlfriend and one ex-teammate would know why.

17

MY PARENTS WERE OUT there in the stands. They'd be cheering for me. They'd want to see me after the game too.

Something inside me twisted tight.

I missed them. I'd spent the last month putting off their calls and texts and telling them I was good, I was fine, I just wanted a little time to get my feet under me before seeing them.

I was surprised they let me get away with it and hadn't shown up on my doorstep yet.

But then, Mom's schedule switched between swing, grave, and days, and Dad was teaching at the university along with his library job. They didn't have a lot of free time as it was. Just getting the same day off together could be challenging.

So I'd dodged having to see them for over a month.

I just…couldn't bear to see them walk away. When I got my head together and actually *belonged* somewhere, then I knew I could see them come and go without breaking down.

"Duncan?"

I stopped dead in my tracks, my hands balling into fists. I squeezed my eyes shut hard, trying to hold back everything that roared and rolled and howled in me like a thunderstorm raging.

Hazard.

"Jesus, would it kill you to answer your texts with more than a single word?" He was frustrated, his voice sort of high-handed with disgust. But I could hear what was below that: fear.

I'd pretty much frozen him out too.

But right here, right before the first game I might actually get to play, the first game I'd be playing not only against my ex-teammates but also against my brother, I was rocked by the realization that it was going to happen.

I'd be playing against him.

Directly. He was fourth line too.

That's why Coach Nowak wanted me to play. That's why he picked this time, this game out of all the others to put me out there with a team that hated me and didn't want me, against the team that I'd turned my back on.

What a clusterfuck.

"Duncan? Dunc?"

He was close. So close I wouldn't have to even take a step to reach him. Everything in me stayed stone still while I decided, did I run? Did I fight?

I inhaled hard, felt the ache in my lungs, the stretch of my ribs. This was my life, my body, my world. This was where I was grounded. Where I belonged. Everything was okay. Everything was fine.

I relaxed my hands, licked my lips, smiled.

"It's about time you showed up," I said with a close approximation of my actual voice.

He blinked and a crease pressed between his eyebrows. Then his eyes, blue and sharp as winter tracked from my feet up to my face.

"You're looking lean," he said. "Have you been eating? Are you okay?"

His gaze narrowed in on how I was favoring the left side of my ribs. Not because I'd been hit during the game. I'd been running in wolf form every night and had taken one too many jumps over an alley wall and had landed badly a few times. Plus, shifting always cost something. For Canidae shifters, our coordination was blown after a shift. Some of the bruises I sported were from me running into things as I struggled to replace the fuel and motor skills magic sucked out of me.

"Is someone hurting you? Is he hurting you?" His scowl was epic and he aimed it down the corridor. After Coach Nowak.

Yeah, no love lost there.

But that was not a fight I wanted Hazard to take on. That was the whole reason I'd volunteered. He was strong, and hell, maybe stronger than I gave him credit for.

Physically, though, I was still stronger than him. It wasn't pride or bragging. It was a fact. Second-marked wolf shifters were physically stronger than first-marked wizards.

"Like I can't take care of myself," I scoffed.

He hooked his thumbs in his belt and gave me another disbelieving look. "Not a good answer. Who hit you?" He nodded to my ribs.

"No one." At his look, I rolled my eyes. "Did it to myself, dude. No big deal. Just a bruise that's fading."

"Uh-huh."

"Don't do that."

"Do what?"

"Treat me like I'm lying." Without realizing it, I'd squared off to him. My arms weren't crossed over my chest. They were hanging loose at my sides, my fists curled.

I was ready to fight. Ready to wipe that fucking scowl off his face.

Because I couldn't take it. Couldn't take his notice, his words, his caring. It was too much. Much too much after so very little over the last month.

I didn't realize I was making a sound. Something caught between a growl and a pained whine. Random was right there. Right in front of me. I could smell him, see him. I could touch him.

Home. Family. Team. Pack.

That rage, that pain, that loss knotted up inside me, rising so hard and fast I had to swallow to choke the feeling back before it came out in tears...or something worse, something darker. Something that rode the edge of madness.

"Jesus," he whispered. He lifted his hand, maybe just to touch my arm.

I jerked, my whole body stumbling backward like he'd just tried to slap me.

"The hell?" he snarled. "Since when? Since when can't I touch you? What the hell happened Duncan, and don't give me some bullshit excuse of walking into a door."

I tried to say something, but words were buried beneath the screaming in my head and the only thing that made sense was to follow my gut, follow my instinct. Stay alive.

Staying alive meant staying away from anything that hurt.

And right now, standing here, seeing him with that look on his face, that storm rising in his eyes, the shift of his body and stance, everything hurt.

The air I breathed, the skin I was in hurt. The ungodly noise in my head made it too hard to think.

So I laughed. It came out hard and weird, and manic, but acted as a release valve on the pressure doubling and doubling inside me, stretching me into a weird painful thing, stretching me out of shape.

"No one," I snarled through clamped teeth. "Touches me unless I want them to. Not even you, Wiz."

His head jerked back, his eyes wide. Like I'd hit him. And maybe I had? In the clatter of sensations spiking under my skin, behind my eyes, in my brain—

—I can't breathe—

—I didn't know exactly what had made him react like that. My tone? My words? That I called him Wiz—his hockey nickname instead of Ran, the name I'd called him for years?

Unable to parse any of it, I spun and strode down the hall, blinking until my vision cleared, until I could hear past the roaring of my pulse in my ears.

I had a hockey game to play. The first one Coach Nowak was going to let me have. It was mine and I wasn't going to let anyone else take it away from me. I would be on my home ice against my team, against my best friend, my brother.

I would play in front of my parents. My real coach. People I loved—

—hated—

—no. People I loved. People who I had to leave behind. People I could not afford to let back into my life, my thoughts, my game because I had made them small and weak so I could feel big. I wasn't that Duncan anymore. Didn't want to be that Duncan.

I had to be something different out there than the Duncan Spark who had worn the Thunderheads jersey and been a brother, a son, a teammate.

I had to be something that could do more than survive. I had to be something that would win at all costs.

MY TEAMMATES CROWDED ME on the bench, all of us geared up. It was impossible not to bump into each other.

Every knock, tap, shove felt like a bullet shot into the middle of my brain.

The contact hurt. Five minutes into the game I wanted to scream at them to get the hell off me. Wanted to see them hurt. See their blood.

But they were my teammates. They were what I had. All I had left to be a part of.

I jerked at every contact, but otherwise tried to ignore them and ignore the pain. All my attention was on the ice, on the players of my team sweating and cursing and fighting through their shifts. On the puck, that small black devil's disk that carried our lives, our future on its hard, flat edge. On the goalie and the net behind her.

Thorn was a demon in the net. What she didn't have in height, and she was six foot even, she made up for in sheer, crazy grace.

She had a way of knowing where the puck was going to be. Since she was sensitive—she probably had some way of tracking the puck the rest of us didn't have.

She'd told me she could sense the inert magic in an object one of the times we'd gone out for beers as a team. One of the times she'd made us all dance with her for luck.

A wash of memories and emotions flooded me.

I shut that shit down with a brutal growl. Those things, what I had once been, what this team had once been to me, didn't matter.

All that mattered was getting that puck past the Thunderheads' goalie.

I was already sweating. If I stopped to think too hard, everything got a little wavy at the edges.

I felt like I had a fever. I was ice cold.

And when it came time for me to jump the board and skate, I did it hard, I did it fast.

I was a left wing, which put me up against my old linemate, JJ, who was also a sensitive. It was weird as hell, but only registered for a moment or two. JJ quickly went from ex-teammate to opponent.

He was who I had to stop, he was who I'd be ducking to get the puck in the net.

"Fuck, look at your eyes." JJ's voice came from far away even though he was right next to me as we headed for the boards to save a pass my center had overshot. "You okay, Donuts? Seriously, are you sick?"

I snarled and went hard after the puck. He was on my heels, fast, ready to slam me into the boards if I didn't move out of the way in time. I was quick, dug the puck off the boards and shot it up ice to my winger who was waiting for it.

And that's when I saw their center move. He was crazy fast. And he was good. Darting in to steal the puck, a clean pickpocket, then flying down the ice, dangling the puck on the edge of his stick like it was magnetically attached. His shoulders were down, his head was up.

He was amazing and so was his team.

His D-men were in position to screen his shot, their big bodies cutting off our goalie's sight line.

He was going to score.

Not if I had anything to say about it.

I shut JJ down, putting my body and stick in the way to close any possibility of the center passing to him.

But it wasn't enough to stop the goal. So I pushed more speed into my stride, crossing the ice to get in the center's way, aiming for him like he was the only damn thing in the world.

He wasn't going to score a goal as long as I was breathing. That was my fucking net with my fucking wall of Iowa crouched in it. This was my fucking team; I hated them, I needed them. I wasn't going to let them down.

I was going to keep them safe, keep them alive, save them.

I crowded up on the center, shut down the shooting lane, and followed him as he winged around the back of the net.

We slammed into the corner and I threw my weight into it to crush him.

His head hit the glass.

The tactile violence, the full-force contact, did something to the pain and rage and horror in me.

Something in my chest snapped. My entire body washed with heat and went loose, like I'd just drunk an entire bottle of whiskey in one long gulp.

My vision tunneled down to red. I wanted to strike, shout, hurl away this pain inside me. I wanted to throw away my lungs, dig my bones free, turn inside out until I'd crawled out of my muscles and skin and rid myself of the constant, constant pain.

I fell to my knees over the top of the center I'd plowed into the boards.

Grabbed jersey. Cocked fist. Hit with everything I had.

Over and over and over.

Even when the players showed up to try to drag me off. Even when the refs elbowed in.

I punched and punched and punched. Breaking a hole in my brain, breaking a hole in my chest, breaking a hole in the world.

And when the stun prod shot lightning through my brain, through my spine, snapping all my muscles into rictus, I laughed and kept drunkenly swinging.

I didn't even know who I was hitting. Didn't care.

"Duncan," the voice was so calm, almost quiet which made no sense because the world was roaring and throbbing, an ocean of hatred and blood and violence, screaming, screaming.

Then she was in front of me. She'd taken off her helmet and her hair, which I knew she usually braided back was pulled free of its bond, hanging over one side of her face.

She was beautiful. I'd always thought so, even though I'd never told her that. Because, you know, you don't go telling the goalie that you think he or she is pretty.

But Thorn was a looker. Strong, tall, funny, brash in a way that made me want to buy her beer and watch her chug.

I mean, she wasn't someone I'd date because we were teammates, and also because she was pretty much out of my league. We weren't ever meant to be. But still. I liked her.

"I've got you, okay?" she said, still so quiet and calm. "You're going to be okay. We're right here with you."

And then she reached out, her hand coming toward me for days, years, centuries. I expected her hair to be blowing in some kind of cosmic wind, but instead, sweat ran down her face, catching on the edge of her straight nose, on the corner of her mouth, dripping off her chin.

She looked like she was in the middle of a hard-played game. Like she had been giving it her all. It was in the narrowed focus of her eyes, the stubborn press of her lips that put little lines beside her mouth and between her eyebrows.

Why was she kneeling in front of me, talking, if we were in the middle of a game?

My brain tried to sort through the input but everything was lost to that wall of water: the yelling, chanting. The taste of sweat in my mouth, the sting of it in my eyes, the smell of blood, fresh, hot, and sticky on my knuckles, splattered on my jersey.

Dreamlike, Thorn's palm landed gently on the side of my face.

Not a slap. Not at all. It was a caress.

The moment her skin touched mine, a crack of something bone-deep snapped in my brain. What followed it was pain so hot, so clean, so fucking *pure* that I was, for a moment, lifted above it, knowing it was agony, but that I was drifting, alive and free despite it.

"Oh." It was a soft, almost broken sound that came out of my mouth.

Thorn's eyes rolled back and her eyelashes fluttered, her body jerking once hard.

Then the world came back and brought with it my horror. My nightmare.

The guy they were pulling away from my feet, the center who was being carefully placed upon a board and moved to a stretcher was my brother.

Random.

Bloody, bruised, broken.

By my hands.

"No," Thorn said. "No, no, no. Don't go there, Duncan. Stay with me. He's okay. He's going to be okay. I've got you. We've got you."

But the thing about being a second-marked is that it's really easy to smell a lie on a person.

I dropped from my knees, to flat on my belly, and laced my fingers over my head. Total submission. They could do what they wanted to me. I wouldn't shift to get away.

I'd hurt him. The only brother I had. I'd torn him apart because I was so angry—

—*lonely*—

—so blind, all I'd wanted was violence—

—*contact*—

—and I'd lost my mind, lost my humanity.

I didn't care when they put me in restraints: wrist, ankle, and a choker that would shock me unconscious if I so much as twitched.

Thorn was yelling, telling them they were wrong about me. The crowd pounded the glass, lathered in a frenzy for more blood.

My Tide teammates were nowhere to be seen. But other people—

—*pack*—

—Coach Clay, Graves, JJ, Watson, surrounded me like a wall, a fortress protecting me.

None of it mattered. I'd probably never play hockey again.

But just as I stumbled off the ice to shuffle down the corridor, I saw Coach Nowak look my way. He gave me a tip of his chin. His eyes brittle and flat, his pupils blown with something like lust.

I had done just what he wanted.

I had taken out the only wizard in the WHHL.

18

THE FIRST VOICE I heard was Dad talking to the doctor outside my room.

Blurry memories floated at the edges of my awareness. The arena, the ambulance, the handler and paramedic, the former armed with a stun prod and tranquilizer gun, the latter with the big syringe full of enough knockout juice to keep me down for days.

"It's not a full dose," the paramedic had said. "Just enough to keep you out while we get you somewhere secure."

"Random?" I asked.

The paramedic shook his head and stuck that needle in my arm, and then everything went black.

And now here was my dad's voice. Asking to be left alone with me. No, not asking, telling. The other voice was deep and authoritative, which meant it was probably a doctor.

I lost track of time, but then Dad's hand was on my face.

"Duncan, you're okay, son. This is going to all work out. If you feel a little disconnected and dreamy it's because they have you on a lot of drugs and fluids and glucose. You're underweight, son. Dehydrated, stressed. You're going to stay here at the hospital at least one full day, to see how quickly you recover."

I opened my eyes and made a little happy sound.

Dad looked amazing. He wore a collared shirt under the red Mr. Rogers sweater I liked to tease him about. His glasses, his hair styled off to the side, darker than mine, but with a slight flip at the front because he'd been digging his fingers through it, all looked so familiar, so much like home.

He was worried, it was coming off him in waves.

"There you are." He smiled, and it didn't wobble even a little. My dad was a rock. I might beat him on muscle and height, but he beat me by a million on mental and emotional steadiness.

Nothing ever threw him. He was the guy everyone else turned to when things went to hell. A steady presence in the classes he taught, the community boards he was a member of, the library he loved, and the life of his family.

He pressed his hand over mine and it was warm. But it also trembled just a little before he squeezed my fingers.

"You're okay, Duncan. Underfed, under-hydrated, under-slept. But nothing permanent. Nothing that can't be fixed."

I wanted to say something, because there was a big thing I was forgetting, something huge and dark that was just on the edge of my memory.

Random.

I sucked in a hard breath and my eyes went wide. My heart started beating really fast too, the machine in the room wild with it.

"He's fine." Dad used his "dad" voice. Firm with reason. No blame, just the truth. I trusted him. He would not lie to me.

But I had hurt Random. I had hit him.

I opened my mouth to scream, but there was no sound.

Only the pinch of a needle and darkness again.

MOM CAME IN, KISSED my forehead. Held one of my hands as she read my charts, then held Dad's hand and kept her palm over my heart.

They talked. I listened in. But every time I heard my name or Random's, I threw myself toward the foggy relief of the drugs.

My teammates came in—Thunderheads, not Tide. JJ and Thorn and Watson and the Terminators all in a row. Each of them touched me, my arm, my shoulder, the top of my head.

Coach Clay was there after they left, looking tired and furious and haunted. He ran his hand over his face and breathed hard into his palm before standing above me and just staring.

I returned the look, though he went in and out of focus.

Finally, he dropped down to sit in the chair next to the bed.

"Forgive me, Duncan."

That was...a surprise.

"I never should have let you stand in for Random. I know what he is. What kind of man Nowak is." His scowl was fierce, as was the baring of his teeth and narrowing of his eyes. "I thought the game, having it, having a win, would trump his need for revenge."

I didn't think he was talking about Random. I swallowed, but even that took concentration and time.

Coach Clay stared off in the distance for a while. I didn't think he knew I was actually following what he said.

Maybe I wasn't. The drugs were strong, and I was doing everything I could to keep reality out there at arm's length, squishy and unfocused.

When I opened my eyes again, I knew it was night.

And I was not alone in my room.

But it was not Dad or Mom or Coach in the room. It was my old defenseman.

"Are you listening to me?" Graves asked.

I turned my head a little. He sat in the chair where, to my fuzzy sense of time, Coach Clay had been only a moment ago.

The shadows in the room had changed, and so had the sounds of the hospital. Time had passed.

I studied Hawthorn Graves, the eldest member of the Thunderheads, and he studied me right back.

Graves had this look in his eyes that always read as second-marked, wolf shifter, until suddenly it didn't. I'd been curious about it before, about what he really was, because even though his paperwork said wolf, the man himself did not fit that mold.

The wolf in me knew that on a level I didn't have words for. He wasn't the same as me. Nor was he something I knew like coyote or fox.

But he was familiar. Recognizable on a spine-deep level.

Like a nightmare.

"Duncan I'm going to say this once. You'll hear me." Graves's voice was low, and carried a bit of an accent that I still couldn't tell if it was from Kentucky, or Texas or some place more Southern. Definitely cowboy of some kind.

I licked the inside of my mouth and moved my lips so I could speak. It was just...the way he looked at me made it clear I had his full attention. All of that hard, strange focus. It made me want to respond. To agree.

I huffed in acknowledgment. I was listening.

"You've made very poor choices," he began.

Well, this wasn't going to be one of my favorite conversations.

"Going to the Tide was stupid, but I understood it. Still understand it." He added a nod, as if he knew I wanted to argue with every word coming out of his mouth.

"Still, it should have been me. Because I would not have broken."

Like a finger snap, the fuzziness, the dreaminess, the distance and soft edges came into hard, cold focus.

"Fuck you."

Hey, first words out of my mouth and they were good ones.

He didn't move, didn't shift his lounging position. "You know why I wouldn't have broken under that asshole's treatment?"

"Because you're an ass?" Two for two. I was on fire.

"Nope. Because I do not deny what I am."

That was news. "Bull."

He raised an eyebrow. "You got something to say? Say it, kid."

"You're not a wolf."

He paused, then nodded. "All right. What am I, then?"

"I don't know."

He leaned forward. "Team looks to me like an alpha. Am I an alpha, Duncan?"

He was something. Power. Chaos. Strength. He had a way of drawing us all together, a way of making us work like we were bound together. Like we were a team.

Those were all things an alpha, a leader should be.

But...

No. That wild thing shifted in his eyes and I knew he was not an alpha.

"Do you know how you can see what I am not?" The question took my brain few minutes to unpack. But when I got it, I finally got it.

"Because I'm an alpha," I croaked.

He nodded, pleased, eyes twinkling. "It's why I thought you'd be able to handle Nowak. Why you wouldn't put up with someone torturing you like that."

I didn't know what to say. If he was going for a pep talk, he was failing spectacularly. I didn't need to be reminded that I was weak. That I broke.

"I failed you," he said.

That was not at all what I expected him to say. I frowned.

"I thought you knew," he continued. "That you're an alpha. But you didn't know, did you?"

I shook my head, and really, it didn't hurt as much as I'd thought it would. Thank you, second-marked healing abilities.

"I forget how young some of you boys are, with how you play out there, all attitude and power." He settled back in the chair.

"I'm not that young. You're just old."

That got a twitch of an eyebrow out of him and a half nod. "Half true," he conceded.

Graves's words, this conversation grounded me. I'd been blown apart, all the bits of me flinging away from my center, arcing out and out, getting farther and farther away from what I was, who I was.

Every choice I'd made, the silence, the shifts, the friendship, the runs, the endless isolation was a bomb that had gone off weeks ago, even though I was still reeling from the shockwaves.

I could own up to stupid decisions. I was the one who had volunteered in Random's place. I was the one who had refused to answer my parents' calls, who had lied to them, pushed them away. I had gone into this team with the idea of cutting all ties with the Thunderheads, with *my* team, my friends, my family.

I knew, in my gut, that if I would have reached out to Coach Clay or Graves or any of my teammates, told them what was going on, they would have been there for me, at my side. They had my back.

We weren't just friends, we were a team, a body, a unit.

We were family.

"Coming around to your senses finally?" Graves asked.

"I fucked up."

"Yes, you did. Tell me how."

"You know."

"That's right. I want to know if you do."

"I thought I had to do it alone."

"Yes."

"I thought they were my team."

"Yes."

"I thought I was just one of them, just like anyone else, equal, not equal-but-different."

"Because?"

"Because I'm alpha." I met his gaze. Hawthorn Graves's hard eyes glittered with approval.

"You are."

"I fucked up because I screwed up the Tide's team dynamic by going there and not being what I could be. What they expected me to be on an instinctive level. What I am."

"That team was already screwed up. You have some choices to make, Duncan Spark." The way he said my whole name put a shiver through me. He had some serious Obi-Wan Jedi shit going on.

I couldn't help but grin at him.

"What's wrong with your face?" he asked.

"Nothing. Just happy."

"You're in a hospital because you lost your mind in the middle of a hockey game. You put your brother in the room next to you. There some reason to be happy I don't see?"

A wave of sickness rolled through me. I had to swallow several times so I didn't just barf into the wastebasket. Random was hurt. I'd beat the shit out of him.

Heat washed over me as I simultaneously started shivering. I was freezing. Burning up.

A hand pressed down on my shoulder, grounding me, keeping the bits of me that were flying apart stuck back together.

199

Graves leaned over me, his eyes softer than I'd seen them before, his expression worried.

"He's going to be fine."

Hearing it from a man I knew wasn't going to just say something to make me feel better, the man making me face my truths, meant everything.

"Breathe, Duncan. You got a lot of life left to live. So does Random."

He exhaled slowly, noisily so I'd pay attention and follow along.

I did. "Which room?"

He tipped his head to the left. "He really is going to be fine."

"How? I...I didn't hold back."

"You forget he's a wizard, kid?"

"Of course I didn't forget."

"Oh? You forget he knows how to take care of himself?"

I narrowed my eyes. "People need to stop telling me what I think about him."

He met my gaze, evenly. I knew this, this right here—what my relationship was to Random, who I was to him, how I saw him—was a hill I'd die on. This was where I drew the line of what people assumed.

Slade had been wrong about me. I made choices to protect the people I loved because I loved them, not because I needed them to be weak so I could be strong. That was clear to me now that my brain was working again. I'd been a fool to believe it was ever in me to do someone harm that way.

Graves's eyebrow twitched. "That's right. People don't get to tell you who you are to him, or who he is to you."

"Damn straight," I said, my voice low, steady, and powerful in a way it normally wasn't.

Alpha.

"Damn straight," he agreed.

I SNUCK OUT OF my bed a couple hours later. Mom and Dad had come in again, and finding me awake, I'd gotten an earful of love and reprimands. Mostly love, because my family knew we all made stupid, hurtful mistakes and we deserved to move past those mistakes and be better people.

Still, I knew how much this mistake hurt them, seeing one of their kids lose his mind and hurt their other kid.

It hurt me too. Killed me.

Which was why I was walking barefoot and bare-assed—the hospital gown not doing much to keep my back door covered—one room over where Random should be.

I didn't knock first. I just stepped in.

The room was identical to mine. He was in the bed, sleeping. It was a couple hours before dawn and no one else was in the room. Mom and Dad had gone home to shower, change, and let their respective workplaces know they were taking some time off.

I couldn't even take another step. I had to get my breathing under control so I wouldn't fall under the panic that raged in the margins of my awareness.

But finally I walked into that room and stood beside his bed. It felt like it had taken me a million years to get there.

"Took you long enough." Random opened his eyes. He hadn't really been asleep.

"How long you been awake?" I asked. All the other things I wanted to say felt too big to shove into words.

"Since you opened the door."

"Oh." I picked at a hangnail and resisted the urge to fidget from foot to foot.

I wanted to run out of the room. It was paramount I get away from him. Get away from the guilt eating at me. I'd hurt him. I'd *broken* him.

"Duncan," Random said. "Sit down, okay?"

I blinked a couple times. Sit. He wanted me to sit. I looked for a chair.

"On the bed, you idiot."

I moved woodenly, pressed first my fingers then palm onto the mattress, my gaze locked on his eyes, watching for even the slightest wince or twitch of pain.

He made a face at me. "Sit."

I swallowed down the knee-jerk reaction to tell him that I was not his damn dog.

But I couldn't say those things anymore because we weren't brothers anymore because I'd broken him. We couldn't be friends. We couldn't be teammates.

I dipped my head and sat on the edge of the bed, facing him. Ready for the punishment I deserved.

"Jesus, you are a mess," he said. His voice was a little raspy, but it was still all him. And fuck me, but I was happy just to hear him talk. To know he was alive.

"Look at me."

But I couldn't move. I couldn't bear to find out what I'd see in his eyes. Hatred. Pity. Loathing.

"Duncan, what the hell, dude? Don't you like me even a little anymore?"

I jerked, my shoulders going all tight and stiff, because of course I liked him. He was my brother. I'd follow him to hell if he asked me to—even if he didn't. But I didn't deserve him. Didn't deserve to have him anymore.

He was gone. We were done.

"I can't—" That was all I could get out. Then there wasn't any more air. There was only guilt, choking and so thick, I thought my lungs would harden from it.

"Stop it." His voice was stronger, certain. "Look at me Dunc. Now."

I did as he asked and lifted my head. How could I not?

"Do you see this?" He pointed at his face, made a small circle with his finger indicating all of it, forehead to chin to forehead. "Do you see my skin? I have a bruise right here." He pointed at the left side of his jaw, slanted his head so I could see it better.

And yeah, I saw it. Zeroed in like it was the most important thing I'd ever see and there'd be a test on it later.

It was a big bruise covering his cheek, but hadn't reached his eye yet. A pointy wash of black stabbed down under his chin and dribbled across his neck. Blood moved, and a hit to the face often colored lower than the impact point.

I didn't remember hitting him in the jaw. But I hadn't cared where my fist was landing so long as I could hit something.

"Random," I said, my voice tightened to a whine. I wanted to hide.

"No. Shut up. We're going to do this my way. My way."

I nodded. Yeah. Whatever he wanted. Any way he wanted to make me pay, I deserved it.

"Good. Now look at my neck." He lifted his face, stared at the ceiling. I did as he asked. Other than that one black bruise on his left side, his skin looked normal to me.

"I—"

"No," he ordered. "I'm not done. Sit there. Look at my arms." He had on a hospital gown like mine. Short sleeves, and that weird industrial blue only the hospital ever used.

I stared at his right arm, including the shoulder when he shoved the sleeve up higher and twisted so I could see it, then the left when he repeated the same move.

"But—"

"Shut it." He crunched up and pulled open the gown in the back so he could push it down to his waist.

"You don't—"

"Look at my body, Duncan. Look at my skin. You see this?" He pointed at his collarbones, his chest, his hard-muscled stomach. "You see any bruises there? Anything at all on his ribs? Breaks? Swelling?" He twisted for that too, to show me his sides.

I opened my mouth, shut it. He was glaring at me. Angry. But he was not done.

He kicked off the thin blanket and dropped his long hairy legs on top of it so I could look at them too. There were a couple smaller, faded bruises on his shins, one on his thigh that looked pretty new, though it was already brown whereas the one on his jaw was a hard, bloody red-black.

"Nothing's broken." He rolled his feet in a circle to show me his ankles were working. "Nothing's broken." He twisted his hands in circles and waggled his fingers at me. "I need to you see this. Need you to see me."

He shoved his legs back under the covers, then sat the rest of the way, pulling his legs up toward him, crossing them like he always did, and squaring off to me.

"Do you see me, Duncan?" He dipped his head to better catch my gaze. "Do you see *me*?"

I let my gaze wander over his shoulders, bare chest, arms. Took my time because what I saw didn't make any damn sense. I'd felt him breaking under my assault. I'd hit him hard, and those hits had connected. I'd been there when they hauled him off the ice on a stretcher. My knuckles still hurt from all the impacts.

"You. I broke you," I choked out. "I hit—"

He nodded, his nostrils flared. "Yeah, you did, you asshole. Jesus, you can land a punch. But c'mon. Seriously, dude? You think I'm gonna lay there and let you pound the shit out of me?"

"But…" The world had tipped off a cliff I wasn't sure how to hold onto it. "How?"

"Magic." He wiggled his fingers again and gave me the biggest shit-eating grin in the world. "Remember? I'm a wizard, Harry."

I blinked. Just. Everything in my head went sort of white noise. How could he have done anything with magic to keep me from hurting him? I'd felt those punches connect. Hell, I'd reveled in them.

"Whoa, okay, you're going a really horrible gray color," he said. "I think you might need to lie down, Dunc. 'Cause if you pass out, I'll have to call people in to get you off the floor. I'm on a weight restriction for the next twelve hours or so."

"I can't— I don't—"

"Right here, dude." He moved over so there was room for me to collapse. He patted the side of the bed by his pillow, shifting to lie back too, on his side.

We'd shared a bed more times than I usually admitted in mixed company. It wasn't a sexual thing—I so didn't want to get it on with a guy I considered my brother. It was more that I'd adopted him, brought the sad lonely little Random Hazard home to my parents. And they'd let me keep him.

He was mine, which meant I was supposed to look after him. And as a kid, I'd had to make sure he was sticking around. So sometimes I hung out in his room talking, or playing video games when my dad wasn't watching. And then I just stayed there, sleeping on one side of the bed while he slept on the other.

SPARK

Mom had told me it had more to do with the fact that I was an only child, and needed siblings, a pack. That it was as necessary as breathing for a second-marked.

I stretched out next to him.

He settled facing me, but took all the pillow, propping it under his head so he could stare down at me judgmentally.

"Tell me."

"This bed isn't even big enough for one of us," I groused.

His eyebrows shifted upward. "Well, if you would have used your words instead of your fists earlier, we wouldn't be here, would we?"

At the reminder of what I'd done, all the words in me dried up.

"No," he said, "no. You don't get to clam up. You have to talk."

"Why aren't you in traction?"

"Not what I wanted to start with, but fine. When you lost your ever loving mind and went insane, I pulled magic around me. It shielded me."

"I didn't see it."

"I don't think you were seeing anything really, am I right?"

"Yeah," I breathed. "Still got in one shot." My gaze tracked to his jaw.

"One punch let me know you'd cracked."

"Or I was just really pissed at you."

"You've never been that angry at me."

I clenched my teeth. Evidence to the contrary was right there on his face.

"That," he pointed at his jaw, "wasn't anger at *me*. You couldn't even see me. I was something else. Or everything else. I was a wall you were trying to punch your way through."

He was very insightful, my wizard brother.

"So," he said. "Talk to me, Duncan. What's wrong?"

I sighed, not even knowing where to start. Suddenly, I was just tired. Tired of all the choices I'd made, all the things I'd done.

Tired with the noise in my head. The doubt.

Sort of tired of being me.

Hazard snapped his fingers in front of my nose and little green and purple sparks flicked and kindled into a tiny flame.

I grinned. "Cool."

"Got your attention?"

"Do it again." I loved when he did magic. Especially the shiny stuff.

He rolled his eyes, but I could tell he wasn't mad. He snapped again, and this time the sparks were red and yellow, the flame a little star.

"Spiffy."

"Talk."

I inhaled, exhaled. "They hate me." I waited for his reaction.

"Just keep going. Say it all. I'll have an opinion when you're done." He settled his pillow into a more comfortable position. "Go."

So I told him. Sometimes I could look him in the eye when I went over something, like making friends with Slade. But other times, most of the time, I stared at my fingers, picking at the seamed edge of the hospital blanket.

I got through it all. And I do mean all. I was good at being truthful with Random. We'd had a lot of years to build that trust.

"Finally being on the ice, playing..." I blew out a shaky breath. I was sweating, and freezing, like I'd just broken a bad fever and still didn't have my feet under me yet. "Just playing the game, Ran. It was..." I let go of the blanket I had destroyed and pressed my fingertips into the corners of my eyes, wiping away the moisture there. "It was like breathing again. And it was hell."

He didn't say anything for a little bit. Long enough for me to get my breathing nice and steady. Long enough for me to clear my eyes and dislodge the weight on my chest.

I finally looked back at him, half expecting him to be asleep.

But he was watching me, frown lines above his nose and crinkling the corner of his eyes.

"Okay. So you're an alpha."

I snorted. "That's what you got out of all this?"

"Well, that and the fact that Nowak tortured you."

"It wasn't torture."

"Bull. Shit."

The look in his eyes was fierce. "If I had done something with those letters, or reported him when he threatened me in the diner…"

"No," I said. "You do not get to second-guess yourself. You do not get to take the blame for what that asshole does. Got it? What he did to me was cruel. It would have been torture if he kept it up, I agree."

"Jesus—"

"I'm not excusing him," I said over his protest. "It was an utter shit move. Against the rules."

"Totally," he said on a hard exhale. "Those prods are only to be used sparingly. Not to physically incapacitate to unconsciousness."

"What he did to me is something I can use against him. But I don't think anyone I go to will listen to me alone. One voice isn't enough. One player isn't enough."

"Can you ask the other players if Nowak ever did something like that to them?"

"We aren't really on speaking terms. Not even when they were speaking to me."

I could go—"

"Maybe," I said, cutting him off again. "I have a video."

He went dead still.

"How?"

"One of the players."

"That's proof, Duncan. Player abuse. Nowak can get canned for that."

"Can he? It's one event. And if you and I go to the commissioner with it, do you think they'll listen to us, or write it off as justified? Everyone knows I like to fight on the ice, that I'm a hothead. Especially after tonight. And you and I are kind of a package deal. They might think we're both out to destroy Nowak's reputation so I can come back to the Thunderheads."

There was a tug in my chest. I still missed being on the team.

"We can give it to Coach Clay," Random said.

"He'd go to the commissioner too. Same problem. The Dead Man pick will make him look biased."

Random chewed on his bottom lip. "Nowak told me he has people. In the league. Even high up. That he can kill any bad press."

"You think he was telling the truth?"

The nod was immediate.

"We need to think this through," he said. "Be smart about what we have. If we want to take Nowak down…"

It was my time to nod quickly.

"…then we need to keep our evidence somewhere safe and not let anyone know about it until we have a plan. I still think we need to talk to Coach Clay. He's on our side."

"I agree. But not yet. I don't know who Nowak has on his payroll, and I don't want anyone to know I have the vid until we know who will make sure it gets seen by the right people."

"I don't think that's a good idea. I think we tell someone. We have to do something, Duncan. So he can't hurt you."

I snorted. "He can't hurt me. I won't let him."

"You already let him."

"Yeah, but I got things figured out now. Alpha things."

"He'll hurt other players. Like that guy, Slade."

"He didn't deserve getting cut," I said. "That was a shit move."

Random was quiet. I knew he was sorry I'd lost a friend, but that was a part of hockey too. One day you'd be set, a part of the family, a part of the team. The next day you were gone.

There had to be a team that needed Slade. He was good.

"Go back to the alpha thing," Random said. "What's your plan?"

"I'm not an alpha. Not yet. It's like…I know what I am, but until I do something with it, claim it and own it, I'm not really that thing yet. I'm still just potential."

"All passing, no shots, no goal."

"Yeah. No goals, no goods."

"So what are we going to do?" he asked.

"We?"

He sighed. "You think I'm letting you do anything without having your back ever again, Donuts? Don't be stupid. We're a team. You and me. No matter where we're playing hockey. No matter where we live. No matter what else happens."

I didn't expect those words, a little high handed and derisive, would do so much to settle all the sharp edges inside me.

"Okay." I swallowed. "You and me. No matter what happens."

"You and me," he agreed like we'd shook on it. "Now, what do you want to do?"

"About?"

"Hockey, alpha, that asshole Nowak."

"Big questions."

"Yeah. But if we figure those out, everything else will be easy street. Start with hockey. You still want to play, right?"

I winced. "They're gonna suspend the hell out of me for attacking you."

"Of course they are. Welcome to the club. But after that. You still want to play?"

He sounded nervous. Like I'd give up on the one thing that made my blood sing.

"Yeah, I still want to play."

"Thunderheads or Tide? Or a different team? If you had a choice."

"If I could pick? Thunderheads. All the way." I couldn't quite meet his gaze because this was one of the things I had to take as my responsibility. "I screwed up with the Tide. I wasn't a good teammate. I didn't, couldn't, figure a way to fit in."

"Like they gave you a chance." He was angry for me, which was nice, but kind of moot at this point.

"Doesn't matter. It's on me. I'm still a Tide. It's my job to find my place there, and make a difference for the team."

"Not every player fits in every team, Duncan. Not even in the NHL. You know that."

"Sure. But I'm an easygoing guy. I can make friends with anyone. You know me. I'm good at…"

"Belonging?"

That one word knocked the wind out of me.

"Yeah," I said, trying not to sound too desperate for that. "Belonging."

"Where do you belong, Duncan?"

"With my team." It was instant, easy. I knew that truth as well as I knew my own heartbeat. "But I can't come back." Which cemented that, in my heart, Thunderheads were still my team.

He snorted. "Coach Clay's been working on how to get you back since the day you walked out, you idiot."

"Really? He… Really?"

"He could just wait until Nowak cuts you, if he cuts you," he went on like this wasn't my life, my career he was talking about. Like it was obvious that at the end of it all I'd be back on the team, my team.

It was that confidence, so casual, just tossed out there like he didn't even have to think about it twice that settled the part of me that had been running hard and fast, flat out, trying to save my family.

Random hadn't let go of me, even though I'd let go of him, thinking doing so would make him safer. I'd expected his anger to be permanent. I'd expected my one chance to be on a team with him to be over. He refused to entertain those thoughts.

"The rules say he can't buy you off the Tide. Not until the next trade right before the actual playoffs," he said. "So if we make it that far, to the playoffs—hell, even if we don't—Coach Clay will put an offer down for you."

I knew what I had to do. I knew what would settle my debt with my teammates. I knew how I could make up for my dumb choices. I was an alpha. It was time to be an alpha. Time to be the Tide's alpha.

I heard him as he rambled on about trades and Coach Clay and handling the press, but so many things were clicking into place that I was having to hold really still while the entire world rearranged itself and settled.

"I can't come back," I blurted out.

"Like hell."

"Not yet. Not until… I'm an alpha, Ran."

"You keep saying that."

"It's big. More than I thought I could handle. But it's why everything went crazy. I'm a part of the Tide. Not the way I was trying to be. But the right way. As their alpha."

It was his turn to blink and wait for words to make sense. "What are you even talking about?"

"I have to go back."

"I think you're suspended."

"Probably. After that."

"No," he said firmly. "You don't have to go back and be an alpha for a team that hates you. This is you trying to save people again, Duncan! Jesus, learn from your mistakes."

"Ouch, buddy."

He was scared for me. It was all over him. But I wasn't in that broken headspace anymore. Couldn't return there if I tried. Denying and ignoring what I was—alpha—had messed up all my signals. On a team full of shifters, it had messed up their signals too.

Hell, I was lucky none of them hadn't just shifted and killed me out of mercy. I knew instinctively that the moment I stepped up as alpha for them, for *me* the team would settle into something different. Better.

He rubbed his eyes. "Sorry. That was out of line. Can't you just...be an alpha here? With me. You know your mom and dad want you home. They haven't even touched your room."

"They haven't?"

"Well, your mom might have painted it."

"Uh-huh."

"And then she said it needed new shades. And a closet organizer. And art."

"Hasn't changed a thing."

"She didn't move the bike in there yet."

"Outstanding."

"There's a treadmill. And yoga mats. And a water cooler."

I chuckled, really the first time my chest didn't feel like it was strapped and buckled down tight. "Good to know nothing's changed. My bed get shoved into the garage?"

"No, it's against one wall. New comforter and pillows."

"Pink with bows?"

"Bows? Your mom?"

"Yeah, what was I thinking? So patchwork quilt or something fuzzy?"

"Fuzzy."

"But the bed's still there."

"Yes. That's what I'm saying. There's still a place for you. Even alpha you. As long as your majesty doesn't mind climbing over some yoga blocks."

"His majesty approves of blocks."

"But?" He was serious again. So was I.

"But I have to take care of what I started, Ran. It's important to me. It's the right thing to do."

"No."

"Yes."

"I thought I was important to you. I thought the Thunderheads were important to you. I thought being here was important to you."

"It is. It still is, always. But so is fixing what I screwed up."

"You didn't start that shit show, Duncan. They wanted you hurt and gone the moment they had you. They didn't want you. They abandoned you. I hate them for that," he added in a vicious whisper.

"Yeah, I wasn't a fan of it either."

"So why the hell go back?"

"For one thing, I owe it to my teammates." I shook my head. "No, you can't argue me out of this. I damaged that team. Not from being there, but from letting Coach Nowak define who I was to them.

"I thought if I worked hard and did what I was told, I'd fit in, no alpha required. But that's not how it works. No one can tell me how I fit, how I belong, what I can bring to the team. That's on me. Nowak sure as hell can't tell me, because he's an asswipe, and we both know it."

"You just told me you did everything you could to fit in. They wouldn't even talk to you." His voice was rising and his eyes were doing that sort of glittery yellow thing they did when magic got the upper hand of his emotions.

He was this close to losing it in some huge, wonderful, terrifying way.

I loved it. Like seriously. My brother was this big ole magic bomb always set to explode. How lucky was I?

Still, it wasn't like him to be this volatile.

I had a quick moment to wonder if maybe I was a part of why. Maybe Random wasn't at his best, controlling his magic, his temper, when I wasn't around.

Maybe I grounded him too. Just like knowing he had my back, was a part of my world, a part of my—

—*pack*—

—family put the ground beneath my feet and rooted me there, strong and steady.

It was a big concept to acknowledge something that had been unconscious between us—

—*alpha*—

—and to accept it now as a conscious thing. My new reality.

It was tantalizing, the idea of being the guy Random would turn to, rely upon. Even more alluring was the idea that maybe that draw was there with my team too. That maybe all those players on the Thunderheads' roster were looking for something in me, and were missing it now that I wasn't there.

Was that possible? Did they need me as family, just like I needed them?

I held that idea, savored it for a good long moment.

Then I put it aside.

Right now, I had something to finish. Something to settle and make right.

Random pushed the blanket off his feet and twisted toward the edge of the bed.

"Where are you going, sailor?" I asked. "This is your bed."

"If you're going to be stupidly stubborn about going back, I have to take care of a few things."

"Like what?"

"The press."

I hadn't even peeked at the media storm I was sure I'd set off when I'd attacked Random. It had to be bad.

First wizard in the WHHL came with a lot of public scrutiny, and not a lot of it had been flattering.

"You gonna give an interview?" I asked.

"Not exactly." He pressed his fingers to the machine by his bed, bent his head for a second as if he were listening to the monitor's innards, then stood and pulled the sensors off his arm.

The machine kept beeping along, monitoring his vitals even though it wasn't hooked up to him.

"No way," I breathed. "Magic?"

He nodded. "We have about four hours before anyone's coming in here to check on me."

"Mom and Dad?"

"I made them go home and get some sleep. We scared the crap out of them. I told them I'd keep an eye on you."

He pulled his jeans and T-shirt out of the duffle Mom or Dad must have brought and slipped into them. Then he put on his boots.

"You going out?" I asked.

"Nope." He shrugged into a hoodie with the cloud and lighting logo over the front and THUNDERHEADS across the back. "We both are. Get dressed."

19

MY BROTHER WAS JUST a little bit of a badass. Not the magic thing. Everyone knew he was a badass with magic.

And if they didn't, they would as soon as they watched one of the dozens of recorded videos of me gone wild and beating the hell out of the magic he had pulled around himself like a violet and steel shield.

They'd know it if they watched his eyes, which were never once afraid of having an unhinged second-marked slamming fists into his head, his stomach, his neck.

They'd know it when they realized those eyes were ferocious, and focused, and angry.

And oh-so calm.

He knew me. He knew my limits.

Better than that, he knew magic. And while he still might not know his limits with it, he was able to manipulate magic to make it tough enough to withstand my onslaught and still permeable enough to let him breathe while inside it.

While all hell had been breaking out around us, shifters and players and the general frenzy of West Hell.

He insisted I watch the video as we walked away from the hospital at a quick pace in the pre-dawn darkness.

I didn't want to, but he was relentless, and so I'd watched, my heart beating wrong rhythms in my throat and ears as I watched myself on the screen do the one thing I'd never wanted to do. Do the one thing I'd promised I'd never do to him.

I went wild. Insane. I became nothing but howling hatred and I aimed it at him with everything in me.

And that…was not enough to break him.

Wasn't even enough to hurt him.

Not enough to touch him.

My brother? Man. He could peel the world apart with his fingertips and tear the pulpy core of it out with his teeth.

Still, watching that video was hard.

I got all the way to the end of it, then shoved his phone back at his chest.

"What?" He fumbled, but caught it before it fell.

I staggered to the bushes beside the sidewalk and barfed my guts up.

Random waited until I was empty, breathing hard and spitting to try and get the sour acid out of my mouth. Then his hand landed between my shoulder blades and my entire body shuddered.

Contact. I was still needy for it.

"You okay?" he asked.

I wiped my sleeve over my eyes, and my mouth and nodded. "Just so fantastic, all around."

His palm lifted and he patted me on the shoulder. "Keep moving. We don't have all day."

I straightened and fell into step next to him.

"You going to tell me yet why we escaped the hospital?"

"Nope." He was watching his screen, and sent off a text.

"Who?" I asked.

"Your mom and dad. Don't want them to freak." He was typing again, then sent again.

"And that?"

"Just some guy I know."

SOME GUY HE KNEW turned out to be Scott Dart, the journalist who covered local sporting events and the WHHL in particular. He, Random told me, out of all the press who had hassled him when he got dropped out of the NHL and thrown down into the stew pit of West Hell, had been the most interested in what Hazard actually said and did, rather than the sensationalism of what he had been through.

Not that Scott was a guy I'd want to get to know very well. He was built too tall and gangly, all legs and overly long arms, his hair gray, but long, swept back, his actual rose-colored glasses perched on the end of his nose.

He reminded me of that comedian who had played the Grinch in the creepy version of the Christmas show.

Also, he fit right in with the whole vibe of the tattoo shop where we agreed to meet him.

So did Random, who was all cool and easy as he sat in the chair, his right arm and shoulder bare, the buzz of the tattoo machine stopping and starting.

It was taking everything I had to remain still. And the artist who had the needle in my right arm, had been smart to give me a stress ball to squeeze with my left hand.

"You don't mind if I snap a few shots?" Dart asked, holding up his phone.

"Go ahead," Hazard said.

Dart pushed off the wall and got close enough to catch different angles of both of us. I worked hard not to let the discomfort show on my face. Because, yeah, I got hit for a living, but these were needle stabs. A billion little needle stabs.

"And you're okay with me recording this conversation?" he asked.

"Yes," Hazard said. Dart shot me a glance.

"Sure."

He thumbed his phone and cradled it in his palm, holding it so as not to block the microphone. "So when did you two decide to get ink?"

I glanced at Random. He was looking at me too. "About two hours ago?" I said.

He nodded. "'Bout that, yeah. But I've been thinking about doing it for a while."

"You have?" I asked. "Since when?"

"Training camp."

"NHL or West Hell?"

"NHL." He ticked his eyes away for a second and I chuckled.

"No. No, no, no," I chortled. "You did *not* expect me to get your number permanently inked on my arm did you? With a little Colorado Avalanche swoop?"

"No." But his color had gone pink. Plus, I was second-marked. I could smell the embarrassment on him.

"Oh, yes you did! Oh my god, Ran, why didn't you tell me?"

"Because I didn't know...you know, if it was gonna last."

"Being an Avalanche?"

"Yeah. I thought maybe after training, if I got put on one of the lines."

I snorted. "Dude, I would have totally gotten your number, whether you made a line or not."

Random shook his head. "Good thing I waited, right? Otherwise, wouldn't you look stupid?"

"Like I'd care. As far as I'm concerned you were NHL, buddy. Doesn't matter how long it lasted, you were there. You were *there.*"

"For half a minute, about."

"Still," I insisted.

"Yeah," he said. "I know."

"Do you miss it?" Dart asked.

I hadn't forgotten he was there—it was hard to ignore a guy that tall and limby. Also his cologne smelled like root beer, and I wasn't sure if it was actually cologne or if he'd just dumped a jug of root beer over his head.

He wasn't talking to me. He was talking to Random. It wasn't a question Random had gotten very often. Most people just asked if he was angry, or frustrated at the rules forbidding marked to play in the pros.

And Random was pro level. It would take a blind rock to not see how much talent he had.

He was going to be a great, a name in hockey that got burned into trophies, and written into books and history. Whether he played in the Hell leagues or anywhere else.

I raised my eyebrows at Random. He was doing that sort of inward search thing he did when he was thinking through what he felt and what he wanted to say.

His eyes, dark blue like the middle of the ocean, flicked up to focus on the journalist.

"Yeah," he said. "I do miss it."

"Would you go back if they asked you?" Dart asked, biting into the meat of the story he obviously wanted to tell.

He licked his lips. Thinking hard again. "I guess we'll find out if they ever ask me." He quirked an eyebrow and Scott chuckled.

"I, for one," the journalist said, "really hope they do."

Random's eyes went a little wide. He had not expected that. Neither had I.

"It would make a grand story, don't you think?" Dart pressed the rose-colored glasses down his nose so he could look over them at both of us. "Almost as good as you two. Want to tell me what started the fight? Bad blood over the Dead Man pick?"

"No. We're solid with that, Ran and I."

"Didn't look like you were solid out on the ice."

I stopped squishing the stress balloon thingy and gave Dart my full attention. I could feel Random tense up, knew he was worried I'd throw myself under the speeding train, or slow journalist, for him. For us.

But I didn't need to do that. I was starting to understand it wasn't always my job to take the hits. Still, this was on me.

"That was all me," I said, honestly. "I wasn't in a good headspace hitting the ice, and I let things get out of hand."

Dart's face didn't change, but there was a shift in his body language. He was suddenly very focused on me and every word I said. I wondered if he was a sensitive.

"You call that getting out of hand? You could have seriously injured Hazard. Those hits were brutal, Spark."

I bristled, but didn't dare move because, hey, needle-in-arm. He wasn't wrong.

"Lucky for me Hazard is smart enough to know when I'm being an idiot." I said it level, calm. It even came out sounding mature, so, bonus.

"Lucky for me, it's easy," Random said. "Because he's always an idiot."

"Hey."

He made a kissy face at me.

I grinned. "And whose idea was the tattoos?"

"Mine," he said.

"Getting them yes, but deciding what they are?" I pressed.

He closed his eyes and lifted his eyebrows. "Yours."

"So if I'm so stupid, you are equally dumb, since you agreed to my idea."

"Just because you're stupid doesn't mean you don't get something right every once in a while."

"See what I have to put up with?" I asked Dart. "The question you should have asked me is not why I punched him in the face, but why it took me so *long* to punch him in the face."

Random's smile spread, making his eyes do that corner arch thing that meant he was really happy.

Good. Because, honestly I'd thought sneaking out of a hospital to get inked while we talked to a reporter was a terrible idea. But he had insisted and it was making him happy.

I owed him this. I owed him more. A full body tattoo if that's what he wanted me to do to show I was sorry.

"What did you pick for tattoos?" Dart asked, still recording, both with his phone and with the sharp eyes of a seasoned journalist.

The woman doing my tattoo leaned back and wiped at my shoulder. "Good enough for him to see," she decided.

I turned my shoulder and knew from the movement I caught at the corner of my eye that Hazard was doing the same.

"His number," I said, showing the 42 with Hazard's name under it and the Thunderheads logo. "My brother's number."

Dart took in the tattoo, red and angry looking, then glanced over at Hazard's arm.

"His," Hazard said, showing off the 9 with Spark beneath it. "Because he's my brother. On the ice. On the same team, on opposing teams. Doesn't matter."

I felt my chest tighten and blew out a breath so I didn't do something like tear up again.

"Same," I said.

Dart glanced between the two of us, then nodded. "Let's get a picture of that ink."

Random and I leaned in toward each other, holding up our rolled sleeves and smiled for the camera.

20

THE BUS RIDE TO Tacoma was odd. I got looks of both admiration and wariness. No one wanted to know they had a teammate who could go crazy at the drop of a glove.

Fighting was a part of hockey, especially here in West Hell. But even so, fights weren't usually because a player had lost track of reality.

Shifting while on the ice showed a loss of control over the magic inside. We were used to that: Canidae and Felidae ready for a tilly. But to see a man lose his shit and beat the crap out of a player in man form?

That was not normal.

I didn't duck their stares, but didn't challenge them either. Just kept my gaze steady, put in my headphones and eventually closed my eyes for the ride.

The league had suspended me for three games. Weird that I got a lighter sentence than Hazard, when I'd done and intended to do more physical damage than he had with his magic the other month.

But he had used magic, and I'd just been a man losing his marbles. If I'd shifted and tried to eat Hazard's head, then I probably would have gotten a five game suspension.

Hockey logic. Gotta love it.

I thought Coach Nowak would have wanted a word with me after we got to Tacoma, but he just told me to get the hell out of his sight and turned to the media waiting for him.

I went back to my hotel, fell into the scratchy sheets, and dropped into a deep, deep sleep.

The team skate had been planned for late morning, so I got there early enough to get changed into my gear and get on the ice before anyone showed up.

I heard them come in, saw some of my teammates walk past the ice to the lockers, saw the equipment handler come out to watch me doing easy laps before he shook his head and walked away.

By the time the team finally hit the ice, I was done with my warm up and had found a spot in the stands where I could watch the team, but not be too close. About half way up, center ice.

The players knew I was there. Coach Nowak knew it too. But I was holding still and being quiet. There wasn't any reason for him to call me out. Ignoring me was more his style, unless I got in his face. And I wasn't going to do that. Yet.

The team seemed frustrated and erratic on the ice. Well-practiced drills came off herky-jerky. Shots on net went wide, high, or hit the pipes with hammer-to-anvil *pings*.

It was easy to see from up in the seats, my head clear for the first time in ages, my arm itching from the quickly healing tattoo.

Being with Random, seeing Mom and Dad when they picked us up from the tattoo shop, had done something miraculous for me. Mom and Dad took turns hugging me and reprimanding me. "We don't sneak out of the hospital at night, Duncan," and "We're going to find you a new apartment. No more living in a hotel."

I felt more grounded, more whole, more *me* than I had since I'd decided to volunteer for Dead Man. I knew who my family was and knew they were with me. No matter where I lived. No matter where I played.

Mom and Dad were driving up this weekend to help me find a "real" place to live. They had been doing a lot of research online and had found a room I could rent from a couple who had turned their basement into an apartment.

Dad was happy because it was just a few minutes away from the arena, which meant less of me having to navigate Tacoma traffic. Mom was happy because one of the owners was a nurse and a second-marked, while the other had played a lot of rugby in college.

Coach Clay had found me and Random and Mom and Dad in the little hole-in-the-wall breakfast place, OMELETTES, OMELETTES, OMELETTES (which served, surprise! Omelettes) and had asked if he could have a word with me alone.

Random had immediately stood, ready to defend me, and Dad had folded his arms across his chest, taking the measure of Coach Clay, while Mom, ever quick to the point simply asked, "Why?"

Coach Clay hadn't flinched from her tone. But she wasn't his mom.

Her tone stopped Random cold, and stopped me too.

I met his wide eyes. It had been years since we'd heard that out of her. Like maybe back when we'd strung a rope from our roof to the neighbor's patio so we could zip line over the metal fence.

"I just want to discuss the game, and no, I'm not going to tell him he should know better than trying to turn a hockey game into a street brawl. I assume the three-game suspension is enough to remind him of that."

I ducked my head, because even though I wasn't his player, he was still my coach. He had chosen me out of so many others to be a part of his team. His opinion of me, his opinion of my game, my actions, and the world of hockey I was trying to navigate meant a lot to me.

"It's fine," I told Mom. "I'll be right back." I moved toward the door, because this place used to be a shoe store or something—all wood and brick, but very narrow and crowded with as many tables and chairs as they could bribe the fire marshals to let them get away with.

The morning air was brisk and welcome, bleached clean from the cool wash of rain that had fallen hours ago, clouds gray and clumpy obscuring any winter blue the sky might have to offer.

Oregon and Tacoma were only about a hundred and forty miles apart, but I swear the smell of the air, the loft of the clouds always felt different.

I moved to the left, out of the way of the door and leaned against the alley side of the building.

Coach Clay followed—not that I could hear him—and stepped past me so he could lean on the brick wall next to me. We were both staring across the narrow space that wouldn't even be wide enough for those tiny electric cars that fit into your back pocket.

"I want to apologize," he began.

I groaned.

"No. Let me talk, Duncan." He waited a second. I stuck my hands in my back pockets and nodded.

"I made a mistake, and that's on me. I should not have let you volunteer. I knew...I *know* what kind of a man Nowak is. What he's been. I thought...well, it doesn't matter what I thought."

"Matters to me," I mumbled.

He stuck his hands in his back pockets too. "All right. I thought you'd slip into that team like a drop of water in a stream and be one of their best players. You have this way about you that makes you easy to like. Hazard doesn't have that. No, don't defend him, it's true. He's more closed off. Prickly. I could see the disaster of letting him be a part of that team from a thousand miles away. You weren't my first choice to send in his place."

He paused then, scowled at the crack in the concrete across from us.

"Graves?" I guessed.

"Yeah," he breathed, and there was more there. Things I could not quite catch before they were gone. "He would have weathered that storm without breaking a sweat. He's..."

"Tough? Better than me?"

Clay rocked his head my way. "Don't jump on yourself just to get ahead of it, kid. I was going to say he's a survivor. And he's been around. Been through a lot of shit. He'd have survived it all."

There it was again, a weight in his gaze, a note in his words that made me feel like there was more to this conversation I wasn't hearing.

"Okay?" I wanted him to explain so I could understand why we were in an alley talking about things that couldn't be changed.

225

"It was my call, and I made the wrong one. You never should have been dropped into the middle of that, Duncan. I was wrong. I failed as your coach."

He shifted his position, one shoulder resting on the wall. I turned to face him. His forehead was lined, and more lines folded between his eyebrows. Tension made the skin around his mouth tight, the skin at his throat twitch. He was angry about this. Angry at himself.

"You couldn't have stopped me." The words were out of my mouth before I had time to think them through. His eyebrows hitched up and his breathing shifted into something less short and angry, but I had said my truth.

I was not backing down now. Not ever again.

"It was my choice to put myself in Hazard's place. I fought you for it. And I won. I don't regret this, Coach. It hasn't been easy, but…" I glanced off over his shoulder, searching for the right words. "I'm finding something there. Something I don't think I would have figured out for a long, long time if I hadn't gone."

"And what is that?" His words were measured, calm. Waiting. Maybe even trusting, hoping.

"Who I am. Who I want to be."

"And who is that?"

I ticked my gaze back to his. "More than a hockey player."

His pupils narrowed, his eyes tightening. I could feel it in him, the beast buried in his bones responding to the beast buried in mine.

Alpha.

He saw it in me. And that didn't bother me one bit.

From the slow creep of his smile, it didn't bother him either. "Holy crap, Spark. Look at you."

I couldn't help it. I grinned. "Yeah." I ducked my head, nervous all of a sudden, standing here in front of a man whose regard I really valued. "Look at me."

He was quiet for a moment or two while I found my shoes really interesting. I was thinking it was time to go back to the restaurant. To my parents. My family. To where I still blended in and didn't stand out.

Because what Coach saw in me...that was all about standing out.

I wanted that. I wanted to be that. But it was still new, a very different thing than me assing around being loud. This was...more.

This was stepping up for more than just others.

This was stepping up for myself.

"You want out of there, you say the word, Spark," he said. "I'll find a way to bring you home."

I swallowed, my chest tight at hearing the warmth and conviction in his words. He would fight for me. And that meant a lot.

But I needed to do some fighting for myself before I dragged anyone else into it. Although...

"So I notice you're down a right winger."

Coach shifted his stance. "Happens I am. Why?"

"I know someone who just got cut. Could give him a shot, maybe?"

"Spark, I like you, but you are not my talent scout, kid."

I smiled. "Whatever you say, Coach."

But here, sitting in the stands and watching the Tide play, I figured I might be a decent talent scout if I wanted to be. Watching the Tide play made it look like they had no talent at all. Every pass was just that much too fast or a hair too slow. Every drill was either one step too far, one skate over the line, one shot too wide.

There were players on the ice, yes. They were going through the drills, yes. But they were not doing any of that *together*. There was no click. No sync. No groove or rhythm that everyone fell into.

I kept my eyes on Steele. He was the Captain. He should be the one pulling them all together. But he just looked tired. Like someone who had been yelling into the wind for so long, he knew it was hopeless to keep shouting.

No one was guiding that team. No one was holding the center of it, grounding it. No one was mashing all the separate pieces together to show it what it could be.

I could see a dozen ways the players would work better together. Could see the lines that joined them, the commonalities that tugged at them whether they knew it or not. The positions they played, the countries they were from, how magic marked them, all played into the game.

Other things too. Who liked pineapple on pizza, who hated ice cream. Who went for the craft beer and who preferred Budweiser. Things that could join them.

Join us.

But someone had to stand up and insist that all those strings could knot together and become this one thing we all created.

Pack.

This could be a pack. It wasn't. Not even close. But there was a subtle pull there, a reaching out that happened now and again. The supportive stick tap, the insult that made someone laugh. It was there, this thing the team could be.

And I knew how to fix it. The Tide could be a team that moved together, planned together, played together.

Every player down there had forgotten one thing: hockey was a hell of a lot of fun. No matter what else I did I was going to show them hockey could be fun again.

"There he is. I thought you were a ghost. You done taking swings at your ex-teammate and causing the media stir of the century?"

I bit back a groan as my heartbeat kicked up into a gallop.

"Hey, Netti."

"Oh," she said, sitting next to me. "You do remember my name. So why have you been avoiding me?"

"I haven't—"

Her eyebrows were deadly weapons, cutting right through my bull.

"Do you know what I thought when I first saw you?" I said.

"How lucky you were to have a great assistant trainer?"

"That was the second thing. The first was how gorgeous you are. And then you started talking and giving me shit, and I couldn't keep my eyes off of you." I cleared my throat.

She was silent. Apparently in shock.

"I wanted to ask you out. I still want that. But this team, my headspace." I tapped my forehead. "Not very healthy right now. And when I ask you out, and I'm going too, Netti Morandi, I am going to be the best person I can be."

She blinked a couple times. "You don't think you're at your best now?"

"I'm getting there."

"And you think I'm going to wait around for you to ask me?"

"I hope so. But no, I don't expect you to."

"And you think I'm going to date you. After I told you I don't date hockey players?"

"Yeah, I'm still working on that part." I smiled.

"Well," she said, her eyes twinkling, her face lit with curiosity. "You keep me in the loop on how that's going for you, all right?"

"It's a promise."

She held her palm out. "Give me your phone, Superstar."

I did so and she thumbed through it and tapped something in. "I've updated your contacts with my info. So you can keep me in the loop. And I better see you in my office after the next practice or I'll break your knees. *Capisce*?"

She handed me the phone, then stood and walked away.

I couldn't stop smiling.

I SAT IN MY car, staring at the apartment building. I shouldn't be here. This was none of my business. The figurative angel and devil on my shoulders were having it out, half of me voting to turn around and forget this, the other half insisting this was important. This was the start of the thing that would make all the rest of my plan work.

Before either shoulder deity had presented the winning argument, my phone buzzed. I pulled it off the dash holder and thumbed it on. Message from Hazard with a link.

I clicked on it. A title lit up the article:

UNBREAKABLE BROTHERS

Beneath that was a picture of Hazard and me in the tattoo shop, each with a fist clenched to hold up our sleeve, tattoos facing the camera, our smiles and the determined look in our eyes just blazing.

I scanned the text, which wasn't half bad. Dart did a quick recap of the fight, of our hospital stay, and that neither of us had come out of it seriously injured. Then he went on to quote us, which would never not be weird, and filled in some opinions of his own.

He thought whatever had happened on the ice had something to do with the Dead Man's draft no matter what we said. But he was sure we were both happy to be there together, at the tattoo place. That it wasn't some kind of a publicity stunt, even though Hazard had called him and offered to give him the exclusive.

He made a big deal about us sneaking out of the hospital, but also letting our parents know what we were doing so they didn't worry.

He said we were in turns annoyed, joking, and tormenting each other. Just like any other brothers.

He said that the fight on the ice had been left on the ice. That we had already gotten over it. And he hoped, for the sake of both our struggling teams, that we had leveled the playing field and were going to put some of that fire into our game play.

Hazard's text popped up.

Good, right?

I texted him back. *You need to lift, bro. Look at that stick arm.* Then I added. *It's good. Yes.*

I got back a middle finger emoji and an angel face. *Don't be alone* he added.

Because that was something we had talked about too. Me pulling away, trying to handle it all on my own was part of my downfall. To make sure that wouldn't happen again, Mom and Dad and Random set up a schedule for who would text or call me at what time of day. When and if any of them didn't get a satisfactory answer out of me, there would be consequences.

They hadn't specified what those consequences were, but from the matching smug smiles, I knew that one: they'd been creative in thinking up punishments, and two: I wouldn't like them.

But they weren't going to have to worry about that. I wasn't going to be stupid. Not again.

I got out of the car and crossed to the apartment. Stopped on the doorstep and blew the air out of my lungs like I was heading out onto the ice for a game.

I rang the bell just as the locks slid and clicked.

"What do you want?" Slade crossed his arms over his T-shirt and scowled at me. His red beard was thicker. Other than that he looked exactly the same as I'd last seen him.

"I talked to Coach Clay. Of the Thunderheads."

"I know who Coach Clay is."

It started to rain, just an innocent seeming drizzle that would soak everything through in a couple minutes flat.

"I sent you his number," I said.

"Bored now."

"I'm going to send it to you again if you delete it."

"Go away, Duncan." He pushed the door, but I got a shoulder on it and leaned.

We pushed, each of us on one side of the door, throwing our weight. It was stupid, but like hell I was gonna lose a door-pushing contest.

"You asshole," he growled.

"Let me talk. Jesus, you're strong." I pushed harder, not about to be outdone.

He let go of the door and stepped back in one quick move. "Fine."

I fell into his apartment, the door slamming loudly against the wall, my knees and shoulder skidding across the carpet.

"Jerk move. What are you, five?" I picked myself up, dusted at my knees. I had landed on my non-tattoo arm.

He was halfway across the room, one foot propped on the ball of his foot, like he was ready to push away in a hurry.

"Talk," he demanded.

"They need a right winger. Fisk got injured and they're looking for someone to fill that gap."

"Plenty of colleges and minors to pull from."

"Or there's you. You want another chance at this game, I just gave you one. Do it or don't, that's your choice. But you would be insane not to want to play for the Thunderheads. They're the real thing, Slade. Hard hockey *and* smart hockey. Clay's trying to pull the league away from the kind of shit Coach Nowak insists on doing.

"You want hockey, real hockey, pro hockey, you stop being a stubborn ass and call Coach Clay."

"And what? He'll just sign me up on the spot because you said so?"

"Oh, hell no." I grinned. "You're gonna have to prove he should give you a chance. I said you should do this. I didn't say it would be easy."

"You think I can just call him?" Every syllable of that was doubt and derision.

"I know you can."

"Why do you give a damn?"

"Because you were right. You're off the team because of me. Nowak knew what that would do to you, knew what it would do to me, and was betting it would all work out just like it did. Still, I owe you."

He opened his mouth, but I narrowed my eyes and growled.

He immediately shut up, his chin lifting. Not enough for me to see his neck, but almost as if he were resisting the urge to bare his throat to me.

Wasn't that something?

I kept my voice level. "You had my back when I most needed it. My first day, when Coach put me flat out on the ice and shocked the hell out of me."

His gaze flicked down to the phone clenched in my fist. I knew he was thinking about the video he had shot of me getting stunned over and over. "You do something with that?" he asked.

"Not yet."

He shifted on his feet, just the slightest sliding of weight from the toe to the side, to the heel. I didn't even think he did it consciously. He was a creature of continuous motion, this one.

His eyes, dark yellow, pulled upward to meet my gaze. No tipping of the chin this time, not a nervous line in his body. He was all fire and edges.

"What are you going to do now?" he asked.

I cleared my throat and then said, in a deep, serious tone: "What I should have done to begin with. Defeat the bad guy." It was such a cheesy line. Such a hero-in-a-movie kind of thing to say. And I couldn't have been happier that I'd finally had a chance to use it.

"You're stupid," he muttered. But he was smiling too. I took it as a win.

"You too, buddy." I waved and headed to the door. "Call Coach Clay or I'll kick you so hard your insides will be on your outsides," I called over my shoulder.

He barked a laugh and flipped me off.

Yeah, it was good to have friends.

21

A WOLF KNOCKED AT the door. Little pig, little pig, let me come in.

Okay, it wasn't quite like that. It was more like, a second-marked strolled into the locker room early, because he'd seen a tiger and mountain lion swagger in there like they owned the place.

Paski and Zima were, in my estimation, the only two on the team who would actively try to kill me on the ice.

Which meant it was time to deal with a little pecking order on this team.

I could smell the other players who were there, could hear their heartbeats if I concentrated with the wolf in me. I knew Big D was in the locker room, and so were the four other wolves.

A couple cats, too, though I didn't think the entire team was here. I didn't smell the coyote, anyway.

Not that it mattered who witnessed this confrontation.

Paski and Zima's lockers were side-by-side and they were talking to each other in that muted tone everyone on this team used. I'd been in plenty of rooms full of hockey players and quiet wasn't really the first description that came to mind.

Big D's back was to the wall, wolves on either side. Busk stood at his left, and our second line defenseman, well, defensewoman, Sava at his right. Big D's cold ice eyes tracked me as I strode across the distance separating me from the felines.

The other wolves were watching every move I made too, interested in what they could sense in me, and what I was going to do about it.

I reached into that place deep in my chest, deep in my brain, where I was more than just Duncan the man, more than just Duncan the wolf. Where I was strong and calm and…

…*alpha.*

It was unfamiliar to pull that awareness around me and to stand there in a confidence that outstripped all the ego and confidence I'd known before. I could be a cocky bastard.

But this was different. This was solid. Unbreakable. As if being this thing, standing in this frame of mind and actually letting this slow, smoking fire burn through me, was new. And at the same time, it was so right that I felt like I was waking up, opening my eyes and really seeing the world for the first time.

"Paski, Zima. How about we go outside and talk about how much I'm going to make you hurt?"

They turned in tandem. That was the most teamwork I'd seen out of them.

Paski was the bigger of the two, heavily muscled, bristling for a fight.

Zima wasn't a pushover. He and I were of comparable build except I was way less asshole.

"Fuck off, dog." Paski turned back to his locker.

I laughed. "Paski, Paski, Paski. You big dumb kitten. I'm not here to *listen* to you. I will *fight* you, but I don't give a crap what you say."

Paski shoved right up in my face. "Wanna go? You don't have the balls to take me—"

I slammed a fist into his stomach.

His breath came out hard, and he bent, but Kitty Two was already swinging at my head. I ducked, came up, grabbed the shoulder of his shirt like we were on the ice, held him at arm's length and punched him in the face.

Physical contact had never felt so good.

He got in a few hits, I got in more, and then Paski joined the fun.

Everything in me was laughter and hot, angry delight. I loved this. A fight. A clear way to make my point with muscle, body, brain. I was made for these kinds of heart-to-hearts, and thrilled that I could have my say.

And I planned to have the last word.

Kitty Two backed off when the tiger decided he was gonna lead the dance.

Every word out of his mouth was a curse, but only some of them were in English. He was just out of arm's reach, so we circled the center of the locker room like boxers in the world's smallest ring.

He was bleeding. I was bleeding. Everybody was just having a marvelous time.

For real. Most of the team was here now. Watching.

No one was jumping in to break it up. Not that I cared. All the more fun for me.

I led with a hard left and then I rushed the bastard, picked him up and slammed him to the floor, face first.

He groaned, and didn't move.

"All right." I spit blood and wiped my mouth. "Anyone else want to tell me I don't belong on this fucking team?"

I stared at Zima. He just crossed his arms and scowled at me. Then he dropped his gaze.

Damn right he dropped his gaze.

I looked over at the wolves. Five second-marked gathered on one side of the room tracking me with curious, almost hungry eyes.

Big D was closest to me. If he wanted a piece of the Dunc, things were going to get interesting. As in, I'd have to shift to wolf, because there was no way I'd be able to take him down in man form. He was a mountain.

"Problem?" I squared off to him.

Was that an actual smile?

"Nyet." His voice was low and rough. "No problem."

He tipped his chin up and sideways. It could have been mistaken as a greeting, that broski chin tip that was a visual "hey" from across the room.

But I knew what it was. Submission, wolf-to-alpha. His gaze slid sideways and then focused on the floor.

"Okay," I said, less uncomfortable with that acknowledgment of my dominance than I expected. "Okay." I straightened out of the slightly crouched fighting stance I'd still been in. Looked over at the wolves next to him.

Busk lifted his chin, grinned at me and slid his gaze to the floor.

The rest, to a man, did the chin tip, glanced at the floor, then when I said okay, went back to getting ready for practice.

Only one wolf didn't chin tip. Sava. She was second-line defense, for a reason. An inch taller than me, with ten extra pounds of muscle she was a force to be reckoned with on the ice. Maybe off the ice too.

"Sava," I said. "We cool?"

She pursed her lips like she'd bit on a lemon. "Like I give one damn which male is pissing on boots around here?"

Oooh. I instantly liked her. "Maybe you do. Things might change if I have any say about it."

"Good. Change that we keep fucking falling asleep in the damn neutral zone and can't keep the fucking puck in our O-zone." She tipped her chin, but her gaze did not waver. "Then you and me got no problems."

"I'll do my best."

"Do better than that."

"Okay."

She nodded and just like the other second-marked, went back to getting ready for practice.

Well, that went better than I hoped. One of my eyes was swelling shut and my throat felt coppery hot from swallowing blood and my fists hurt, but otherwise, everything was coming up Donuts.

I turned to the other people in the room. All the rest of were fourth-marked Felidae shifters except for Nadreau, the coyote.

The cats were mostly ignoring me.

"Anyone else have a problem?" I faced Nadreau.

He wiped a towel over his hair, and smirked. "Naw, boss. I got no problem with you. You teach Paski the rules, I'm smart enough to know how this wind blows." He lifted his chin, eyes averted.

One of the cats, Ledes, a leopard, sniffed. "C'mon, Spark. We've been waiting for you to step up since you got here. Took you forever. Asshole." He threw a roll of tape at my head, which I caught.

Tabor Steele strolled into the room. "For fuck, people. Who the fuck is fighting? Why the fuck is Paski sleeping in the middle of the room?" His eyes, the very angry eyes of our captain zeroed in on me.

He cataloged me from head to foot, then grunted. "About damn time."

"What, that someone take Paski down?" I asked.

"That you got your head out of your ass and alphaed up."

"Why the hell didn't you say something?" I yelled, throwing my hands in the air. "It has been weeks of utter misery since I got here. I blame you." I stabbed a finger at Steele.

Steele sneered. "Not my fault you're an idiot."

"*I'm* an idiot? You're the captain!"

"I bet you didn't even figure out you were an alpha until today."

"No. That's not true." It was almost true. I'd only figured it out when Kudrar had been hurt.

"So, what? Back when Kudrar got hurt?"

I didn't like his tone. It was mocking. He was also correct.

"Yes," I mumbled.

That got a huge smile out of him. "You suck so bad, Spark."

I rocked one hand back and forth. Fifty-fifty agreement on that one. "I refuse to captain this team."

He leaned back and squinted. "Good. Because I'm the only captain on this team. You want to take my position, you're gonna have to take me out."

"I just said I don't want your position."

"Good."

"Good."

"I'm serious, Spark. This C…" he tapped at his chest where there would be a C if he were wearing his jersey, but right now was nothing but green T-shirt with a hot dog on it, "…isn't up for grabs."

"I don't want to be captain," I said slowly. Clearly. "But I'm the only alpha here, hot dog."

"Good," he said, a little more quietly. "We've needed that, I think. The centering."

"Sure. Right." I had no idea what he was talking about. I nodded wisely. "Centering."

He gave me a weird look, then stepped past me. "Suit up, Spark. No one on this team gets out of practice. Not even goons with three game suspensions."

The rest of the players laughed and jeered. Another roll of tape flew at my head and a random glove hit me in the chest because I wasn't fast enough to catch it.

It was all so very juvenile. It was the first fragile strings of a new beginning, a knot just beginning to pull tight.

And I stood there grinning like an idiot, loving every minute of it.

I WAS SIDELINED FOR the next three games.

Game one against the Calgary Rustlers was a loss from the first period. Down four to zero, we never climbed out of that hole. They sent us off the ice with a six-zero on our record.

I waited for the team in the locker room after the game. Gave them a little shit, then told them we'd pull it together in the next game. A lot of eyes were on me, either trying to read how much oil I was selling, or wanting to believe in a miracle cure.

Since I believed what I was saying, a few of the players gave me short nods.

Steele paused in stripping off his gear. "I expect everyone at practice tomorrow morning early. Because that shit on the ice will not stand. You too, Spark."

"Like I'd miss it." I drank down the last of my cola. "Someone has to score all the goals."

This time they threw jock straps at me.

Early practice was better. We were settling in with the kind of plays we could create, who had speed, who had ice sense that could pull a line together. We had all shown up an hour early to run some easy drills, and Steele called the shots.

He really knew how to put the dick in dictator. But it was good. It was what a captain should be doing.

The Tide was starting to feel like a team. A little too quick to lash out, a little too slow to forgive, but still a team. It wasn't anywhere close to the genuine family loyalty and close-knit *esprit de corps* of the Thunderheads, but maybe it would get there someday.

Or maybe this was as close to a family as this team could be under a coach like Nowak.

At the end of practice, before Coach Nowak and the assistant coaches showed up, everyone skated past me and tapped my skate, my ankle, my leg.

Next game? We lost. But we lost it in the third after being ahead by one for most of the game.

It wasn't much, but it was improvement.

The last game was on the road and I was not allowed to travel with the team.

So I bought a six-pack of beer and knocked on a door.

"Kill me now," Slade said, when he found me loitering on his doorstep. "You and I are not friends."

"Sure we aren't. Wink, wink."

He scowled and gripped the door, ready to slam it in my face.

"I brought beer. And ordered pizza. You don't have to be my friend to be hungry."

The door paused. He heaved a mighty sigh. "Why did I ever talk to you? Why was I so nice to you?"

"That was nice?"

"I'm never getting rid of you am I?"

I held up the beer. Jiggled it. "Extra cheese, extra meat on the way."

I could see he was trying hard not to tell me how much he loved and admired me.

"Fucker." He stepped aside and once I scuttled in, he slammed the door behind him.

It was set up like most apartments, with the kitchen open to the living room. I didn't bother stopping off at the refrigerator since the beer was cold, and instead made my way straight toward the couch.

Correction, couches. As in three. Or at least I thought there were three pieces of furniture under the heaping piles and piles of pillows. All kinds of pillows. A smorgasbord of colors and fluff and size. Mountains of colorful, squishy accents.

"Uh…this is…"

"Shut up."

"…cozy." I grinned at him.

He narrowed his eyes. "You know what?"

"No," I said. "Wait. Don't throw me out. I love pillows too. I mean maybe not as much as you do, because, dang, Slade. This is some pillow collection. What are we up to here? A hundred. Hundred fifty?"

"Screw you. I like pillows."

"Yeah, I can see that buddy. But maybe it's more than like. Maybe you should just admit that you like-like pillows. You love-love pillows. You maybe want to marry pillows."

"Shut up and give me a damn beer."

I pulled a beer out of the cardboard carrier.

"What do you call a metric ton of pillows anyway?" I asked as I pulled a beer for myself. "A Stay Puft of pillows? A System of the Down? A pillow kilo?"

"It's called a shut up or get the hell out of my house." He twisted the cap, took a long swallow. "Why are you even here?"

"Game tonight."

"So?" The sneer was spot on.

"So, I wanted to watch it with someone."

"We are not friends. We are not hockey watching buddies."

The doorbell rang and I shoved the rest of the beer into his chest, then moved quickly so he had to grab it before it fell to the carpet.

"Sure," I said, over my shoulder. "We are not friends." I opened the door, took both pizza boxes from the guy on the stoop, and strolled back into the living room. I deposited the boxes onto the coffee table which was, surprisingly, pillow free.

The scent of crust and cheese and various meats and garlic wafted into the room. My mouth watered. "Can you smell this? Oh, my god. Better than sex."

Slade dropped his head back and closed his eyes, face toward the ceiling. "If I eat the pizza and drink the beer, will you leave?"

"Yes." I pushed a couple dozen pillows onto the floor so I could wedge myself into the corner of the couch. "After we watch the game and braid each other's hair."

Slade groaned. "You suck."

"What?" I said with mock offense. "Just for that, no hair braiding for you, buddy." I leaned in, grabbed two slices from the top box, folded them together goo-to-goo and took a bite. "Sit down. The game's about to start. Oh, my god, this is amazing. I'm a genius. Gimme my beer."

Slade grumbled something that might have been "asshole" but was probably "classroll" as in I was classy and he liked how I rolled.

Then he sort of wriggled his way down into the pillows by first lying on top of the pile and then turning and flipping them until he was not only covered, he was practically iglooed into them.

He still, amazingly, had enough mobility and reach to snatch a piece of pizza.

I got my own beer off the table where he'd left it.

The TV mounted on the wall clicked to life. It was already tuned to the hockey game. I didn't point out that he'd been watching it before I'd arrived.

We sat there in silence that became more comfortable the longer it stretched out. The game was on, and the Tide weren't doing too badly so far. Of course only a few minutes into the first had passed.

"Fucking Steele," the pillows known as Slade grumbled. "Thinks he can just wait for someone to give him the puck. Sniper punk ass. You're not fucking Ovechkin in his fucking office. Move!"

I laughed, then grabbed a second beer and third slice of pizza.

End of the first and the game was tied zero-zero. Not an exciting score, but it meant the Tide hadn't given up goals.

"You call Coach Clay?" I asked as I looked for the perfect combination of pillows to prop up my arm so I didn't have to lift the beer to my mouth.

"No," he grumbled.

"Slade. Don't be that guy."

"What guy?"

"The dumb guy."

"Did you show anyone that video of Coach Nowak?"

There was a stretch of silence where we watched the Tide totally blow puck possession in the neutral zone and have to chase back to defend the net.

"No," I finally admitted.

"Who's the dumb guy now?"

I grunted. "I will. I'll do it. I'll show what he did to me."

"When?"

"When it's right. When it's smart."

"It's always smart to report abuse, dumbass."

I shifted my arm so the beer tipped into my mouth. "You think Lundqvist will ever figure out that back pass?"

"Which one? Husband Lundqvist or wife Lundqvist?"

The husband and wife were hell on fire when they were in sync. But right now they were out of step, just a half second off with every pass, every play. It was frustrating because it was so clear that they were good together out there, great together out there.

"Husband," I said.

"It's not just him. Everybody's off out there."

I made a sound of agreement.

"You stand up and make yourself known yet?"

I looked over at him. Nothing but two bright eyes twinkling out from the shadows of the pillows.

"Something like that."

"Something?"

"Exactly that," I clarified.

"So you told them you were going to be the alpha of the team."

"Nope. I just told them what I was. Alpha. They could do with that what they wanted."

"How did Paski and Zima take it?"

"On the jaw, on the nose, on the eye."

"Lots of head shots there."

I shrugged, which jiggled the beer. But since it was only half-full, I caught it before it rolled into disaster. "They took it in the ribs and gut too."

"Wish I'd seen it. They are a pair of asses."

I lifted my beer in a toast, and took a drink.

We both turned just as the announcer yelled out, "Goal!"

And there it was, on the screen. The first line of the Tide on the ice, whooping up a celebration. We'd scored a goal.

"About damn time," Slade muttered. "Now let's see if they can finally win one of these."

I raised my beer in another toast, and he did the same.

THEY DID NOT WIN. But they pushed it into overtime to a shootout, so that was something. That was almost, *almost* the team they could be.

I was back in my apartment, that homey little room close enough to the arena Mom and Dad were happy about, with the sounds of my nice neighbors moving around on the floor above me. Even though I had my own space, people who knew me were nearby. People who had invited me to watch a movie with them anytime I had a free evening. It was nice.

I had just crawled into bed when Random sent a text.

Bullshit call in the third. Good game. U would have made that shootout goal.

I grinned and texted back: *Damn right I would have.*

U good?

All good.

Miss you.

Same.

And that was that. But that was perfect. He was there, reaching out to me, I was reaching out to him. I no longer felt so alone. Even though we weren't on the same team, we were still teammates. Still brothers.

I pressed my palm over the tattoo that had finished the itchy phase and healing phase and was now in the cool new tattoo phase.

His number was there. The stupid 42 that my dad had told him was his favorite number when six-year-old Hazard had asked. Hazard thought 42 stood for the four of us and then the two of us, as in he and me: brothers, Mom and Dad: parents.

It was, when I thought about it, kind of sweet in that lost-boy way that Hazard used to have.

It had been several years later that we'd both asked Dad why his favorite number was 42. He told us because it was the meaning of life.

Yep. My dad had made a *Hitchhiker's Guide to the Galaxy* joke. Because he was a total nerd.

Hazard kept the number. And hey, maybe that was also the meaning of life: hockey, brotherhood, family.

22

THE NEW GUY'S NAME was Bill. It wasn't a bad name, but after being around so many players from so many different backgrounds and countries, I was always surprised when a Sam or a John or a Bill showed up.

Bill was dark-haired, tanned, and bearded, his face cut narrow, his cheekbones too sharp. He had these Mountain Dew colored eyes that hit something deep within me when I shook his hand for the first time.

"Wow, dude," I said. "Those eyes."

"Yeah?" he asked. "Was going to say the same thing about you."

We let go of the handshake but stayed squared off, neither of us giving ground.

There was something about him.

The second-marked stopped what they were doing to watch us. As soon as we went silent, they made their way across the room and stood next to me, behind me, all of them announcing with Canidae body language that they were on my side, not his.

And that's when it hit me.

I was staring at an alpha.

Wasn't that interesting? I was probably supposed to do something here.

"Uh, so I'm sort of new to this." I rubbed the back of my neck, thinking. The wolf in me wasn't pushing yet, wasn't angry yet, but with all the other players—

—*pack*—

—surrounding me, the ties that bound me to them, and each of them to me thrummed with heat, trembled with two dozen heartbeats, two dozen minds focused through me because I was—

—*pack*—

—alpha—

—*brother father home*—

—their teammate, and this is what I did. I stood between them and harm. The warmth and power of my pack filled me, calmed me, centered me.

Dude. Sweet.

"You're alpha, right?" I asked.

He nodded, those lime-yellow eyes steady.

"Okay, good. That's good. So, um...*grr*, and *rawr*, I guess." Why was I making claw fingers at him? Talk about awkward.

"Look. I sort of just did this whole big thing where I told the team I was gonna alpha them. Not captain, because we have one of those, but I wasn't gonna be ignored anymore. You know?"

I had his full attention. It was intense.

"Right, so this is new for the team and new for me, and if you want to fight me, fine. I could go for a scrap. But alpha of the team is not on the line. I'm going to let you mess with what we've got. It's a little raw and we don't quite know how we all fit. But we belong. That's the big thing. That's the important thing I won't let you fuck with.

"You can belong here. There's room for you. But there's only one alpha on this team. That's me." The wolf pressed just beneath my skin, my eyes, my voice, my words putting a little power behind that statement.

"And if I have a problem with that?" Bill asked.

I opened my mouth to tell him we'd probably have to fight or do some kind of shootout on the ice. I mean, what did alpha wolves who were also hockey players do to prove superiority? Compete for the best trick shot?

I didn't have to say anything because Big D moved out from behind me and planted himself in front of me like a damned colossus.

"You have a problem with Spark, you have a problem with me."

There was nothing like staring up at a six foot five mountain, who looked hungry for blood.

The Canidae behind me made noises of agreement. Even a couple of the cats chimed in which was kind of funny. Cats were so not interested in pack politics since they all thought they were the gods of the air they breathed and earth they walked. Husband Lundqvist did the whoop-de-doo circle with his finger to show just how much he cared about wolves and pack relations.

I grinned and rolled my eyes, because this team was ridiculous.

"Cats," I said. "Whatcha gonna do?"

Bill blinked, and a sly smile curved his lips. It did a lot to soften the edges of his face. A sense of happiness and contentment rolled off him. It was a young sort of happiness. Almost puppy level. I'd misjudged his age. He was several years my junior.

"Can't live with them," he said, "can't trust them with a can of tuna."

"Oh, fuck off, Kibble and Bits," Wife Lundqvist said.

"You understand how this works?" I pointed at myself, pointed at him.

"I have some idea." He tipped his chin up, but his eyes held mine. Maybe that was the way an alpha gave ground. Worked for me.

"Good enough," I said. "Welcome aboard. Welcome to the team."

We shook again.

That broke the tension, smoothed all the ruffled fur. Everyone went back to dressing for practice. Bill took the place where Slade used to sit, right next to me. I kept an eye on him, curious. I wondered if he and I were anything alike.

He smiled easily. Fell into the locker talk that had finally started to be a regular thing around here. No one would guess this had been a silent, grim place just a few weeks ago.

As I watched the team respond to him, studying him just as closely as I was, figuring out what he was, who he was for the team, I was proud of what I'd helped make happen here.

This was a family. Well, the beginning of one. And I was proud of them accepting a new member with open minds. Or at least not with closed fists.

I had made that happen. That made me happy.

I glanced up and saw Steele looking at me. I raised an eyebrow in question and he gave me a thumbs up.

Yeah, that made me happy too.

"SPARK," COACH NOWAK BARKED as I was headed down the hall to see if Netti was in. "My office."

He was already walking away, storming, really, down the corridor. I followed, tracking the mood coming off him.

Fury.

He stood behind his desk and gripped the back of his chair, squeezing hard enough to pop tendons over yellow knuckles. "Sit."

The wolf in me, the alpha in me riled. I clenched my teeth and swallowed a snarl. I was not a dog. I didn't follow his commands.

"Naw, I'll stand." I tossed my helmet and gloves into the open seat and leaned on my stick. I didn't have my skates on yet. "Problem?"

The vein in his temple throbbed and his skin tone went ruddy. I waited to see if this was going to be a fight. I wouldn't mind. Had been wanting to get a few payback shots in for a while.

"You showed your real colors in the last game you played. Tried to kill the wizard." The chair creaked in his grip.

I waited, careful to keep my emotions off my face. I was getting better at that.

"You are a bad penny I can't shake. And you're dragging this team down."

"Trade me," I said like I didn't care.

"I'll do whatever I want with you, understand? I *own* you."

Boring. "All right. If that's all you wanted, I'm going to practice now."

"I know about the video."

An icy sheet of panic froze over my skin.

"What video?"

"You know exactly what video, Mr. Spark."

I waited.

"What do you want for it?" he asked.

It took me longer than it should to parse those words.

He knew I had the video of him shocking me almost to death. I hadn't told him about it. The only other people who knew it existed were Random and Slade. Random wouldn't have told anyone without talking to me first.

So Slade was the narc. But why would he tell Coach Nowak about it?

"What?" I said.

"I can be a reasonable man." He squeezed the chair harder, wood snapped. "Negotiate. What do you want?"

"I want you to play me."

"When hell freezes over," he growled.

"You won't be in the league that long. When that vid gets out? You're done." I picked up my gear. "You can kiss your career good-bye, Coach."

Just that fast, he was on me. The punch to the head came faster than I could block.

Pain exploded through my skull. He might have thirty years on me, but he still knew how to hit.

Fucker.

I blocked the second hit. A snarl rolled up out of my chest and I slammed an elbow at his face, caught him hard, fast in the jaw. His head snapped back and he stumbled backward.

Satisfying.

I stepped toward him, but paused. This was his office. He could have hidden cameras. This could be a set up.

I spread my hands wide and took a couple more steps back, headed to the door, wanting no more fuel for his fire.

Nowak pulled himself together. He shook with fury, his face red hot, sweat peppering his skin. The seam at the shoulder of his suit jacket was ripped, his nose bleeding.

He rushed, grappled, and fucking boarded me against the wall.

I could knee him. Punch his ribs into splinters. I could throw him to the ground, maim him. Break bones. Smash his skull.

I could kill him.

A dark, hungry, *angry* part of me wanted that.

But it would be my end. The end of being human, of being alpha, of being me.

I was angry, but not stupid. Furious, but not suicidal.

I didn't push, didn't fight. I just held eye contact as he pinned both my shoulders against the wall. I could *see* him. See the rotted, twisted heart of him.

He was nothing. Weak. Alone.

I was all, pack, family, protector, teammate. The faint lines tied to me, these new knots of emotion and strength and power, these fragile connections thrumming with hearts and souls bolstered me, shielded me.

"You show one fucking second of that video, Spark," spittle hit my cheek as he yelled, "and I will bury you!"

Why had I ever been afraid of him, cowed by him? He was nothing.

"Take the shot, Nowak. I'm here for the hockey." I held eye-contact. Refused to look away.

Hatred twisted his features. The beast just under his skin squirmed to get free. There was madness in the too-wide eyes. There was insanity in the way he bared his teeth.

And then he stepped back. Kept moving until he was up against the side of the desk then stalked back behind it. Like he needed that heavy piece of furniture between us so that he didn't jump me again.

Not that it had stopped him before.

I remained where I was. Watched him yank his chair out away from the desk. Watched him sit.

He clenched his jaw, but refused to meet my gaze.

"Get the fuck out of my office."

I picked up my helmet and gloves and left.

The arena door burst open with a rubber stamp punch as I strode outside, breathing hard. I needed air, needed sky, needed the smell of something other than the concrete of the arena, the sweat, the stale scent of ice.

The team was with me, their concern, their worry riding those new ties. It tasted like butterscotch and peanut brittle in my mouth.

I thought calm thoughts, filled myself with blue sky and clouds, soothed their worry. I was fine. We were fine. Everything was fine.

I pulled out my phone and dialed.

"Clay." Coach Clay's tone was clipped, but warm. A wave of homesickness washed over me.

"So I was thinking," I started.

"Spark?"

"Who did you think it was?"

"You've never called me before. I had no idea."

"Oh. Hi. It's me. Duncan. You should update your contacts list."

"Get to the point, kid. I'm aging."

"Two things. One, you need to reach out to Icarus Slade."

"The right wing?"

"He'd fill the hole you have in the third line."

"You know what I'm thinking?"

"That I'm brilliant?"

"That I don't remember asking for your advice."

"Lucky I gave it for free, huh?"

"Why are you pushing Slade at me?"

"It's…" I scrubbed at my jaw. "All honesty, Coach?"

"I prefer it."

"He's a good guy. A fantastic player. All fire and fight. I like him and he got cut from the team because of me. He shouldn't get the shaft just because Coach Nowak wants to bust my skull."

There was silence on the line. It went on long enough I pulled the phone away from my ear and made sure we were still connected.

"Coach?"

"Has Nowak hurt you?"

"Okay. Here's the second thing."

"Son-of-a-bitch," he seethed.

"Just. Listen. I have a video. Slade had his phone out on that first day I showed up for practice."

"All right?"

"I mouthed off, so I got a bag skate. Then Nowak pulled out his stun prod."

The breathing on the other end of the phone disappeared. He was holding his breath.

"He used it on me. A lot. Not just once."

"How many times?" His words were tight, stretched thin.

"Until I passed out."

An animal roar blistered through the connection. There was a loud *pop* and then the call went dead.

Holy crap. Had I just witnessed Coach losing his shit? I so had to tell Random. This was epic. Now I wished I'd done this in person. I'd never seen him go violent face-to-face.

I dialed back. It rang and quickly dumped to voice mail.

I pocketed my phone and took a couple minutes to run the conversation back through my mind. From Clay's reaction, he hadn't known about the video. So Slade hadn't told him.

My phone rang.

"Duncan?" Not Clay. It was Graves.

"Hey, Gravedigger."

"So. Clay's phone is demolished. He's going to talk to you on my phone now. On speaker."

In the background I heard, "Oh, for fuck's sake, Haws. Give me your damn phone."

"You're on speaker, kid," Graves said. "Talk."

"Uh…Coach?"

"I'm still here." His voice had a lot of gravel in it. "It's just Graves and me in my office. You can talk."

"Okay, like I was saying, Slade is going to get picked up by a team. I'm sure of it. You'd be smart to reach out to him first and fill that third line hole."

Clay went silent again, but not for long. "I'll talk to Slade."

"Yes!"

"Tell me about the video, Duncan."

"Coach Nowak doesn't want me here. He punished me for taking Hazard away from him. I let it go too far."

"Duncan. This is not your fault."

"I know. But I should have been smarter about what he might do. I'm used to mouthing off to you and getting sentenced to meditation retreats."

"Noted. Has anything else happened? Has he hurt you in any other way?"

"Nothing I have on video."

"Bad answer, kid," Graves said. "Hold on."

It sounded like the phone was set down, then I heard movement. Someone was pacing. There was a thump like a fist hit a wall, the bang of something metal taking a blow.

I couldn't tell what was happening and wished I was there in the room with them. Sharing something like this over the phone really sucked.

Then I heard Graves's low voice, the tone of it soothing even if I couldn't hear the words. The pacing stopped. There was breathing, one too ragged that finally slowed to match the other's tempo. It was only for a minute or so, then they were back.

"I'm taking over the questions now," Graves said. "Coach Clay is sitting right here. *Sitting*," he instructed, "Right. Here. In his chair."

I heard the chair creak and moan as Clay apparently did as he was told, then Graves was back again.

"You have a video of Nowak using the stun prod on you after a bag skate. Were you shifted?"

"No."

"You blacked out?"

His matter-of-fact tone put me at ease. Made this seem like less of a trauma, and more of a problem we could solve.

"Yes."

"Is the vid on your phone?"

"Yes."

"Send it to me. I'll wait."

I navigated to my downloads and forwarded the file to him. I heard a ding.

"All right. I have it. Now, have you watched it?"

"No."

"Do you know who filmed it?"

"Slade. Um, Icarus Slade. He was a player on the Tide."

"I'm familiar. Nowak did other things to hurt you. Physically?"

"Yeah. Just a scrap or two. Nothing worse than any other hockey fight."

"He hit you." Graves's voice was still matter of fact, but there was a cold, steel edge creeping into it.

"Yes."

"Anything else?"

"It's...no...I don't think it counts. Nothing else."

"Let me decide if it counts."

"They, um...he...everyone ignored me." It sounded like the stupidest complaint. Something a kindergartner would say.

"How?"

"No one spoke to me. No one looked at me. I wasn't allowed to run drills even when I was on the ice. No one touched me. I know those are dumb things to bring up—"

"Stop," Graves said. "You are a Canidae shifter. A wolf. You need a tactile environment."

"Yeah, but it's not like I need a team hug fest."

"Not what we're talking about here, kid. Okay. Now, I want you to know I've heard you. Coach Clay has heard you too. We're with you on this. All the way. Understand?"

I felt my shoulders drop. "Yes."

"Who knows about the video?"

"Slade, me, Hazard..." I heard Coach sigh, "...you, Coach Clay, and Nowak."

"What?" That was Coach Clay. "Oh, fuck no. Pack your bags, Spark. I'm coming to bring you back."

"That's not going to happen, Coach." I could tell, even over the phone, that my tone of voice surprised him.

"You don't get to decide what happens here," Coach said.

"Yes. I do. This is my career. And right now, this is my team. Nowak isn't going to do anything to me now that he knows the video's out there. I'm just as safe here as I would be at home."

"Underestimating Nowak is a fool's game, Duncan. You don't know the lengths he will go to make a problem disappear."

"See, I think I really do."

"I'm taking that video to the commissioner," he said.

"All right."

"All right? That's it? That's all you have to say?"

"You can take it to the commissioner. Maybe he'll listen to you. Maybe he won't. But no matter how it shakes out, while I'm on this team, I'm playing hockey. Nowak can't touch me. Not with what I have on him."

He exhaled, the sound of it loud. "Jesus the balls on you, kid. Don't do anything stupid."

I laughed.

"Duncan." His tone was firm. "I'm not leaving you there. Remember that. You're a Thunderheads. You will always be a Thunderheads. You're coming home."

"Yes, Coach."

"And if he lays a damn finger on you, you will call me."

"On your broke-ass phone?"

"I'll get a new one."

"Okay. And you'll call Slade?" I asked.

"Dog with a bone."

"Is that a yes?"

"Yes."

"Thanks, Coach."

"Stay smart, Spark."

I ended the call and texted Slade's number to Graves. That done, I headed into practice.

23

SLADE TEXTED ME RIGHT before the game that night. *A-hole*

I sent him back a kissy face, a thunder cloud, and a chicken drumstick, because I was hungry.

Clay called

And? I texted.

I'm going down 2 try out

Good. Don't be a jerk. I'll kick your ass if U fuck w/ my team.

You mean the Tide?

I ignored him. As I was ready to leave the locker room, he texted again.

I hate owing you

Sort yourself out, Diva.

He sent me a donkey and a golf flag in a hole.

I chuckled and threw my phone in my locker.

HALF WAY THROUGH THE first period, Keller, our second line left wing, took a shoulder to the head. It was a dirty hit that sent the Vancouver Brass player to the sin bin.

Keller got off the ice under his own steam, but it took a player on either side to guide him. Dr. Jerkwad took him back for concussion protocol.

We were down a man. By the end of the first period we were down a point, one-zero.

Nowak refused to play me. He screamed at the defense, he insulted our forwards.

Me, he ignored.

"We got this, boys," I said when he left the locker room and we were all standing, ready for the second period to begin.

The women growled.

"And ladies, of course," I said. "You know I have faith in you. You're carrying the damn team with that power play kill."

Wife Lundqvist, lion, yawned, baring all her teeth as she flipped me both fingers. Our female defenseman, Sava, wolf, pushed her hair out of her eyes and made a kissy face at me.

"The Brass aren't as fast as us, aren't as focused," I said. "We can shut that shit down."

"Damn right we can." Steele finished his energy drink that smelled like grapes and hospital cleaner. "If we get the fuck off our heels. Keep your eyes on the prize, people. Take every shot, stay on the puck. We play our game, we win."

There were a few grunts of agreement.

"This is our ice!" I yelled. A few people startled. I stood up on the bench. "Our ice!" I waved my hands over my head. "Our win! Fuckin' take it, Tide! Bury them! Drown them. Drag them down to the bottom of the sea, arrr, Mateys!"

More faces turned my way. The cats look nauseatingly unimpressed with my makeshift cheer.

"Fuck you all," I said with a huge smile. "You do whatever the hell you want. I'm going out there to win us a fucking game. Because the fuck with all this losing fuck. The fuck with it."

I hopped down off the bench and punched Bill in the shoulder because he was sitting nearest me. He grunted and punched me back. And something inside me shifted, settled.

Clicked.

I gave the next guy in line a slap, which he returned, and *click* there was that connection again. I made my way across the locker room, thumping chests, bumping fists, slapping backs, shaking Wife Lundqvist's hand because I was not stupid. I knew which lion to be afraid of.

Even Paski, who treated me with grudging respect now that I'd handed him his ass, went in for the high-five.

Click, click, click.

The beast in me vibrated with joy. I was going to hit that ice and break this losing streak. Even if I had to do it on my own.

But I knew I wouldn't. Because we were a—

—*pack*—

—pack.

EVERYTHING IN ME WAS on high alert. Sounds were extra loud, lights cutting and bright. My heartbeat thumped in my chest, my pulse sang in my ears. I could feel other heartbeats too, hot, fast, deep, calm, ready for this battle. Ready for this win.

My team. My pack.

I jumped onto the ice and skated, warming up, shedding some of that extra adrenalin and getting my head clear. We were a man down with Keller out for the night. Nowak had no choice but to play me.

I didn't have time to worry about it. It was time to play. Our first line stayed out on the ice and the rest of us found our places on the bench. I sat with the fourth line, squeezed water into my mouth and focused on the game.

Coach Nowak stalked the bench behind us. A boiling creature of hatred, pacing, pacing.

And then, the game was on.

Twenty minutes had never gone by so quickly. The Brass had found their spines and their speed during the break. They were putting us through our paces, hoping to put on so much gas, they'd leave us gasping for air in the gutter.

We matched them, play for play, speed for speed. Pushed hard. Pushed them harder. Fast plays, bone-cracking checks.

They made the mistake of losing track of the pass in front of our net and Husband and Wife Lundqvist cut through their D-men like two hot blades through butter, racing down the ice in a breakaway drive. Tape-to-tape and Wife Lundqvist buried that puck through the five hole.

The lights went off, the horn sounded, and we were on our feet shouting our lungs out.

Fourth line, and I was on the ice, taking this fight shoulder to shoulder with my team, my pack. I threw myself into scrum, got in front of the net to swipe for the rebounds and garbage goals.

I outskated their wingers, and taunted their D-men. I played like this was the one and last chance I'd ever have to play hockey again.

The final seconds dribbled fast, faster off the clock, chasing the zero. I took a shot at the net from the blue line. Time ticked and time tocked its last. Hammer-on-metal chimed out as six ounces of vulcanized rubber blasted the crossbar.

The audience let out a disappointed groan as the period horn blared.

It was good to know we had some fans out there.

The locker room was charged up. Lundqvists espousal got another round of back slaps and fist bumps for burying that goal. Wife Lundqvist gave us all hell for standing around while the lions did all the work.

The connections between us grew a little stronger, the threads wove a little tighter. For this moment, for this game, we were a greater whole and greater players than we could ever be on our own.

I wanted to bask in it. Laugh and jump around. Because I knew we were finally there for each other. Finally ready to do more than play. We were there to win.

Steele slapped my shoulder. "Hit the net, not the pipe, Spark."

"Yeah, yeah. Thanks, Captain. I'll make a note." I mimed writing on my palm with my middle finger and he laughed.

Everyone was talking. Everyone was giving someone else shit. It felt good. It felt right.

The new guy, Bill, looked up from taping his stick. "Nice job out there." Like I needed the not-the-alpha-right-now's opinion.

Okay, actually, I liked his approval too.

We were finally on our way to being awesome, and I couldn't wait to get there.

Coach Nowak did not join us in the locker room. That was strange. As the minutes flew by, everyone started watching the door, waiting for him. It wasn't like him to leave us alone. To skip a chance to deride and threaten.

With only two minutes left until ice time, the tension in the room built and built. Brooding instead of laughter, growls instead of chirps.

No. I wasn't going to let Nowak ruin this. His absence was tearing us down faster than his presence. Dick.

"You know what this game is worth?" I asked all those dark, grim faces. "You know what the win is worth?" I waited until eyes turned to me. "Pizza, buddies! If we win, pizza's on me."

Silence.

"What kind of pizza?" Steele asked. "Pizza pockets? Microwave DiGiorno?"

I made a rude sound. "Aw, hell no. This win, *our* win is Pie Town all the way."

Nadreau lifted his head. He wobbled a hand back and forth. "Meh."

"You have no taste. It's the best damn pizza in Tacoma." Or at least I assumed it was. I'd heard them all fighting about it on the bus back when we played the Brimstones.

"You buying the beer?" Big D asked as he swabbed the visor of his helmet. "Because a win is worth pizza and beer."

"No," Bill said. "Beer's on me."

I stared at Big D, but pointed at Bill. "What he said."

The noise went up in the room again. The tension broken.

Bill gave me a quick grin. "New guys like us gotta stick together. Right Spark?"

"Donuts," I said.

"Dollar," he replied.

"And yeah, Dollar," I said, "guys like us stick together."

"I don't care who's buying," Wife Lundqvist raked fingers through her sweaty hair to keep it out of her eyes. "I want that win."

THIRD PERIOD WAS A whole new game. We came out hot. Line after line powered it up for the grab, the assist, the rush. We picked more pockets than a Dickens street urchin and put the heavy in heavy-hitter.

We *roared.*

Nowak was there at one side of the bench behind the backup goalie. Nowak was grim and red-faced, but silent, which was weird. All of the plays were being handled by the assistant coach.

I decided to ignore Nowak and keep my attention on the game. The rest of the team followed my lead.

Game stopped on a power play. A Brass player lost his cool and fast as a shot, shifted into a snarling, snapping hyena.

Big D had been all over him pushing and yammering insults at him, but he did not shift. He backed away from the beast and our massive wolf took a knee, his gaze searching and locking on mine.

The part of him connected to me surged, too wild for a moment. I breathed in, breathed out with him, for him, and that line between us went solid, smooth, steady as iron. His hard breathing calmed and the smile he gave me was villainous.

We absolutely smothered the Brass.

Five minutes left in the third, Steele dropped a juicy slap shot that slipped right through the goalie's legs.

We were one up. We were in the lead.

We whooped and pounded sticks as first line pummeled Steele with joy, bumping helmets, hugging, before winging by the bench to slap gloves as we leaned out for them.

I jumped out with the fourth line, heavy on the defense, pushing for the net, but making sure they couldn't get anywhere near our goalie.

Time crawled. We sweated, we dug deep. We played for every inch.

The Brass swept the puck up the ice with two swift passes.

We soared after them like trained fighter pilots, gunning them down, crowding the lanes, clipping their wings.

A quick pass, another, and they had a hole. They flung past us, putting on speed I hadn't seen all game.

I hauled ass toward the net. Head up, stick extended, eyes on the goal. Like it was water in a desert, like it was air in an ocean, like it was pizza and free beer.

The guy I was covering smacked the puck through a forest of legs to his buddy on the far side of the ice.

We were all still barreling to the blue line, crossing to our net. Bill's, I mean Dollar's, opponent caught the pass and didn't hesitate. He bent his stick in half and sent that puck screaming to our goal.

The seconds were going, going...

Dollar was just out of reach to foul the shot.

I wasn't. I put on speed and leaped, like a man standing on a cliff who had nothing left to lose.

I hurled my body between the puck and our big Iowan giant, Johnson, in our goal.

Like a wall. Like a boulder. Like a mountain. Like a goddamned alpha.

The puck slammed my left thigh just above my knee.

Holy fuck that hurt.

I groaned and tried to push to my feet. There were too many legs, too many razor-sharp skates, too many sticks and players colliding above me.

If I didn't move, I'd be mincemeat.

My left leg refused to take my weight so I got to my knees, looking around desperately to orient myself to the play.

But there was no play. There was only celebration.

Teammates tackled me, tackled our Iowan giant, slapping, shouting, yelling.

"Yes!"

"Fuck yes!"

"Atta boy, Donut!"

"We won!"

"We fucking won!"

"Fuck the Brass!"

"Holy shit, that block!"

I laughed and shouted back at them, piled into the clambering hug, the collision of bodies, sweat and sore muscles. It was pack.

It was joy.

It was hockey.

I glanced over at our bench. Coach Nowak was nowhere to be seen.

24

A MAN STOOD IN the middle of our locker room. He wore a suit, styled his gray hair short, and brandished a watch I thought I could pawn to pay my rent for the next five years.

I had never seen him before.

Before I could open my mouth, Money Guy gestured to the room.

"Sit down, please. For those of you who haven't met me, I am Tomas Gosden, the owner of the Tide."

We all shuffled into our places, and waited.

"It has been brought to my attention that serious accusations have been made against Coach Nowak. Until this is sorted out, he will be temporarily suspended."

Clay. It had to be. He must have taken the video to someone he trusted. Or Slade had beaten him to it.

No one spoke. So I did.

"What does that mean for the team?"

Mr. Gosden stared at me hard and long. Maybe he was trying to remember my name or maybe he knew exactly who I was because he'd seen me on my knees being electrocuted.

My face caught fire. Embarrassment, guilt, and anger flashed through me.

I held eye-contact and squared my shoulders. If Slade or Coach Clay had flipped me out of the frying pan so I could burn in the fire, I'd do it with eyes wide open and no regrets.

"Duncan Spark," he stated. Not asked. He knew me.

"Yes, sir."

"I need you to come with me. The rest of you, please remain here. I'll have a word with each of you before you go home. Your assistant coaches will be here shortly. Food is being delivered."

Food. So this was going to take some time. I stood and nodded briefly to Steele.

The captain nodded back and took the reins. "Let's get out of this gear and hit the showers," he said.

Everyone got moving. Dollar cracked some kind of joke that got a chuckle or two.

They were okay. They weren't in any danger.

I just kept repeating that as I followed Gosden down the corridors to Nowak's office.

He walked in like he owned the place, which, yeah, he actually did.

"Take a seat, Mr. Spark. Water?"

"Yeah. Thanks." I dropped into a chair. He opened a small fridge in the corner and handed me the cool bottle.

"You've made quite a stir in the league this year, Duncan. May I call you Duncan?"

"Sure."

"I want to go over how I see this playing out." He walked around the desk, glanced at the chair, and decided to rest his fingers on the back of it instead of sitting.

"There are a lot of ways to get ahead in this league. But this is your first year. You were vastly overshadowed by the wizard on your team. You were not the strongest player on your previous team, but you are smart enough to know that if you volunteer for the Dead Man, all eyes will swing to you. Suddenly, you're the star. You have traction in history."

Everything he said was wrong, but I'd listen until he was done. I drank water and kept my eyes on him. I wanted to know his angle before I jumped down his throat and told him he could shove his assumptions up his ass.

"What did you think you were getting out of releasing the video to the public?"

"I didn't release the video to the public."

"Do you know who did?"

"No."

"It's not a secret, Duncan. Icarus Slade released it. He was cut from the team and he's using this, this trumped up video, to throw Coach Nowak under the bus."

"Have you talked to Slade?" I asked. "Have you looked him in the eye and told him he's a liar like you've looked me in the eye and told me I'm a manipulative, cheating narcissist?"

He let out a breath and ran a hand over the lapel of his jacket before pulling out the chair and easing down into it.

"No, I haven't. Not yet. I want to hear the truth from you. What you know. What Coach Nowak did or didn't do. Anything you saw happen to other players."

Slade had told me I wasn't the only player Nowak had put under the stun. Knowing that Nowak had hurt my team for no other reason than to establish dominance set fire to the anger in me.

No one touched my team like that. No one hurt them. Not while I was standing. Hell, not while I was on my knees.

"I have not seen him abuse the other players on the team. But I've been told by Slade that it's happened."

He blinked once, slowly in that way only sensitives did. He probably could tell if I was lying.

"Continue."

"I mouthed off to him, he gave me a bag skate and then he shocked me unconscious. I was new to the team but I was following his directions. There was nothing in my behavior that should have earned me that many shocks. I didn't even shift."

"Did you tell anyone?"

"The trainer and assistant trainer knew. They have my medical reports, though I think they've been falsely edited. I also told Slade, Random Hazard, my ex-coach Elliott Clay and also Hawthorne Graves."

"You should have gone to the authorities, Duncan. The police, the league commissioner. Whatever the nature of the threats, you should have followed up with the correct action."

"Yeah, well. Here we are."

He pinched the bridge of his nose, then sat back in the chair and made keep-going circles with his hand. "Then what happened?"

"I was an outcast from the team. Coach Nowak wouldn't allow me to run drills, didn't let me play. The team could not make eye contact or physical contact of any kind. They didn't speak to me. Well, Slade spoke to me, but that was it. It was solitary confinement in a crowded room."

"Did you tell anyone about this at the time?"

"No."

He shook his head. "How does a man with a mouth like yours stay quiet about these things?"

"Excuse me?"

"I've seen you play, Duncan. Especially when you were with the Thunderheads. You were always running your mouth like it was the last piston that would win the race."

He said it in such a normal, coach-like, or in this case, owner-like way, I forgot I didn't trust him and smiled.

"Yeah, I'm friendly and outgoing like that."

He tapped his fingertips on the desk. "I wish you would have brought all of this to someone in an authority position when it first started. I don't know what your relationship was with Elliott Clay—"

"We're solid. He's a great coach. I'd play for him for the rest of my life, if I could."

"And yet you didn't tell him what was happening for weeks?"

I rolled a shoulder, uncomfortable with his question and my answer to it. "I thought I should handle it on my own. I know being a part of a team doesn't mean it's going to be easy and friendly all the time. I get that I have to earn my way, prove my way."

His eyes shifted, taking in my face. Maybe it was the seriousness of my tone. Maybe it was that I was telling him a personal truth.

"Do you think you made the right decision?"

"No. Not even close. But it got me here, playing the game with a great team. Plus, we just won against the best team in the league. Gotta love that, right?"

He tapped his fingers again. "I'm sure you and I will need to talk again. I can't say what will happen from this point forward, but I want you to know that I intend to see this to the end and to make sure there are no other incidents like that video. I won't allow torture in my locker room."

It seemed like the least he could do, but at least he was doing something. "Thank you, sir."

"I'll be talking to the team and staff. But until I gather all the facts on Coach Nowak's alleged behavior…" He held up his hand when I started to protest.

"I've seen the video," he said. "What he did to you was out of line. You have my sincere apologies for what was done without my knowledge. However, it is an entirely different set of consequences he will face if this was a one-time incident as opposed to being habitual behavior. Understand?"

"Yes, sir."

"It would be in both your and my interests if you do not involve the press further. I'd suggest getting a lawyer, Mr. Spark. These allegations will bring out the sharks." He leaned forward, offered his hand.

"Off the record, I wish you would have spoken up the moment it happened. I wish you would have come to me. But I'll respect your reasons for not doing so. This is my number." He handed me his card. "I'll be in touch, Spark. Call me if you need anything."

I shook his hand. It was warm, dry, and strong. The handshake was firm like his words, not promising everything would work out, but promising to be as fair as possible about it.

"Is that all, sir?" I asked.

"For now. The pizza and burgers should have arrived. You might want to eat before they're gone."

I stood.

"One more thing," he said when I reach the door.

I looked at him.

"If you could stay on this team, or be on any other team, where would you choose to be, Mr. Spark?"

My insides twisted. The Tide were my team. My pack. But…

But even though I felt like I had made a place here and had done good for this team, it wasn't the same as being a Thunderhead.

I hadn't been kidding when I said I would play under Coach Clay for the rest of my life.

No matter what my brain told me—that I belonged here, this was my team, these were my pack mates, I was their alpha and couldn't leave them—other images overrode those thoughts.

Dollar was an alpha. He already fit in with them better than I did in a much shorter time.

He *belonged* in a way I still hadn't mastered. Like that drop of water in a stream thing Clay had talked about.

My team, my pack *liked* him. If I left, they'd be more than fine. They'd be better.

Being an alpha meant doing the right thing for my pack. The right thing for my pack wasn't me.

I knew where I belonged. Had known my pack from the first moment I'd dragged Hazard down to tryouts. That was family. It would always be family to me.

"If I had any choice, I'd play for the Thunderheads, sir," I said. "Second to that, I'd stay on the Tide. But not if Coach Nowak continues his career here."

"Remember what I said about the press. Send in Tabor Steele to see me next."

"Yes, sir."

The smells of soap and pizza met me when I got back to the locker room.

Showers were done and a pile of empty pizza boxes were stacked up on the floor near the garbage can. The full pizza boxes covered a table set up against the wall. I aimed for the full boxes.

"The fuck, Duncan," Steele said, crowding up in my space, his hand on my shoulder. "Why didn't you say anything?"

He was pale and a little sweaty in his street clothes. He should have had plenty of time to cool down from the game, but he looked sick.

There were no reporters in the room, just the team.

I chewed and swallowed my bite of meat lover's, then wiped the back of my hand over my mouth. "You saw the vid?"

Several people held up their phones.

Great.

I shrugged. "I was the new guy, right?"

"You didn't think we would believe you?" Big D came up close too. He bumped his shoulder into mine. Left it there.

"Would you have?" I was starving, so I stuffed my face.

"Yes," he said. "I would have believed you."

The pizza stuck in my throat along with emotions I hadn't expected.

The other wolves drew near, reaching out to pat my back, touch my arm, telling me they would have believed me too. That might have looked strange to some people, but for a second-marked, for me, it was heaven.

"Thanks," I finally said. "I wish the whole thing would have gone down differently. I made dumbass mistakes."

"We all did," Steele said.

"Well, not me," Dollar chimed in. "I wasn't even here."

Paski, my favorite tiger in the whole hockey jungle, threw an empty beer can at his head, he caught it, threw it back, and just like that, normalcy had been restored.

Dollar was good for them, good for the team. I was not blind to how many players smiled when they looked at him as if they didn't want to look away.

I wondered how long he would remain content to stay in the sidecar while I alphaed us down this road.

"Mr. Gosden wants to see you next, Steele." I shoved the rest of the pizza in my mouth and accepted the beer Zima pressed into my hand.

Steele nodded and headed out the door.

"So that game tonight, boys and girls," I said. "What a game."

"Hell of a game," Nadreau agreed holding up his drink for a toast.

I popped the top on my beer, lifted it. "To the Tide! May it continue to roll right over those Brassholes."

The toast was echoed, other beverages lifted. Then we all took a long, deep swallow.

I STAYED UNTIL THE last player left. It took that much time to return my messages. Random, Mom and Dad, and Coach Clay had all called. I ignored everything from the press, even Scott Dart's offer of a low-key conversation if I were ever in the mood.

Every other player on the Thunderheads left a text. Most were worried, some were furious. A few wondered why the hell I wasn't home with them this very minute and threatened to drive up here to get me themselves.

I hated to worry people, but the outpouring of concern and support was pretty humbling.

Somewhere in the middle of all of that, I got up the guts to watch the video.

It made me sweat, made my heart race to watch Nowak shock me over and over.

What I didn't know was that he'd kept shocking me even after I was unconscious.

But it wasn't my out-of-control spasms that made me sick to my stomach. It was the look of joyful hatred on Nowak's face.

If there was evil in this world? I'd just seen it.

I made it to the bathroom before I lost what was left of my pizza dinner. Then I washed my face, turned off my phone, and left.

There was no question that vid threw Nowak in a bad light. It might even be brutal enough to damage his reputation and get him suspended for the rest of the regular season.

Did I think it would cost him his job? Naw. The league thrived on scandal and violence. It filled seats.

We were the freak league, and that was what freaks did.

I walked across the parking lot, content in the quiet, content to have some time alone with my thoughts. Just as I reached my car, I felt someone watching me.

I paused, my car door half-open and scanned the shadows.

"You're welcome." A flash of yellow eyes, and Slade moved under the lamp post, hands in his pockets, red hair a flame of its own.

"Could have warned me you were going public with the vid," I said.

He shrugged and started my way. "You could have warned me you called Coach Clay and told him he should pick up my contract."

"You leaked the video before I called Coach Clay. Didn't you?"

"Does it matter?"

He stopped on the other side of the open door. There was something different about him. Then it hit me. The relaxation in his muscles, the stillness of his hands, the evenness of his breathing.

He looked happy. No, he looked content.

"He's signing you, isn't he? Coach Clay? You dog, you!" I smiled. "You're gonna be a Thunderheads. It's a great damn team. The best."

"Yeah," he said.

"I got your back, Icky."

"Hate that name."

"Gonna use it forever, Icky because we are BWFFFs: Best Wolf Fox Friends Forever."

A smile cranked up one side of his mouth, revealing teeth. "You are the dumbest thing in the universe."

He exhaled and stared up at the sky like he could see the moon and stars through all the clouds and darkness.

"Thanks. For all of it. Everything."

"Do right by them," I said. "Best team you'll ever be a part of, I mean that. Don't throw it away."

He nodded, still looking at the sky. Finally, "See you around, Donuts."

"See you around, Icky."

I got in the car, and he took a couple wandering steps away. He was still staring at the sky, a smile on his face, when I drove away.

25

THE KNOCKING WAS NOT going away. I shoved my pillow over my head and threw my arm across the top hoping whoever was out there would take their Girl Scout cookies, save-the-environment, have-you-found-Jesus elsewhere.

It was the jingle of keys and click of the lock sliding that got me out of bed and storming across the room.

Who had keys to my apartment? The owners of the house. Maybe there was an emergency?

I'd made it to the fully-furnished living room before it hit me.

My Dad had asked to keep the spare set of keys in case I developed a desire to own plants that needed watering while I was on the road. I was just now realizing his ulterior motives.

My Dad was sneaky like that.

Before I could do anything more than cross my arms over my bare chest, the door opened and sunlight streamed in, January pale, bringing a puff of cold air.

The chain caught and stopped the door.

"Huh."

I grinned at my dad's voice.

"Duncan? Are you awake, son?" He didn't yell. He knew second-marked had great hearing. "Honey, try his phone again."

I heard Mom fiddling with her phone. My heart was beating so strong and happy, I couldn't stand it anymore.

I bounded over to the door. "Hey, hey." I unlatched the chain then threw the door wide. "Hi. Hi, Dad. Why are you here? Hi, Mom. Hey, Ran. Hey, you guys. Come inside. Come in."

I moved back, but didn't get far. Mom and Dad rushed me at the same time and folded me up in a hug. They held on tight, not saying anything, just breathing, just holding me.

I closed my eyes and hummed, content like I hadn't been in weeks.

They were worried. They were angry, and maybe a little afraid. I could feel all of that rolling off them. I could feel their deep, endless, unquestioning love for me too.

That was a lot of pretty strong emotions before coffee.

Random was furious and pale as a sheet. He pressed his lips together and shook his head, his eyes watery.

Why was he on the verge of tears?

"What's wrong?" I asked, suddenly worried. "Why are you guys here? What happened?"

Mom made a little sobbing sound, then squeezed me hard enough it hurt.

Dad pulled away just enough to press his hand on the back of my neck, keeping me there, safe, so he could stare straight into my eyes, so he could make sure I heard him. Really heard him.

"You always tell us if someone hurts you. Do you understand me? You always reach out to us. You always answer us when we reach out to you. If this ever, *ever* happens again, in any way, shape, or form, you tell us as quickly as you can."

Oh. *Oh.* This was about the video. They had watched it, and had seen me hurting and helpless.

"But we talked on the phone last night," I said. "You know I'm okay. I've been okay. That happened weeks ago."

"It happened almost two months ago, Duncan," Mom said. "Almost *two.* We should have known. You should have told us, baby."

Uh-oh. When Mom went all soft and started calling me baby, there were gonna be tears galore. I could count on my hand the times she'd broken down and cried about anything, much less anything I'd done.

"Mom, it's okay."

"It is not." There was flint in her tone. "Not okay."

"Okay, right. It's not okay. But it's over. I'm in one piece. I'm still in one piece. I'm still your baby."

My dad shook the back of my neck like he wanted to strangle me just a little.

Like Mom with the tears, I could count on my hand how many times Dad had ever been angry. Really angry. He just wasn't made like that. He was always calm. Reasonable.

The video had shaken them hard and now they needed to know I was whole, I was safe. "Let's sit down. I'll make coffee. I'll tell you. All of you. Everything."

Dad gave me one last long look, then let go, making space so Mom could do the same. She squeezed me then surveyed the room quickly like she had to make sure everything else was where it belonged. "I'll use your restroom," she announced, crumpling a tissue in her fist.

Dad held her hand until she had walked too far for them to reach, their fingers dragging to the very tips.

"Is she okay?" I asked Dad.

"She will be. We'll get through this. We just need to come to a better understanding of what we can handle alone, and what we can handle as a family. Now—" he waved toward the kitchen "—I'll make some coffee and see if you have anything here for breakfast. If not, I'll get us some food. Because this is not a conversation for empty stomachs."

He left for the kitchen and I heard water running and cupboards clicking open and shut.

"I am so pissed at you, releasing that video when you were still here, still where he could hurt you," my favorite brother-friend said. "I should kick your ass."

His eyes had that glitter of gold. He was holding onto magic by a thin thread, by spider silk.

I gave him a moment, watched him cautiously as he stood there, fists at his side, eyes blazing. My brother who could break the world with the snap of his fingers.

"Go for the knees," I suggested. "You're too short to reach my ass."

He blinked and opened his mouth. Then he laughed.

And I laughed too.

He rushed and grappled me into a hard, lingering hug.

"I never want to see that again, do you hear me, Duncan?" he whispered furiously in my ear. "I can't see you like that. Can't see anyone doing that to you. You gotta look after yourself better than that. You gotta let *us* look after you better. You can't be alone. Away from us. Do you understand? You're the only...the only brother I h-have. I—I c-can't..."

"I know," I said stopping him before the panic and stuttering got worse. Before all the memories of his childhood took over his brain.

No one had loved Random when he had needed it the most. Not his father who had died when he was born. Not his mother who abandoned him.

Only us. Only Dad and Mom and me. We were the ropes that kept him tied to this world. We were the tape that patched him up, and showed him what family could be. What love could be.

"I was stupid," I said, still holding him because every muscle in his body was stiff, and he was breathing too hard.

He was almost in a full panic attack. But I could make this better.

"I need you too, Random. You're the good angel on my shoulder."

He coughed at that, sort of a hiccup, sort of a snort. But I knew the words helped. Eventually he pulled back and so did I.

"I'm not," he said.

"An angel? Sure you are."

"No, I can't be. Because devils don't have angels on their shoulders."

I smiled. "This devil does. I told you about the vid."

"Yeah. But when it went viral in seconds, while you were in the middle of a game with him with no one at your side, at your back? Jesus. I about lost my mind."

"Let's sit down. Dad's gonna feed us, and I'm starving."

He wiped at his face, scrubbing off sweat and a little wetness at the corners of his eyes.

"You even have any food?"

"Nope. Think we'll get pizza?"

"It's six o'clock in the morning." He slumped down onto the corner of the couch dislodging a pillow. "You're gonna be lucky if we get a dry toast."

"Well then," Dad said as he strolled into the living room. "Coffee's on. I'm going out to get a few things for breakfast. No talking about the big stuff until I get back."

"No big stuff." I plopped down next to Random, shoulder to shoulder. "What are we allowed to do while you're gone?"

"Drink coffee and talk about hockey." He gave us both a smile, then was out the door.

That didn't sound like such a bad way to start the day at all.

LUCKILY, DAD FOUND EGGS and sausage and hash browns and threw together a huge bowl of fruit with yogurt on the side. We all drank enough coffee the high emotions were sanded down by the sheer force of caffeine.

I couldn't stop yawning. Three hours of sleep on the heels of a life-changing night, and now all curled up in the comfort of my family was knocking me out.

"So what are you going to do?" Mom asked. She was snuggled against Dad on the loveseat. His arm draped across the back of it, and he ran his fingers absently through her hair, which she'd left loose instead of in a ponytail.

"I'm not sure. I'm alpha of the team. It needs that. Needs someone to keep all the emotions and actions in sync. It might sound weird, but I feel right being with them. Being a part of the team."

"You are not playing for Nowak," Random growled. "Fuck him."

Mom and Dad hummed their agreement. My family had no sympathy for Nowak and could muster no love for his team.

"I can't just quit. I came here because I was drafted."

"No. *I* was drafted. You threw yourself in front of a bullet aimed at me."

"And I'd do it again." My voice was calm. There was a confidence and finality to my words. If he was second-marked he would have bared his throat right then.

Instead he scowled at the coffee table. "I know."

Okay, maybe he could read alpha language.

Neat.

"We'll hire a lawyer and get some advice." My father: the voice of practicality. "I think we will need to talk to Mr. Gosden. Also, we should contact the league and see if they are investigating how widespread this kind of abuse may be. With that information, we'll decide if we're going to sue the coach, the owner, the team, or the league."

"Wow," I said. "You kind of went all the way there, Dad."

"It might be the WHHL, but it is not without laws, Duncan. Even if other players don't step forward you have a very strong case for litigation. We're not going to let this be swept under the rug. That does no one any good. If there's going to be good hockey in this league, we need good rules that protect the players upheld."

"Can't I just forget all this and play hockey?"

"That's a good question," Mom said. "Can you? Forget this and play?"

I closed my eyes again, lids too heavy to bother fighting anymore. It would be a long, hard road if I took legal action against anyone.

No one wanted a litigious player on their team, so I'd probably be out of a job.

But standing down and doing nothing? No. That wasn't in me. There were other players who had been hurt. They might not be able to stand up and take the hit, but I could. I was strong enough, and I had my entire family at my back.

Plus, I liked the idea of making Nowak squirm.

"Duncan?"

"I'm awake!" I sat up in a rush. "Lawyers, lawsuits, got it, got it. How do we start?"

"I think we start," Dad said, bemused, "by letting you and Random get some sleep."

I looked over at my softly snoring brother. He was drooling on one of the fancy pillows.

"You're a genius, Dad," I sighed.

And the *smile* he gave me. "I am aware."

26

WE WERE ALL CRAMMED into the tiny kitchen when my phone rang. Dad was ordering Thai food for a late lunch, Mom was making tea, and Hazard was texting his girlfriend.

Me? I was just standing in the middle of all of them, damn happy with my life.

I recognized the number from the card Gosden gave me.

"The Tide owner." I held my phone so Dad could see. He nodded.

"Hello, Mr. Gosden," I said.

Mom and Random both turned their attention to me. Mom made a stabbing motion. At first I thought she wanted to kill Gosden. She rolled her eyes.

"Speaker, Duncan," she said quietly.

Oh. I held the phone out and pressed the speaker button.

"Duncan," Mr. Gosden said. "I hope I haven't caught you at a bad time."

Random moved up beside me and slung his arm over my shoulder.

"No, sir. How can I help you?"

"I need you to come by my office, let's say in an hour. We need to discuss your contract and your place on the Tide."

My stomach dropped like a bomb and exploded in nervy fire. He was going to cut me. He was going to take me away from my pack. A small earthquake trembled inside me, threatening my footing.

Random squeezed his arm tighter around the back of my neck. Mom put her hand on my hip. The earthquake quieted.

"Yes, sir," I said. "What is your address?"

He recited it, and Dad wrote it down on the back of the Thai menu. We ended the call and that was that.

"We'll have just enough time to eat before we drive over there," Dad said. "Good thing we picked the Thai food place on the corner."

"Wait. No. Wait," I said. "Dad, you don't have to, all of you can't—"

"Duncan." Mom's nope-to-the-most voice stopped me dead. "We're going. We're all going."

There was zero arguing with her when she gave me that look. Random squeezed his arm on my neck one more time. "You're stupid," he whispered in my ear.

I shoved his face. He grinned and plopped back into the chair, phone out, thumbs flying.

"Okay. So should I wear my suit?"

Mom frowned, but Dad spoke first. "Always show respect for the game, no matter the circumstances."

"So go with the suit?"

"Go with the suit," he agreed.

MY HANDS WERE ROCK solid. Not even a tremble. But the rest of me was a big sweaty mess. It was January in Tacoma, Washington, cold, wet, gray. And I was sweating like I stood under a desert sky.

"You don't need to go in there with me," I said. Again.

Dad looked at me in the rearview mirror. "You're not going in there alone, son."

"But all of you is too much. I know you're here to support me, and I appreciate that. But I'm capable too. I need to know you trust my decisions."

And wasn't that the hard truth of it?

"This isn't about trusting you," Dad said. "Of course we trust you."

"But we don't trust Gosden," Mom said. "One of us should go with you."

"That's fair," Dad said. "Whichever of us you want. But you don't go alone. Fair?"

"Fair. Random Hazard," I said in my best Pokémon trainer voice, "I choose you!"

He looked surprised, then his expression darkened. "Good. Don't worry, Mr. Spark. I'm going to record the conversation so the bastard can't use it against him."

Wow. Vengeful much?

"Sean, Random," Dad reminded him for the millionth time. "You can call me Sean."

Random cracked his neck then his knuckles. His eyes went bright as steel.

"Uh…maybe I should pick Dad."

Random gave me a look that said he'd fight me.

"Ha-ha," I said. "I am just kidding, buddy. You and I can handle this. We got this. So, um…" I opened the car door. "Ran and I will be right back." I got out, gave Mom and Dad a thumbs up, then straightened.

"Dude," I said glancing over at Random, "could you scowl any harder?"

He did.

"Wow," I said. "That's…just wow."

He started toward the building and I fell into step on his left, just like we always were on the ice.

I could feel the anger vibrating off him slowly diminish. It was why he made such a good centerman. His instincts were spot-on when it came to the game around him. He always knew who was where, what obstacles were in the way, and what needed to happen in the moment for our team to win.

The guy at the front desk directed us to Mr. Gosden's office. I had a vague impression of the building being large, the decor expensive, and the time it took for us to reach his office a minute or so. But none of those things stuck with me.

What stuck with me was the scent I picked up right before I walked through the open doorway.

Cedar and sunshine, salt and honey.

Gosden sat behind an enormous black desk, trophies lined up in a glass case at his back. But he was not the familiar scent.

Sitting on a couch at one side of the room was the last man I'd expected to see here.

"Coach Clay," I said. "What are you doing here?"

He stood and I managed to rein myself in enough that I didn't tackle him with a hug. Because: maturity.

We shook hands while Hazard introduce himself to Mr. Gosden.

"You should have told me sooner," he said, quietly. "The moment it happened."

"Yeah." I swallowed. "I've been hearing a lot of that lately."

He let go of my hand and nodded to the chairs in front of Gosden's desk. Random was already sitting there, studying Coach Clay.

He didn't know why Clay was here. But I could guess. He'd signed Slade, and was probably here taking care of the details with the Tide's owner.

I shook Mr. Gosden's outstretched hand, and took my place next to Hazard.

"I want you to know," Gosden started, "that I've taken the video very seriously. I've spent time with each player on the team, and the decisions I've made are built upon more information than what you and Mr. Slade have brought to light."

"Sir?"

"What I'm saying, Mr. Spark, is that I haven't ignored what happened to you here on this team, under Coach Nowak's care, and ultimately under my care. I do not condone it. Steps have been put in place to make sure it does not happen again. We are offering counseling to any player who asks for it. If you want to pursue counseling, it's available to you."

"Thank you, sir."

"The reason I brought you here, however, is to tell you in person I have fired Coach Nowak. He will no longer coach the Tide."

A hot wash of—Panic? Delight? Vindication?—ran like rapids across my skin.

Hazard straightened in his seat. He was radiating joy, joy, joy.

"Okay. Uh, thank you for telling me, sir." This drastic of a decision told me there was no way the other players had remained silent about their treatment by Coach Nowak.

Thinking of the team, my team, being tortured by that asshole, pushed me solidly into the anger zone.

"Who are you replacing him with?" Because that mattered. Nowak was arguably the worst coach in the league, but he was not the only one who had been accused of brutal on-ice, or behind-the-scenes practices.

"I'll be stepping in his position until I find a suitable replacement," Gosden said.

Both Hazard and I went totally still.

Gosden sighed. "I have coached before. For several years. Don't these kids read their history?"

Coach Clay grunted. "I'm lucky if they read the playbook."

Gosden and Clay exchanged a battle-weary look, then Gosden continued.

"I was the winningest coach the second year I led the Fargo Flurries, and took the trophy the next year. So, for the interim, I'll be the one stepping in for coaching duties. If the right person with the right resume wanted to make a change…"

"Nope," Clay said.

Oh, so *that's* why he was here. Gosden had reached out to see if Clay wanted to change teams. It was actually a genius move. Bring in the coach of the team who Nowak hated the most and have him turn Nowak's team around. It was a nice story and would have packed the arena to capacity.

"…*if* the right person with the right resume shows up, I'll hire on a new head coach. Until then, it's me."

"Have you announced it to the team?" I asked.

"I will tonight. Then the press will hear about it shortly after. And that's the other reason I wanted you here. Elliott?"

Coach Clay moved to stand next to Gosden's desk. Yellow-haired, surfer-relaxed Clay in a gray jacket, jeans and a T-shirt with a taco logo, was a sharp contrast to the silver-haired square-faced Gosden who appeared twice as put together in a navy button-down under a dark tailored jacket.

Clay smiled. "The Thunderheads are picking up your contract, Duncan."

I heard Random's sharp inhale.

Then, for a moment, there was nothing. Not even the thrum of my own heartbeat, not even the voice of the wolf within me.

I hadn't jumped off the cliff. I'd been kicked in the chest and was falling off a mountain. Off the world, off the universe.

Coach Clay's words stretched out and netted me back to myself. "You don't have a say in this, Spark. I'm down a winger and Mr. Gosden and I have agreed to transfer your contract back to the Thunderheads."

"But," I heard my mouth say from a distance, "what about Slade?"

"What about Slade?" he asked.

"Is he still a Thunderheads?"

Clay tucked his hands into his jean pockets and held eye contact. His eyes were ice-blue, but somehow they were warmer than fire.

"Slade's career is his own, Duncan. You two don't come as a matched pair." As an afterthought he pointed between Hazard and me. "Neither do you two. This is hockey, boys. Not a dating site."

"Yes, Coach," Hazard and I intoned together.

Random bumped my shoulder with his own.

I was instantly vibrating, on fire, burning to yell, run circles, tackle someone in giddy glee.

Instead, I wiped my sweaty hands on my slacks, stood, shook Mr. Gosden's hand, then turned and shook Coach Clay's hand again. "Thank you, Coach."

"Thank me by not half-assing the neutral zone coverage, Spark."

I grinned. Because this was it. This was home, looking me right in the face. And this time I wasn't going to let it go.

27

"YOU SURE?" HAZARD LEANED against the corridor wall, trying to look casual and not like he wanted to grab me, stuff me in the trunk of a car, and drive me across state lines.

"Yes. Stay out here. This is something I need to do alone."

He scowled.

"You'll be right here," I pointed out. "Even with your puny wizard hearing abilities, you'll know if something goes wrong."

"Fine," he agreed. His eyes flashed gold.

Wizards. Such drama queens.

I slapped him on the shoulder and made a face at him. Then I turned and walked to the Tide locker room to face my soon-to-be—

—*pack*—

—ex-teammates.

They heard me coming. Of course they did. I could feel them, all those strings connecting us, tying us together. I could taste their worry, their anger, their disappointment, and it was my own.

They were my team, my pack, my hockey heartbeat. And I was leaving them behind.

The wolf in me howled.

I strolled into the room. Everyone was here at their lockers because practice would start in about a half hour. They were all looking at me. Even the cats were paying attention.

"First, don't interrupt me, because I can't do this twice." I swallowed, my mouth already too dry. The wolves shifted, uncomfortable and wanting to be near me.

Steele nodded. "Go ahead."

"I hated you. All of you. Because you were our rivals on the ice and because you targeted my brother early in the year and tried to take him down. I couldn't forgive you for that."

I held Steele's gaze until he flushed and looked away.

"But I thought I could come here and find a way to at least tolerate you so we could play hockey together. So we could be a team.

"I did not expect to fall in damn alpha love with you assholes."

Paski scoffed and Husband Lundqvist chuckled.

The tension broke and bled out of the room.

"I blame all of you for that. Mostly Paski and Zima, who gave me such a warm, friendly welcome, I could feel it for days. And partly Kudrar, who was the first to nut up and fucking shake my hand. And totally the rest of you who have been dealing with a shitshow around here all year and haven't given up on this game, this team, or each other.

"I'm proud as hell to be a Tide." I blinked, and there was wetness at the corner of my eyes. "And I'm proud as hell of this team.

"But this is the end of the line for me. I'm going home, boys and ladies. Back to the Thunderheads."

I knew they'd been told, but there was still anger and shock running through our pack connection.

"Today's the day I say good-bye. C'mere, Dollar."

Bill looked surprised, but he strolled over. I guided him to stand next to me. Then I draped my arm over his shoulder.

"All right, team. This here is Bill, also known as Dollar. He's the new guy on the team, and he's an alpha. I find myself threatened by his presence."

Bill snorted.

"*Threatened*," I said louder, "by his presence. So we're going to fight for the right to be alpha of the Tide."

Bill tensed under my arm. I could feel his heartbeat rise. Not in fear. No, he liked this idea of taking me down. As a matter of fact, he *loved* it.

Before he got it in his head to punch me, I stuck my free hand toward him handshake-style. "Dollar Bill, I declare a thumb war."

The room came unglued. Everyone surged to their feet, surrounding us as if we were in a boxing ring, hooting and whistling. Bill and I broke apart, and circled each other, bouncing on our toes, throwing fake jabs like we were about to go for the heavyweight championship.

Bill was grinning like a fool. I was pretty sure I was too.

Steele pushed his way through the bodies to drop a hand on our shoulders. "All right, gentlemen, I want a fair fight. No kicking, no lifting, no hitting below the belt. No eye-gouging, ear-biting, or hair-pulling. Ready?"

We leaned in and clasped hands, thumbs up.

"Go!"

We stared straight into each other's eyes and intoned the pre-game chant. "One, two, three, four, I declare a thumb war."

I winked at the alpha in front of me, tipped my chin, and let my eyes slide to the battle of the thumbs.

I lost, of course.

Bill was a terrible sport and rubbed the victory in my face with plenty of insults.

I laughed at him and made my rounds, a hug here, a back-slap there, a handshake or two, soft "good-lucks" and strong "good-byes".

Bill was right behind me, touching a shoulder as I let go, getting that wolf head tip, making the pack connections I could already feel fading away inside me.

My wolf keened at the loss. At the loneliness. It hurt.

And then there was a hand on my shoulder—

—*Brother, pack, home*—

—and another on my neck—

—*Father, pack, home*—

—and one on my arm—

—*Mother, pack, home*—

—and one more on my other shoulder—

—*Coach, pack, home*—

Because of course they were all here: Random, my parents, and Coach Clay. They were my pack. They were my family.

They wrapped around me, held me close, got me moving out of the room. Which was good. The world had gone a little watery and no matter how hard I blinked away wetness, I still couldn't see.

"We got you," Random said. "You're ours. You're *mine*, and I'm never letting you do something this stupid again."

I coughed a snotty laugh and wiped my leaking face all over his shirt. He pushed my head away and told me I was disgusting. Then he magicked up some floating lights that popped like bubble wrap when I poked at them.

"Let's get some food before we hit the road," Dad said. "We've already packed your stuff and spoken to your landlords."

I wrapped one arm around Mom's back, and one around Random's and followed my family home.

28

"HOW MANY?" WATSON ASKED me as Hazard and I strolled into the locker room.

"Eight," I said. "Yeah?"

Hazard nodded. "Five local reporters, three from out of town."

"They're probably here for the Brass's new lineup," Watson said.

"Yeah," Troiter added. "Dead Man drama is so who-the-fuck-cares now."

"It was always who-the-fuck-cares," Slade, the asshole, said.

Watson leaned forward to give him a high-five and Slade slapped his hand.

Slade fit in here like an egg in a carton. Just one more misfit on Misfit Island.

"Yeah, everyone wants to talk about Nowak's fall from grace now. Bastard," Jada said. "Hope we never see his face again."

I thought we'd be seeing his face until the next exciting scandal rocked the league. Or at least until the league followed through with their investigation.

For his part, Nowak denied doing anything wrong and said the video had been altered. His story was pretty much what I'd expected: I'd been in cahoots with Slade, and it was all a plan to get him fired and for me to renege on the Dead Man.

My lawyer, a sharp woman who was the wife of someone my mom knew from work, told me to tell the press it wasn't something I could comment on until the league finished looking into it.

So that's what I did.

Hazard pulled off his T-shirt and sat on the bench, getting his gear together. The flash of my number on his shoulder still made me smile.

It wasn't that the last two months with the Tide felt like a dream—because nightmare was a more appropriate description—but coming back here and having the team treat me like nothing had happened, nothing was different, made my time with the Tide feel fleeting.

The ties that had bonded me to the team as an alpha were completely gone now. Sometimes I thought I could catch a faint echo of a feeling from one of the players, but it was more memory than real.

Things like the tattoo on Hazard's arm, the tattoo on mine, reminded me of the difference he carried now as compared to when he had first joined the team. I carried some differences too.

I was not the same man who had volunteered to protect my little brother. I was more. And it was time I stepped up and let the team know exactly where I stood.

"Look," I stood in the center of the room, facing the benches. "I need to say something."

The whole team was here, all in various states of dress. No one paused in their prep, but I had their attention. Thorn even turned down the music.

"Since this is my first game back with the team, I want you all to know that I am going to play my ass off out there. Tonight, and every night. Or day, you know, when we do day games."

Someone snorted.

"You're going to play your asses off too," I went on. "And if you don't, you're not going to answer to Graves. You're not going to answer to our captain, Lock. You're not going to answer to Coach Clay."

All eyes were on me now, narrowed, waiting.

"You're going to answer to me."

Silence.

"So, um...*grr* and *rawr.*" I curved my fingers into claws. "I'm the alpha of this team. I'm your alpha now."

Blank looks. Finally Balstad spoke up. "Is this, uh...a wolf thing? Did I read about this in that vampire novel?"

"You know how to read?" Yoffie asked.

Humans.

I rolled my eyes. "It's a second-marked thing, and a hockey thing. It's a team thing because it will affect the team dynamics and it's a...me thing."

Lock, our captain, who was a fourth-marked jaguar shrugged. "We know."

I swallowed a couple times to get my throat spitted up enough I could talk. "Know what?"

"We all know you're the team alpha," he said like it didn't mean much to him. Which, fair point. Jaguar shifters didn't follow the whole "pack" thing in general.

"So...that's settled? Just...tell you what I want and you agree? I want a million dollars."

Someone booed. A sock flew at my head.

"We all know you're the heart of the team, Donuts," Random said.

"Yeah," one of the T's, Tetreault, agreed. "We were dead without you, dude. Did you see our last three games? Even Thorn couldn't save our asses."

"Yours maybe," the other T, Troiter, said. "Because of the size of it. As in it's big, brother. You have a large ass."

Tetreault threw a roll of tape at his face, the music cranked back up, and I was promptly ignored.

Except for the second-marked in the room. They were silent, watching me. One by one, they held eye contact with me, tipped their chins up, showing their necks, then slid their eyes to the side.

I nodded at each of them. So they knew I saw them. So they knew I would be there for them. The alpha of this team. The heart.

And that first thrum of lines reaching, connecting, growing, and knotting sang out in my mind, a shout, a victory cry, stronger than any tie I'd had with the Tide players. The whole of us, the all of us vibrated through my chest like a hundred instruments holding a single note, a thunderbolt of song.

Graves watched me. His eyes never wavered as I met his gaze. He tipped his chin a half-millimeter, barely a movement, really just an acknowledgment. And then he winked.

I laughed and shook my head.

Hazard looked my way and gave me a plain, happy smile.

And I knew I was home, and there was no place in the world I'd rather be.

There was, however, one more person I wanted to see.

I pulled out my phone, and sent a text to Netti.

Been thinking, I sent.

I only had to wait a second before she answered.

Is that what you've been doing? What about?

You.

Smooth.

I want to take you on a date. Netti Morandi, will you go out with me?

You still a hockey player?

Sometimes. When I'm on a date with you I'll be something better.

What's better than being a hockey player? Being an alpha?

No. Being your man.

She didn't reply. Not for several long minutes. I chewed on a hangnail and waited.

Finally: *Sweet save, Spark. Think you can follow through?*

For you? Always.

The next text was a time and date. And a nice restaurant between Portland and Tacoma.

"Yes!" I yelled. I jumped up and started dancing, while the wolf in me howled.

"What is wrong with him?" Lock asked.

"I want a new alpha," Troiter said. "This one's broken."

"I got a daaate! I got a daaate!" I crowed.

"Oh, god," Slade said. "Poor woman."

"Naw, buddy, she's the richest in the world. She's got me!"

Watson made a gagging sound and Slade mimed sticking his finger down his throat.

"Will you all knock it off," Lock demanded. "Donuts. Sit the hell down. We have a game to play."

I stopped mid-boogie, and dropped down on the bench. "Yes, Captain." Since dancing was out, I started singing. "Hungry Like the Wolf" of course. Loudly, and off-key.

Everyone groaned and threw things at my head.

I couldn't have been happier with this team, with myself, with my life.

And I would do everything in my power to make sure this feeling would never end.

COMING SOON

THORN
WEST HELL MAGIC - 3

ACKNOWLEDGMENT

THIS BOOK WAS A lot of fun to write, and I certainly hope it was a lot of fun to read! Several lovely people helped make Duncan's story shine.

I'd like to thank my amazing cover designer, Kanaxa Designs, who somehow made me fall in love even harder with the second cover than the first. How did you do that? It's magic, isn't it?

Thank you also to my wonderful copy editor, Kimberly Cannon, for catching my grammatical errors and pointing out the finer details of hockey rules. Huge thanks to Skyla at Indigo Chick Designs for saving my bacon on the print format once again. You're brilliant.

Big thanks to my sharp-eyed beta reader Dejsha Knight, who went above and beyond (two or three times) to give me such valuable feedback, and also to my incredible proofreader, Eileen Hicks, for turning this project around in record time.

Shout-out to my hockey sisters, Deanne Hicks and Dejsha Knight. It wouldn't be the same if I couldn't share the joy and excitement with you. Let's watch more games, girls!

I'd like to give a tip of the hat to Patrick Swenson of the Rainforest Writers Retreat, who always creates fun, productive, word-writery events and community. Spark got its start at last year's retreat.

All my love to my husband, Russ Monk, for his unfailing optimism and encouragement. Thanks for all the games, that crazy Route 66 road trip, and for keeping track of hockey stats.

To my sons, Kameron Monk and Konner Monk, thank you for your support, watching LetterKenny with me, and for being the best part of my life. I love you both.

And to you, my dear reader. Thank you for strapping on your skates and pushing off onto the ice to give Duncan's story a go. I certainly hope you've enjoyed the game!

About the Author

DEVON MONK is a national bestselling writer of urban fantasy. Her series include West Hell Magic, Ordinary Magic, House Immortal, Allie Beckstrom, Broken Magic, and Shame and Terric. She also writes the Age of Steam steampunk series, and the occasional short story which can be found in her collection: A Cup of Normal, and in various anthologies. She has one husband, two sons, and lives in Oregon. When not writing, Devon is drinking too much coffee, watching hockey, or knitting silly things.

Want to read more from Devon?
Follow her online or sign up for her newsletter at:
http://www.devonmonk.com.

Made in the USA
San Bernardino, CA
30 June 2020

74554962R00185